Montana Blues

◆◆◆ ◆◆◆ ◆◆◆

Ray Ring

◆◆◆ ◆◆◆

Writers Canyon Press

Tucson, Arizona

2023

Publisher's Cataloging-in-Publication Data
(provided by Five Rainbows Cataloging Services)
Names: Ring, Raymond H., author.
Title: Montana blues / Ray Ring.
Description: Tucson : Writers Canyon Press, 2023.
Identifiers: LCCN 2022919383 (print) | ISBN 979-8-9869383-0-1
    (trade paperback) | ISBN 979-8-9869383-1-8 (ebook)
Subjects: LCSH: Black people—Fiction. | Racism--Fiction. |
    White supremacy movements--Fiction. | Murder--Fiction. |
    Thrillers (Fiction) | Mystery fiction. | BISAC: FICTION /
    African American & Black / Mystery & Detective. |
    FICTION / Mystery & Detective / Women Sleuths. |
    FICTION / Thrillers / General. | GSAFD: Mystery fiction.
Classification: LCC PS3568.I567 M66 2023 (print) | LCC
    PS3568.I567 (ebook) | DDC 813/.6--dc23.

ISBN 979-8-9869383-0-1 (trade paperback)
1st edition

Cover photo by Todd Klassy (Montana)
Author photo by Steve Sweeney (Montana)

Writers Canyon Press
www.WritersCanyon.com

Previous novels by Ray Ring

Arizona Kiss *(Little, Brown and Company 1991)*

"A well-crafted tale of sexual obsession, treachery and violence ... in its own distinctive shade of noir." — Times Literary Supplement, London

"A rattlesnake of a book: its plot curves and coils and finally strikes, unforgettably." — Barbara Kingsolver, bestselling literary novelist

Peregrine Dream *(St. Martin's Press 1990)*

"A stylized detective mystery ... fast-paced and sensuous ... The intense heat of the desert, its brilliant light and color, radiate from every page." — The San Francisco Chronicle

"Sharp characterizations, vivid nature descriptions, and love of the land are wrapped up smartly in a well-conceived plot." — Kirkus Reviews

Telluride Smile *(Dodd, Mead & Company 1988)*

"A neat little detective thriller (and) a wonderfully bittersweet and entertaining satire of the state we all know and love." — The Denver Post

"The behavior of affluent Americans in a modern ski resort is rendered flawlessly." — Newsday

~

All of Ray Ring's novels are available at RayRing.com.

For Molly and Henry

ACKNOWLEDGMENTS

Linda Platts, my wife for more than thirty years, and Molly and Henry helped with editing this novel. Linda has been especially patient and dedicated, editing many drafts over the years. Also I benefitted from edits by fellow authors in a Tucson critique group: Liz Gunn (who passed in 2022), Mike Hayes and Susan Cummins Miller. Wayne Hare, founder of The Civil Conversations Project, read a key draft and helped me be considerate and accurate. More people were helpful in many ways. Thank you.

PART 1

DAWSON

CHAPTER 1

In the promising light before sunrise, he gears up for the long swim, doing stretches and jogging on the sand where Long Beach meets the ocean. This is the day he turns eighteen and he's thinking about the challenges in his life and how nearly ten years have passed since the wreck.

The sun inflames the eastern horizon. He wades out, wearing only swim briefs and a swim cap and goggles, no wetsuit. He wants the shock of the chilly water, a form of intimacy with the ocean. He begins swimming straight out from shore — long-reaching strokes, deep steady breaths, climbing the swells and swooping down through the troughs, warmed by his internal fire. Roughly a half-mile out, he angles south, measuring his progress by landmarks along the shore that are barely visible now, mainly the top of the twenty-story Galaxy Towers. After a while, he pauses to scan the surface for any sharkfin, turns around and swims north. He guts it out for his goal, swimming four miles.

Back on shore, he puts on the Hawaiian shirt and walks

up the bluff to the grassy park along Ocean Boulevard, overlooking the water. Resting on a park bench, he pulls out his phone and re-reads the email from the Montana State University football coach. It's an offer — a scholarship for a university education if he goes to Montana State and plays halfback for the football team. He's been strong running the ball for the Cabrillo High team, and six universities that need a halfback are interested in him. Montana State offers the most financial aid. He gazes at the water shimmering out to the horizon and stretches out his thoughts.

Playing hard to make the dead proud, ever since I lost my parents. Yeah, that's part of it.

Heading back to the house he shares with Aunt Cecie, he rides the 121 bus through the array of skyscrapers downtown, then the 191 bus inland, across the concrete-banked LA River. The views coarsen with industrial buildings and parking lots filled with cargo containers for the Port of Long Beach. In his short-of-money neighborhood, Upper Westside, as he walks the last blocks to the house, he kids around with a group of big Pacific Islanders who've played football with him over the years toughening up his game.

He knows Aunt Cecie will have her special apple cobbler ready for his birthday. She's letting him make the decision. He pauses on the front porch and sends an email accepting the Montana State offer. He'll sign the contract and have the official phone talk when the Montana State coach schedules it. He's thinking, guess I'll find out what winter is.

CHAPTER 2

They released him from Montana's Deer Lodge prison when they got tired of trying to break him. That's how it seemed to him. Two guards and a captain — good ol' boys but not the worst — opened the cell door after the morning count.

"Dawson Koloko, step out."

He took his time obeying the command, a few seconds to make his point. Tossed his essentials into a paper bag and buddy-hugged his cellmate, Billy Redcherry, "Thanks for everything, Billy. I'll be in touch."

He stepped out to the unit's hallway carrying the paper bag. The guards relocked the cell and walked him through the world of steel and concrete and shatterproof glass, past many White convicts who tracked him with their eyes. Some said versions of *good luck* and some yelled the standard racial slurs. A few flicked cigarettes that had been smuggled in, the embers hitting him like hot bullets.

Of course the prison bureaucracy required procedures

and paperwork, then the guards walked him all the way outside, where the wind riffled the Montana flag. He saw the whole sky crackling blue and the mountains shined by snow. He breathed the cold fresh air. The twenty-first of December — he'd remember this date. The lawyers were waiting for him by the flagpole. MaryAnn Meloy hugged him, with tears on her cheeks, and Langdon Burns gave him backslaps.

"The governor made it a big deal, announcing your pardon at his prayer breakfast," Burns said. "Covering his ass with religion."

Beyond the lawyers, a crowd had gathered — roughly a dozen journalists, and a few crusaders who held signs about reforming the system. Some of them wore masks even though the latest predatory virus was almost tamed. The journalists came at him with questions and cameras and microphones, and he gave them what they wanted, brief answers that were honest enough, until one said, "Now that your lawyers proved you didn't kill your girlfriend, who —"

"Nikki Fontaine," he cut in. "That was her name."

"Sure, Nikki Fontaine. Who do you think killed her?"

"Maybe the Montana cops will figure it out someday."

He looked for Rose while he dealt with the questions. Wondering if she'd show up for this. He spotted her standing by herself behind the crowd. Her hair was different now — blond, not black. She seemed further disguised by her long wool coat and large sunglasses. Most people wouldn't recognize her as Nikki's identical twin.

Rose, he thought, maybe you haven't given up on me.

Burns leaned in with the Texas drawl and the tailored Western suit and the slim-brim cowboy hat, very much the hotshot reversing wrongful convictions across the country. "What we proved is, Montana's crime lab bungled the original evidence," Burns told the journalists. "Put this in your stories: At eighteen, Dawson lost five precious years along with his football scholarship and his chance to be drafted for pro football. Other convicts assaulted him repeatedly just because he's a Black man. He's limping on a bad leg where they stabbed him a while ago. He should be compensated for damages — meaning, money."

Burns enjoyed talking like that, the drawl and the poking of hornet nests.

"What's your percentage, Burns?" somebody asked.

Burns ignored that question.

MaryAnn did the champagne toast, "Here's to justice!" — a joke. Her public-defender sense of humor. She flashed more of it with her Frosty Snowman sweater and the sassy purple streak in her hair. "Here's to *correcting* justice!"

"Dawson," another journalist asked, "are you heading back to California?"

"I'm heading any direction that looks good. Haven't done that in a while."

He watched Rose turn her back and walk away, the wind riffling her hair same as the flag. The crusaders took over the press conference, talking about the system's bias against people of color. He went along with the lawyers, walking toward the parking lot. He saw Rose get into the driver's seat of a newish pickup truck. He walked toward her but she peeled away, her tires shrieking.

"Is that Rose?" MaryAnn said. "The blonde? If you haven't heard, along with brightening her hair, she's married to the sheriff now. Probably she still thinks you're a murderer."

"Hell," Burns said, "probably half of Montana still thinks you're a murderer. We shocked them out of their boots — but it's more difficult to change their minds."

CHAPTER 3

H e rode in the front passenger seat of MaryAnn's Volkswagen, a sleek all-wheel-drive with the heater vents blowing. Burns sprawled across the back seat and MaryAnn stomped the gas pedal. That Montana sport — driving fast on icy roads.

He watched the prison get smaller behind him. Waves of snowdrifts and evergreen forest stretched all around. He buzzed his window open to feel the wind that was faster and colder with the speed of the car. The colors were so intense his eyes almost hurt. The air smelled so fresh it almost choked him. That quickly, he was about to overdose on freedom. He buzzed his window closed, to protect himself, and heard Burns making a phone call about some Georgia case, Burns telling some assistant, "Book me a suite in the Atlanta Four Seasons for the week after New Year's."

"Dawson, there's good coffee in the thermos," MaryAnn said. "And cinnamon rolls in the bag. Your aunt couldn't make the trip from Long Beach — she says have fun and call her when you can."

MaryAnn understood that he needed to not talk. He thanked her and looked at more Montana scenery, the beautiful emptiness that could fill up a person. Some of the mountains were rounded off, kind of gentle, and some were jagged, looking like accidents. In the side-view mirror he saw vehicles behind them — a prison habit, looking around to see if anybody was a threat. Roughly seventy yards back, there was an older SUV, maybe a Chevy Suburban, that had only one daytime headlight shining. It made that SUV distinctive. When MaryAnn slowed going up a mountain pass, the one-eyed SUV slowed about the same, and when she increased her speed going down the pass, that SUV maintained the gap, as other vehicles passed them or dropped back or turned off. Maybe it meant nothing.

They went over another forested pass and down to a valley where subdivisions grew. The clutter increased and they came into Bozeman, the trendy town where he'd done his college football until the cops hit him with the bad rap. MaryAnn lived in Bozeman and Burns had become a part-time resident for pushing the appeal and squeezing money from the system.

Probably Rose still lived here too.

Some of his thoughts were too much to say out loud. Yeah I'm going to figure out who killed Nikki and framed me. And Rose, I need your help.

CHAPTER 4

*F*lying from the LA airport to Bozeman to begin his college football adventure, it's his first time above the clouds. When he lands, he discovers a town of White people dressed for hiking. Bobcats — that's what they call the Montana State University team. The late-summer football practices begin on grass that's lush compared to Long Beach grass. One of the other Black recruits, cornerback Ka'Deem Adams, feels so out-of-place, Ka'Deem quits and goes home to Chicago. And right away, two Bobcats catch his attention. They're identical twin sisters on the cheerleader squad, often practicing beside the football team.

He asks around and learns, they're Nicole and Rosalette Fontaine, going by their nicknames, Nikki and Rose, same age as him but a year ahead in college. He sees Nikki and Rose are fellow athletes — they're small and slender but muscled, the flyers on the squad, getting flung around and held aloft by the beefy cheerleader guys. They spend hours practicing flips and other tumbling and balancing as if gravity doesn't apply to them. And they have an intense look with their blue eyes and straight black hair that whips as they make their moves. When they finish each practice, for fun they do easy cartwheels on the grass and strike a pose, arms spread — ta-daah! They're laughing, chitchatting and wisecracking. So they're only serious sometimes.

One restless night around 2 a.m. he's surprised to encounter the twin sisters as he walks from his dorm exploring the quieted campus. In a construction zone where campus streetlights are off, he hears whispering and laughter, and he walks through the darkness toward the sounds and makes out the twins hanging around a flagpole. They're barefoot, wearing gym shorts and t-shirts, despite the nighttime temperature drop. Their jackets and shoes are heaped on the sidewalk, out of the way.

"Nikki? Rose? It's me — Dawson Koloko."

They shush him, "Shhh!" He lowers his voice to whisper, "What are you twins doing out here in the dark? This late?"

They answer interrupting each other:

"Today's our birthday —"

"We always do something wild on our birthday —"

"We're going to climb this flagpole —"

"Vow of silence, Dawson!"

They wiggle their fingers at him, imitating spiders, and start climbing, opposite each other on the pole. Only their bare hands and feet touch the pole — they get traction with skin against the smooth metal as they race upward. He watches them become vaguer shapes blending with the dark *sky. The pole seems about thirty feet tall with no flag at the top, probably somebody removed the flag because of the construction zone and lack of lighting. He gets ready in case they slip, he might be able to slow their falling. Right.*

Then he can see them descending and hears the squeaking of skin against metal. "Give us space," one says and she releases from the pole to land in a barefoot crouch on the concrete. Then the other one lands. In the darkness he can see their grins, their teeth glowing white.

"Vow of silence," one of them says again.

"You never saw us here," says the other.

And they run off.

~

About twelve hours later, during the afternoon practice, one of them approaches him as he takes a water break. In the daylight he can see her much better. Her eyes are even darker blue the closer she gets. She gives him a little poke in the arm. "Thanks," she says.

"For what?"

"Keeping the flagpole stunt our secret. You've got some grit yourself, Dawson. And that's a nice smile on your face."

She's poised, inches from him, looking up into his eyes, in her sports bra and gray-and-blue gym shorts, maybe not the 2 a.m. shorts. Sweat gleams on her skin and dampens her hair. The elastic wraps on her wrists emphasize her muscles. The flecks on her are fragments of grass. "Are you Nikki or Rose?" he asks, even though he thinks he knows.

"Nikki."

"OK Nikki. When you added that twist to your backflip a few minutes ago, and you kept wiping out, I thought you might hurt yourself or give up. Then you landed it, cool."

She smiles too, and shrugs, "It's who we are."

He sees the sharpness of her face, her lips finely edged. He's been around many tight-bodied attractive cheerleaders, and he tells himself, it's not her looks, her spirit is what's zinging me. Sure. Since last night, he's been wondering. "How come you twins go wild on your birthday?"

She hesitates as if she's deciding whether to trust him for this too. "Rose and I have an unusual family story," she says. "Our mother died giving birth to us. ... So we honor our mother on our birthday by doing risky stuff, like climbing flagpoles." She pokes him again. "We don't talk about it, don't want to burden anybody with it."

He fills a paper cup from the water jug, rinses his mouth, spits the rinse to the side, and sips slowly while she waits for a response. He's aware his own t-shirt is soaked with his sweat, wondering how he appears to her. "Both my parents died when I was eight," he tells her. "They were on their motorcycle, caught in a crash of many vehicles, not their fault. I got into football then, it was good for me."

She's looking at him differently now.

He keeps it casual, "Nikki, we could go out after practice. Rose can come too, if that would make it less risky."

"Just you and me," she says. "One date. Our tryout."

CHAPTER 5

While he was in prison, Bozeman had boomed with new condo buildings that attempted to be sophisticated and new trophy homes and new stores selling high-end stuff. The lawyers took him to a bank for cash and a debit card linked to an account they'd set up, because freedom often required money. Then a car-rental place where he used the Montana driver's license he'd acquired when he came here for football. The clerk asked him, "How about a Ford Escape?"

He liked the sound of it. "An Escape? Perfect." He slipped behind the wheel and began driving imperfectly, following the lawyers to a mall, to shop for what he needed, the modern basics — clothes and a phone and a tablet computer. In the hordes of Christmas shoppers propelled by Christmas music, people stared at him, maybe they'd heard about Dawson Koloko on the loose. As usual for Montana, only one Black person in view.

He told the lawyers he needed private time to call his

aunt. Not the whole truth. Separating from them, he cut through a store to buy pocket-size binoculars and walked out an exit and scanned the parking lot.

He spotted the one-eyed SUV idling near where he and the lawyers had parked. Using the binocs he studied the White guy in that SUV — pale blond beard and a winter cap that had a bill shading the rest of the guy's face and downward flaps covering the guy's ears. The license plate wasn't visible, wrong angle. The guy had binocs too, aimed this direction. Almost amusing.

He kept an eye on that guy while he called Rose, a number he knew from five years ago. The number had been disconnected — at some point Rose had cut ties.

Then he called Aunt Cecie in Long Beach. Video call. Cecie's face appeared on his phone, Cecie crying happy tears for once. "Dawson, you're out! I saw you on CNN. You're looking fine but that prison haircut needs a tune-up. If I was in shape to travel, I'd take the next flight to Montana to be with you." Cecie held up her right hand so he could see the bandage, "I fell off a ladder," she said, "stringing Christmas lights. Fractured some little bones. Need to pamper this girl for a while."

He unfurled his smile. "Cecie, you never fell off any ladder," he said. "Another dog bite?" Cecie's job — LA County animal control officer, the bureaucratic term for dogcatcher — seemed to require occasional bites.

"Mmm-mm. It wasn't a bad dog," Cecie said, "but the bite got infected. They're treating me with a frequent IV drip, super antibiotics. No indication of rabies. When are you coming home? I'm eager to give you a good long hug."

He knew what she meant. Guards in the prison visitation room had a rule: No more than five seconds per hug. "I'll be home soon," he said. "After I finish some work related to my case."

"You mean *Rose?*" Cecie said.

"Partly."

She ended the call with her go-to advice — a principle she'd made up, "Always remember, Dawson, do it right and do it strong."

He walked off his own tears approaching the guy in the one-eyed SUV. The guy peeled away, same as Rose had sped off from the prison press conference. He wondered, is that guy somehow connected to Nikki's murder?

~

Zhao Noodles, a brightly painted unpretentious restaurant on West Main, was his next stop, for more than lunch. He'd come to Zhao Noodles with Nikki and Rose often. Today with the lawyers he chose a table where he had a view of the guy in the one-eyed SUV, who'd tailed him here and was parked across the street. Lin Zhao, the owner, still hustled around working the tables and the front counter. Lin congratulated him for getting out of prison, and answered his questions about Rose.

"No," Lin said. "Rose hasn't come in here since Nikki got killed, and I don't have her current phone number or her address. Sorry, Dawson."

"You know a lot of people, a lot of customers, Lin — can you find out how I can reach her?"

"I'll make some calls while you're eating," Lin said. "You want your usual — spicy stir-fry?"

"My usual, five years ago. Excellent, Lin."

He remembered sitting at this table with Nikki and Rose. Their laughter, their eyes flashing. Now the lawyers tried to talk him out of looking for Rose and whoever killed Nikki. "Focus on your future," MaryAnn said, "not the past. We're buying you lunch, enjoy it."

"I have the feeling," he said, "if you two know how to reach Rose, you won't tell me."

"Rose lives with the sheriff now," Burns said, "so her address and phone are private. Listen, if you get into any new trouble with Rose, that would make it more difficult to negotiate a lucrative settlement. Just chill, Dawson."

He wasn't in the mood to chill. The seasoning in the stir-fry woke up his taste buds, which had been put to sleep in prison. When they finished lunch, he talked more with Lin, one-on-one. Lin had a newspaper open on the counter and tapped a finger on a story about a Chinese restaurant in Idaho getting torched, a hate crime. "The virus going up and down, have you heard some people call it the China virus?" Lin said. "Some of them hit this place," waving at the plywood over part of his front window. "Savages. About Rose? I called a friend who delivers hay to a stable where she boards her horse. Sometimes he talks with her on the phone about the hay. Here's her cellphone number. I can't get her address."

"Thanks, Lin." He laid three twenties on the counter. "To help cover a new window. I'm guessing a lot of cops still come in for your mooncakes, have you heard any new angles on Nikki's murder?"

Lin pushed the twenties back to him, "I'm rooting for you, Dawson. The cops talk about how they totally messed up the evidence in your case. Nothing else new."

Standing outside the restaurant, he called Rose and got her *leave a message* recording. The sound of her voice hit him hard. The last time he'd heard her talk, she was testifying against him in the trial. He didn't leave a message — that would be too easy for her to ignore.

~

Fresh snow in the air began to stick. The lawyers wanted to continue chilling at today's Bobcats football playoff game, as if he'd enjoy a triumphant return to the stadium where he used to perform. He went along thinking it could be a chance to confront the guy tailing him. They parked their vehicles in a lot near the stadium and joined the crowd walking by the snow-dusted statue of a wild bobcat and through the metal detector that limited weapons in the stadium. His bad leg, the sort-of-healed shank wound, ached. The cold was getting colder.

Most of the fans were going up the concrete ramps to the stadium's seats. The lawyers started up a ramp and again he separated from them with a half-truth, "I'll get us programs for the game." Glancing behind him, he spotted the guy from the one-eyed SUV, tailing him on foot now. He pretended he didn't see the guy and bought several of the magazines providing info about this game. Tucked the magazines inside his belt, hidden by his shirt and jacket — some degree of protection from any blade jabbing or slashing at his gut. Another prison lesson.

Behind an upward ramp he found the out-of-sight narrow concrete stairs going down. He'd taken these stairs two at a time when he played football here. He limped down the stairs now, down to the steel accordion gate that prevented access to the tunnel.

He heard the fans up in the stands beginning to cheer and the usual *rah-rah* music. He found the key tucked between the gate's frame and the concrete wall, same place the key was kept five years ago. The key worked and he slid the gate open enough to squeeze through. He left the gate open and limped into the tunnel that was more concrete with pipes and wires stretching along it. Until this moment he hadn't realized how much the stadium's innards resembled a prison.

He took off his cap and sunglasses, going by the dim light of the wall fixtures that had little cages protecting the bulbs. The tunnel turned left and then right. It smelled musty. He heard faint noises — footsteps in the dimness behind him. Good.

CHAPTER 6

For the tryout date after that first talk at practice, Nikki shows up in front of his dorm driving her spunky little Jeep. He climbs into her passenger seat thinking how lucky he is. She's wearing a yellow shirt that quits an inch above the jeans belted around her hips. As she reaches for the stick-shift, her hand brushes his leg. She suggests a sunset hike on a mountain on the edge of town. It's the dirt trail going up to the big letter M, a landmark formed by whitewashed rocks the Montana State students maintain. She hikes fast in front of him, pointing out the view of the valley.

"That's the Madison Range over there. And the Gallatin Range to the left, and the Beartooths in the far distance."

Up in the clearing for the M, she lands on a bench and he lands beside her, facing the valley from this high perch. When the sun is about to meet the horizon, it casts low-angle light that makes the rivers and ponds shimmer — reminding him of the Long Beach sunsets shimmering the ocean. "See those green buildings south of campus?" she says. "That's the apartment complex where I live."

On the bench she keeps brushing him with her hands and other parts of herself. As darkness comes on, the other hikers leave and the air cools. The night sky glows with more stars than he's ever seen before. He's tingling all over and hard in his jeans. He rests a hand on her bluejeaned thigh, feeling her firmness and warmth, but attempts no other moves, worried he might blow it.

She has two headlamps for the hike back to the Jeep. Then she drives him to Zhao Noodles for dinner. She touches him more as she gossips about strangers at other tables. "That guy dining alone? Dressed like a lumberjack in the denim shirt and knee-high boots? That's a designer shirt, and his boots aren't scuffed at all. The twinkle in his earlobe? Probably a diamond. I bet he's a relocated techie working remotely."

After dinner she drives him around, roaming as the conversation dwindles with the unsaid question. He's thinking maybe she'll veer off to some lovers lane or to her apartment. Instead she stops at his dorm. Still in the driver's seat she gives him a look and pats his knee, "We better say goodnight, Dawson." He realizes she's not even going to kiss him. "You're a big teddy bear," she says, so direct, "and I can tell you're a virgin. Not what I expected. OK, no rush."

Watching her drive off, he's thinking, she's not as loose as I've heard. Or not as loose with me as she might be with other guys. Maybe that's her respecting me.

CHAPTER 7

He limped around another corner in the tunnel under the stadium and came to the workshop. The light switch was where he remembered. He flicked it and brighter light came from overhead tubes that flickered, some problem in the circuit. The rest was also as he remembered. Tool lockers, steel workbench, a barrel full of deflated footballs and fractured helmets and torn pads. He used to come down here to repair his own gear — the broken clip on the shoulder pads that fit him better than other pads, the frayed chin strap on his lucky helmet. Now he looked around for any tool he could use as a weapon. No tools anywhere he could see. Padlocks on the lockers.

He stood by the barrel of damaged gear and took off his jacket so it didn't restrict him. His shirt hanging down still concealed the magazines tucked inside his belt. The fluorescent tubes kept flickering on and off like underground lightning. He listened. Heard only more of what was above him, the cheering fans and the music that meant the game was about to kick off, muffled by the layers of concrete. Probably many of the fans up there cheered for him five years ago.

~

His first game here, his first play, he's charged up positioning beside the quarterback, Reggie Mills, who's from Oakland. Reggie begins the cadence, with the whole offense cocked in stances, ready to go against the big Boise State Broncos defense. On "blue thirty-three hut hut" the center hikes the ball and everybody becomes a blur. Reggie rolls right, handing off to him. He cuts left and every step and hip fake feels good as he keeps the run angling forward — ten yards, twenty, cutting the last angle on the safety, crossing the goal line. Touchdown. Shocking his teammates and the fans and Coach Charlie Maguire, the guy who'd recruited him. "Fifty-eight yards!" Coach says. "That was awesome."

A week later, he catches a Cal Poly punt and breaks loose, crossing the goal line with a tackler hanging on him. Which causes Coach Maguire to gush another, "Awesome." His teammates start calling him Awesome Dawson.

~

The guy tailing him on foot came around the last corner of the tunnel.

"Whoa," the guy said. "You're a big nig."

He assessed the guy — about six feet tall and two-hundred-and-a-few pounds, pulpy nose from past fights, the beard so pale it was almost transparent, pale blue eyes that resembled zeroes. And the dufus hat and the need for racist labeling. Might as well turn that insult around, "White man, it's possible to be too White, and you're achieving it. Who are you and why are you tailing me?"

"Gee, I'm only looking for the snackbar."

"Did Rose hire you?"

The guy stepped closer and said, "Who's Rose?"

"If that's not it, then I guess you killed Nikki? And now you're worried that I'll be hunting for you?"

"Who's Nikki?" The guy slipped his right hand inside his jacket, "This has to do with prison, fool."

He didn't wait for the guy to finish pulling some weapon that evaded metal detectors. He grabbed a helmet from the barrel and threw it hitting the guy and threw another helmet and charged reaching for the guy's right hand that had the blade out now. A white plastic blade. He captured the guy's wrist and forced the blade outward and felt and heard *thump-thump-thump* around his belly and realized the guy was stabbing him left-handed with a second blade. He grabbed the guy's left wrist too and pressured both wrists and made the guy drop the blades. Then he jerked the guy around and up like a barbell overhead and threw him down on the concrete floor. Kicked whatever part of the guy was available. Give the guy credit for scrambling away.

He listened to the guy retreating through the tunnel. Couldn't run after the guy. The quickness lasted only a few steps anymore, with the bad leg. He collected the blades and the dufus cap off the floor — manufactured blades, not homemade. There was a market for sharp durable plastic blades that could pass through metal detectors. Then he opened his shirt and looked at the cuts in the magazines he'd belted to himself. Pulled the magazines out, checked his belly. Four of the cuts had penetrated his skin and there was bleeding, but the cuts were shallow.

He went after the guy best he could with the limp and the cuts. Up the concrete stairs to ground level. He saw the guy staggering through the crowd, probably a delayed reaction to getting thrown down and kicked. Other people noticed the guy. A cop appeared and began assessing the guy's condition and the guy collapsed. Another cop appeared. Cops packing pistols, acting authoritative. He walked the other way and glanced at the injured guy trying to wave off the cops.

~

He had nowhere else to go, so he tried to blend in with his lawyers in their seats close to the fifty-yard-line. He filled the open seat between them and shared their blanket as insulation against the falling snow.

"These seats cost a fortune," Burns said. "Scalpers jacking up the price. If we were any closer to the field we could intercept passes."

He heard a woman's voice begin singing the national anthem over the loudspeakers. He pulled some of the blanket up around his shoulders and scanned the stands looking for cops looking for him. He didn't expect cops would believe anything he said about the guy with the blades. He didn't trust cops to do anything right.

The teams lined up for the kickoff on the snow-dusted field. This Bobcats playoff game was against the Jackson State University Tigers, to determine who would advance to the championship for second-tier college teams. The Tigers, from Mississippi, were mostly Black players. A contrast because this Bobcats team was only one-third Black — the usual ration of talented players brought in from distant cities, mixed in with Montana White-boys who could run, catch and throw well enough to give the fans some of their own to root for.

The Tigers kicker did his thing. The football bounced unpredictably. The Bobcats ran it back a few yards. Soon he understood, the Bobcats quarterback had a good arm and one of the running backs had some moves. But the team lacked creativity. A run left. Then a run right or up the middle. Then a pass. Then repeat.

He used his binoculars on Coach Maguire and saw the same hairdo tinted silver, the same red cheeks that, according to gossip, bloomed with booze.

The cuts in his belly hurt. Shallow cuts could hurt more than deep cuts because nerves tended to be near the surface. The year-old shank wound in his leg was deeper. I'm one of the walking wounded, he thought. There are many of us. Then he told himself, *man up*.

In a while several cops appeared on a walkway to his left. He aimed his binocs at them. They seemed to be surveilling the crowd in general.

"What are those cops doing?" Burns said. "Somebody in the stadium needs a defense attorney."

"Everybody needs a defense attorney," MaryAnn said.

He told them, "Walking up the ramp, I noticed a guy who seemed to be having a medical problem. Maybe the cops are reacting to that. Maybe they're looking for some friend or a relative of the guy."

The game on the field accelerated. Every time the Bobcats scored, the stadium crew fired a cannon at the snowflakes in the air.

CHAPTER 8

One day Nikki drives him through Yellowstone National Park, a day-trip from Bozeman, to see the geysers and the bison, such magnificent shaggy beasts. She counts down to their first kiss, timing it to coincide with an Old Faithful eruption a few feet away, laughing about the obvious symbolism, "Three ... two ... one ... go!" The steamy water gushes up as her lips touch his, tender, delicious. Another day she ropes her canoe to the roof-rack on her Jeep and drives him up to Hyalite Reservoir, in the national forest. They launch her canoe and float out amid peaks that hold some of last winter's snow. She shows him paddle strokes and then she rolls the canoe deliberately, dumping them into the frigid water close to shore, what a rush.

On Peets Hill, the most popular trail in Bozeman, she surprises him again — "Cheerleader move!" — springing up to perch behind his head with her legs dangling down his chest, her thighs clamping his ears, not a come-on, kidlike fun. Her voice wafts down, "The view is better up here." So he walks the trail with her on his shoulders, greeting other hikers like that.

More and more he likes her spontaneity and liveliness. She opens him up for real conversation. When she orders a mocha in a coffeeshop, and he shakes his head at the barista indicating no mocha for him, she gets him to talk about money, how his football scholarship barely covers his college costs. She wraps her hands around his hands, a safe intimacy, and she offers to cover the costs of the dates.

"I'm not rich," she says, "but Rose and I get a share of Jules's royalties."

He asks, "Who's Jules?"

Her fingertips roam his palms, lighting him up. "My father," she says. "An oilman, drilling oil and gas wells. He's always encouraged me and Rose to call him Jules — the three of us as equals."

He's thinking of her mother's death in the hospital delivery room. She buys a mocha for him and he decides to open up more about his parents. "They owned a motorcycle-repair shop near the LA airport. I lived with them in the apartment attached to the shop, for my first eight years. They were kind to me."

That evening on a stroll through campus, sharing a bag of popcorn, she keeps it going, "You lost your parents in that motorcycle wreck, and I had no mother after I was born. We're both shaped by that. You're lucky your Aunt Cecie stepped up for you, acting so strong. Rose and I are also lucky — we have Jules, even if Jules spends most of his time in the oilfields. But ... you know how twins compete with each other? Rose and I compete for Jules's attention, trying to outdo each other being wild." She nibbles kernels one by one. "The math professor Rose is dating? Rose isn't really into that prof, she just wants Jules to tell her to knock it off." She confesses, she's majoring in art history. "That's utterly testing Jules's patience."

Which inspires him to reveal more. "I fool around with clay, sculpting animals, inspired by my aunt's dogcatching job," he tells her. "Not as challenging as art history." Provoking her to elbow him.

Of course there are uneasy moments, the inevitable conflicts. He wonders if he can interest this Montana White woman long-term, once he's not new to her. She jokes, can she really commit to a quiet Black guy who doesn't care for bluegrass music? The complications of a mixed-race couple, that can be exciting too. They're allied against the stares. They imagine they can deal with any opposition.

~

As the dating lasts into autumn, Bozeman's leafy trees turn bright colors amid the constant evergreens. Nikki takes him to an ice rink, attracting more stares. She's skilled on skates, zooming around in tights, and she teaches him. Once he's skating forward without falling down, she skates around behind him and hugs his waist to match her strides to his, synchronizing with him. Which is sexy.

That night in her apartment she says, "I'm tired of you being a virgin."

He tells her, "Me too."

She puts a headlamp on the nightstand and clicks it for a red glow and turns out the other lights. "I'll take the lead," she says. "Let's go easy, Dawson." She seems relaxed peeling off the tights and guiding his hands to undress the rest of her. He sees the fading bruises on her hip, the damage from a cupie stunt at a game two weeks ago — a cheerleader guy flung her upward and she stood on the palms of his raised hands, then that guy wobbled and failed to break her fall. She undresses him slowly ... and pulls his hands to her bare shoulders and down, inviting him to travel his fingers over her pale skin and her pale fingers explore his dark skin. He feels the growing connection to her flesh and her desire. Time slows and then, still standing, he's together with her, lips to lips, belly to belly. She nudges him onto the bed and kneels straddling him, her breasts barely touching his chest, drawing him into her and with subtle cries of effort and pleasure she gives all of herself to him as he gives all to her.

The golden feeling afterward is also new for him. There's more lovemaking as their friendship strengthens. One night as they lie naked and spent in a double sleeping bag on the roof of her apartment building, she brings up her flings with a few other Black players in the past, not shying away from that either. "I intend to have a special life," she says. "Making love to men who are so different from me, that seems special. I'm starting to think, you and me are more than special." She hears herself getting lovey-dovey and instantly cracks a joke.

Their togetherness attracts even more attention.

Especially when the university poses them as a couple, in their uniforms, and the photo lands on the cover of the magazine for the game against the archrival University of Montana Grizzlies. The text with the photo says, "The Bobcats' top runner, Dawson Koloko, and top cheerleader Nikki Fontaine are sweethearts — despite their very different backgrounds." Code for "despite the racial divide." Lots of people notice that.

~

Who can ever forecast a murder? When football season climaxes with a victory over the Griz, the full-on Fontaine twins aim their grins and their blue eyes at him, both talking at once, as they tend to do.

"Some Bobcats fans —"

"The hardcores —"

"They're taking over a sports bar in the Big Sky resort, next Saturday night —"

"They're inviting cheerleaders and players, charging everybody else a couple hundred dollars to get in, raising money for Bobcats football —"

"We rented a condo in Big Sky for the party night —"

"It'll be a blast!"

The condo looks good when they check in around noon. He and Nikki share the bigger bedroom, with a view of the ski mountain, and Rose gets the bedroom facing the forest. The afternoon is for skiing — Nikki and Rose on the expert runs and his first lesson on the beginner run. At dusk the party cranks up in the End Zone Saloon, a short walk from the condo. There's a band with dueling electric guitars and a mash of the wealthy fans who bought into mingling with players and cheerleaders. Everybody's dancing and feasting on ribs and drinking any booze within reach. No coaches in sight. The bartenders must be paid off, nobody gets carded.

Around midnight he starts to feel dizzy. The walls spin. He's about to pass out. Nikki walks him back to the condo.

Then, according to Rose's testimony, Rose walks into the condo around 2 a.m. and discovers Nikki strangled on the floor and him unconscious beside Nikki, as if he passed out drunk after committing a rage-fueled murder. There's evidence to make it believable — mainly scratches on his face that he can't explain when the deputies shake him awake, and shreds of flesh under Nikki's fingernails, which they test for DNA and match to him.

He thinks Coach Maguire will back him when the bust comes down. Turns out, Coach's priority is Bobcats football, straight-arming any bad publicity. Coach lines up with the cops and the Bobcats boosters — the same people who pay for football parties and stadium improvements and Coach's bonuses, people who want the Montana v. Dawson Koloko case tidied up quickly so none of this shit sticks to them. Coach never comes to the county jail to visit him while he waits for the trial. Coach never shows up in the courtroom. Then day after day, year after year Coach never sends so much as a word of support to his prison cell once he's doing a rest-of-his-life sentence. Nothing from Coach.

CHAPTER 9

The halftime show of the playoff game interrupted his thoughts. University officials staged a ceremony on the snowy field, handing a plaque to a famous Bobcat-for-life — Alonzo Davis, now a pro with the Seattle Seahawks. The crowd applauded while the scoreboard showed videos of Alonzo making plays. The current cheerleaders climbed each other to imitate Lady Liberty waving the torch, and the marching band wearing snow boots made organized noise, the Bobcats fight song.

Toward the end of halftime, Alonzo noticed him in the stands and yelled, "Awesome Dawson!" — that nickname teammates gave him during his single Bobcats season. Alonzo hopped the railing between the field and the seats and made a big deal out of greeting him, like it was up to Alonzo to welcome him back to the freeworld. Alonzo's grin was flashy but not convincing. A flying drone with a camera projected Alonzo and him up on the scoreboard, and Alonzo made it more dramatic with an exaggerated hug. Some of the crowd cheered, not a lot, most of them wondering about the justice system — was it a mistake to lock him up or a mistake to let him out? When the drone zoomed off, he introduced Alonzo to the lawyers. "Nice work," Alonzo told them. "And Awesome Dawson, I knew you weren't guilty." Then Alonzo peeled off to sit with prominent people who hadn't been convicted, up in a heated skybox.

He watched Alonzo beginning to party up there, then he watched Coach Maguire's current team jog onto the field for the second half. He had an urge to leap down and grab Coach, do some payback for abandoning him five years ago. But he knew it wasn't that simple. Some players did commit crimes thinking they were so exceptional they could get away with anything. Even his Black teammates had suspected he was guilty. Including Alonzo.

The game ended after sunset, a Bobcats win. He felt sympathy for the losers, another indication that football didn't mean much to him anymore. He watched the cops in the stadium pulling back to direct traffic. Nobody else tried to stab him and no cops busted him.

"We'll celebrate more tomorrow," MaryAnn said. "For tonight, are you OK being alone in a hotel room?" Her and her freckles and her purple-streaked hair. She read his thoughts and scrambled for her phone. "If you'd like some tending, after five years without, call the number I just texted to you. Bozeman's best escort service. I hear the women are clean, all vaccinated."

He told her, "One more thing on my wish list today. My cellmate, Billy Redcherry, he's doing time for robbing an heiress's safe. She deserved to be robbed. Billy had a lousy lawyer — he deserves better."

"Send me Billy's info," she said. "I'll look into the case, but no promises."

Solo, he drove his rented Escape to a drugstore for first-aid supplies, then to the hotel in Bozeman's version of downtown. No vehicle tailing him now, or none he detected. The hotel was five stories of timbers and glass and chemically rusted metal, built while he was in prison. The only available room was ground floor — vulnerable to anybody walking up to the window and breaking in. The door was flimsy, one good kick or a prybar, all it would take. Tomorrow he'd move, and he'd keep moving around to make it harder for anybody to locate him.

He stood at the bathroom counter for the bright lighting and the mirror, and opened his shirt to inspect today's wounds. Scabs forming in the bloody cuts. He applied alcohol and antibiotic goop, gauze and tape, then he inspected the plastic blades and the cap he'd taken from the attacker. Nothing indicated who the guy was.

Mirrors in prison reflected poorly. In this hotel's glass mirror he could see that his hair was still tight curls, naturally reddish-brown, and yeah, as Cecie said, the prison haircut was bad. His face — widely set brown eyes, blunt nose and chin, lips on the thin side — had hardened. Same for his body. He'd been in good shape for football, a six-foot-one juggernaut, and in prison he'd bulked up more, all the pushups and crunches and barbells necessary for his survival. The biggest change was the attitude in his eyes.

He started to call the escort service, and decided, not tonight. Thinking of Nikki. He dropped to the floor and did pushups until the belly cuts overruled his routine. He switched the TV to nonstop news, looking for himself. He watched a segment of medical experts discussing how the latest virus could reassert or a new virus could attack anytime. Then video of him at the prison press conference saying, "I'm heading any direction that looks good."

He kept the news on, in the background, and spread his case file on the hotel bed — evidence assembled by the Bozeman sheriff's detective and the prosecutor, not the lawyers' briefs about *blah blah blah*. Photos of the crime scene, Nikki's body sprawled on the rug, all too familiar. Close-ups of her neck, the mottled bruises where the killer choked her. Her lips swollen and bluish-white from lack of oxygen, her tongue protruding, her eyes red from burst capillaries, another sign of a bad struggle. The crime-scene reports and witness statements, also too familiar.

Some of the photos showed Nikki alive with Rose before the murder. He focused on those photos and called Rose's cellphone again. This time she answered.

He wanted to talk but couldn't.

"Who is this?" she asked. As if she suspected it was him. He listened to her breathing until she hung up.

Exhaustion crept into him. He left the documents and photos on the bed and took a defensive position, sitting on the floor in a corner where nobody could get behind him. Fell asleep like going off a cliff. Challenged again by prison dreams.

~

Nighttime in the cell, playing poker on the bunk with Billy Redcherry while the usual prison noises go on and on — unmedicated schizophrenics and agitators yelling and TVs and tunes played loudly against the rules. For gambling chips, he and Billy are using pictures torn from magazines.

"I'll bet a Buckingham Palace."

"I'll match that with Beyoncé in a bikini."

... Sunny morning in the prison art class. He's applying his attitude to handfuls of clay, sculpting another dog's head. This time a mutt with a golden's floppy ears and eyes that express a history of abuse. Only a hint of fear and meanness, a dog not yet ruined by the abuse ...

... Afternoon in the prison yard, several years into his sentence, his first brush with the huge White guy who has shown up recently. Perry Sebastian, dirty blond and built like a TV wrestler, standing across the yard with some suckups and a booming music player, probably another violation of rules. The music sounds strange in this setting. Chesty singers, a full orchestra. An opera?

Sebastian strolls over to him, accompanied by the suckups, one carrying the boombox. Sebastian's neck is tattooed with musical notes. Sebastian gestures to have the boombox turned down, and says in a gentlemanly tone, "You must be the Africoon from LA. That's Giuseppe Verdi's anvil chorus. Beautiful music."

"Long Beach," he tells Sebastian.

"Forgive me," Sebastian says. And to the suckups, still the gentlemanly tone, "This one came all the way from his urban jungle to play Montana football. Dawson Koloko. The sound of the jungle in his name. Mister Koloko imagined, if he played football well enough, we'd forget what he is. Mister Koloko even fucked a White cheerleader."

He decides not to tell them, modern racists should come up with better dialogue. They raise their fists to show him the numbers tattooed on their knuckles — 4 0 6, the area code for Montana phones. Those numbers are also the name of their prison gang, pronounced 4-oh-6ers. They're laughing the way people who enjoy cruelty laugh. He keeps his face blank, remembering Aunt Cecie's refrain, do it right and do it strong. They pull back. But later that day, near the cellblock's shower room where there are fewer witnesses, he hears opera music again. Sebastian and the other two come around a corner rushing him with clubs made from broomsticks, letting him know it's going to be severe but not immediately fatal. "The 406ers demand respect!"

A month later, in the prison laundry, they come at him with the first shank and more opera.

~

He woke up sweating, saw the darkness continuing outside his open curtains, 3:14 on the clock. "Sebastian, where are you now?" he wondered aloud. Because Sebastian got out of prison a while ago.

He forced his thoughts toward Billy Redcherry and used his computer to transfer money from his new debit-card account to Billy's prison account.

Then he put on his new jacket and cap, eased out of the hotel and began walking, almost for sure nobody following him now. He walked aimlessly through the winter night, his shoes crunching on the snowy sidewalks, his breaths puffing little clouds. He got into a neighborhood of houses that twinkled with Christmas lights, everybody else asleep.

CHAPTER 10

In the prison chow hall, Billy Redcherry takes the seat next to him and jokes about the slop on the cardboard plates, "Perpetual macaroni-and-cheese — the chef needs antidepressants." Billy leans closer, cautious about others hearing him. "Dawson, if you get a pardon and start your hunt, you'll need a gun. An untraceable gun. You'll also need intel on who's doing what and why. I know a Bozeman guy who deals in both — guns and intel. Leon Jackson. Tell Leon you're a buddy of mine, he'll do business with you. If Leon is still breathing when you get to him."

"Leon got the virus?"

"Yeah. Leon was a tech for hospital equipment, but when the virus hit and they ran short of facemasks, it ruined him. Long covid. He had to retire from that career. Now he runs a junkyard and he's one of us — a decent criminal."

~

Second day out of prison. He fired up the Escape at dawn, aiming to try Billy's contact for guns and intel. The snowstorm had moved on, leaving a foot of fresh powder on the ground. Sunrise came on without generating heat.

He found the junkyard past the town limits, where regulations withered. Grizzly Salvage. Within the fence he saw hundreds of vehicle carcasses — more of the wrecks that defined the world. He limped through the rows of destroyed Chevies on the left, Fords on the right, Toyotas in the next row. He heard coughing and found the source, a middle-aged White guy using hand tools to pull a bucket seat from a wrecked Audi. "Leon Jackson?"

"I only use my last name for signatures."

He noticed the roughness in Leon's voice, the labored breathing. A phone rang and Leon pulled it from a pocket. "Grizzly Salvage, Leon here ... what year Dodge Ram? Yeah, we got a tranny for it."

While the phone talk lasted, he studied Leon's high-mileage face and style, classy for a junkyard — the bomber jacket bearing the logo of the Bozeman hospital, good cargo pants and smooth leather boots Leon had polished.

"If you come for the tranny after today," Leon told the customer, "I won't be here. I'm moving to Boston. Tell the gal in the office, Leon said three-fifty."

Leon clicked off the call and nodded, "Dawson Koloko, everybody in Montana knows who you are. ... What do you want in a junkyard?"

"A gun and intel. Billy Redcherry steered me to you."

Leon resumed coughing, spit in the snow and rasped, "Aftermath of the virus — I'm not a spreader. Billy who?"

"The Cheyenne-tribe safecracker locked in the Deer Lodge prison. A couple others in prison also mentioned you. Nate Sensovia and Little Frank Nixon."

"Describe Billy — persuade me you know him."

"Little Native guy, granny glasses, a crumpled ear from getting bashed by a security guard at a Google exec's mansion. Billy donates half his take to tribal groups. We got tight in prison when a Whitey gang targeted both of us. We put in a request to be cellmates."

"What do you need a gun and intel for?"

"I'm investigating to find out who killed my girl-friend." He watched Leon pull out an inhaler and suck a blast, and went on, "I can't buy a gun in a store yet, because it'll take a while to erase my felony from the databases. And I want a gun that can't be traced."

"I don't have time," Leon said. "You heard me tell the caller I'm moving to Boston? I'll be in a clinical trial there, treatments not approved for the wider public."

"I might not have much time either. Yesterday a guy stabbed me, at the Bobcats stadium. Mostly he stabbed magazines I'd tucked under my belt. He said it's related to prison, then he ran off. I don't know him or why he wants to kill me. I need the gun and intel for both problems — to find whoever killed my girlfriend, and to not be killed by that guy or what he represents. Maybe they're related."

"OK. Lickety-split." Leon led him to an old Mercedes painted primer gray, popped the trunk and pulled out things wrapped in oily rags. Three pistols and an assault rifle, the kind madmen preferred for spraying classrooms and churches and grocery stores. "The last of my guns inventory," Leon said. "The serial numbers lead nowhere."

The Smith & Wesson pistols were a popular weapon around Long Beach, called *nines* because they fired 9-millimeter bullets. These nines had seen some use. The triggers and slides worked smoothly. *Ka-click. Ka-click.*

Holding the nines, one in each hand, he asked Leon, "How much for these?"

"For you — a friend of Billy, and what the system did to you — no charge."

Fist bump.

"I'll throw in two boxes of ammo and a cleaning kit," Leon said, leaning into the trunk and pulling out more things. "And *this*." A bulletproof vest. "If you get into gunplay," Leon said, "this vest will work better than football magazines. And the intel? I can give you an hour of research, phone calls and the Dark Web, right now. Your girlfriend was Nikki ... what was her last name?"

"Nikki Fontaine. Nicole." He spelled the names. "And I need to find her sister, Rosalette Fontaine, goes by Rose. Rose showed up at the prison when I got out yesterday, maybe she has new ideas about the murder. I have Rose's phone number but I need her address, to approach her in person — better than a phone call. Her address is hard to get because she married the sheriff."

Another blast. "My pharmacist says I'm using this inhaler so much, it'll make my breathing worse," Leon said. "My pharmacist is a wuss."

~

He wanted to try the nines while Leon worked the intel. He walked to a truck carcass dragged against a hillside and pocked with bullet-holes. Loosening up with stretches, he settled himself and squeezed off a shot. Felt the kick. His gun knowledge didn't come from gang-banging in Long Beach — Aunt Cecie took him to firing ranges and taught him to shoot. Same as learning to talk and read, Cecie said, got to learn guns, it's another way we communicate, a language of modern times. He cracked off more shots, trying both pistols. Snowflakes appeared in the air again. As the gunbarrels absorbed the heat of the shots, flakes melted on the steel. His accuracy improved.

Then he cleaned the guns and limped over to Leon's intel department, an old RV resting on cinder blocks. On the way he made friends with the junkyard dogs — a pair of Belgian Malinois, big and growling. He gave the dogs peaceful vibes and extended his hands, palms down, and they relaxed a notch and sniffed him.

Leon said, "You get dogs."

He saw Leon sitting in the RV's dining booth with two computers and a heater powered by an outdoor extension cord. "My Aunt Cecie is an LA County dogcatcher. She taught me things. What do you call these dogs?"

"Duck and Goose. I got some intel for you. The immediate threat, as you suspected, it's the prison gang, the 406ers. They always have some of their gangsters running around outside the walls, in between doing time, coordinating with those in prison. The guy with the blades yesterday, he's one. They still want you dead. Their head honcho is pushing it. Big guy with musical notes inked on his neck, uses opera audio to mind-fuck his victims. Guess you know Perry Sebastian?"

"Sebastian ran the attacks on me in prison. He got released before me. He doesn't play opera just to mind-fuck victims — he's also a fan of opera."

"Sebastian is a maniac."

"A gentlemanly maniac. Where can I find Sebastian, before he and his gang find me again?"

"I got nothing on where Sebastian is. People are intimidated by him." Leon paused again for coughing. "Also nothing new about the murder of Nikki Fontaine, but I got better intel on Rose. She dropped out of college after Nikki was killed. Bleached her hair blond and changed her last name to Faber. Most people don't connect her to Nikki's murder now."

~

Nikki, talking family stuff again as she drives him somewhere: "Rose and I are from two oilfield bloodlines — the Fontaine family based in Montana, drilling oil and gas wells, and the Faber family based in North Dakota, building pipelines. Our father is a Fontaine, our mother was a Faber." She stops for a red light and sketches some architecture on a paper napkin. "This is what Rose and I were raised on — a drilling rig," she says. "The Eiffel Tower, Montana-style."

~

"Faber was their mother's last name," he told Leon. "She died giving birth — twins was too much for her."

Leon nodded. "Rose started over. She works on horseback for ranchers and government agencies. And she didn't exactly marry the sheriff, it's worse than that — she married the sheriff's detective who sent you to prison. Kurt Vandyke. In a Las Vegas chapel, no publicity. Then Vandyke persuaded voters to elect him sheriff."

"... I didn't know Vandyke is the sheriff now. I still want to talk with Rose, in person."

Leon gave him the unlisted address where Rose lived with Sheriff Vandyke, and said, "I leave for Boston on Tuesday to try the virus clinic. I can only do one more thing for you," pulling out a flask, dull metal with dents. "Peppermint schnapps, my personal antifreeze."

He noticed Leon's fingernails had a bluish tinge that indicated a shortage of oxygen. He accepted Leon's flask, took a sip that tasted like a candycane.

Leon reclaimed the flask and sipped and said, "Too many ghosts in these smashed vehicles. If I was you, I'd definitely steer clear of Sheriff Vandyke."

"Probably that won't be possible. I expect I'll be meeting the sheriff at his headquarters," checking the time, "about an hour from now."

CHAPTER 11

He felt like that mythical Greek sailor who went from island to island gathering intel and dealing with what threatened him — witches and a man-eating one-eyed giant. He'd read about Odysseus in a prison library book about classical battles. Other convicts had torn out the last page of the Odysseus chapter, and he didn't know if the sailor made it home.

With his pistols stashed in the Escape's glove compartment, he drove toward the meeting with the sheriff, and tuned in satellite radio news, included with the car rental. Listening for any news related to his case. They were reporting the trend of White bullies attacking Asian-Americans across the country, trashing restaurants and some actual beatings. The usual White supremacy groups encouraged the attacks, supposedly as retaliation for the virus from China, and mainly because Asian-Americans would never be White enough. A demagogue leading a movement called White Pride warned all owners of

Chinese restaurants, "Go back to where you came from. Take your virus and your noodles with you." Classic line.

This meeting was in the county's Law and Justice Center, very funny. The lawyers waited for him at the entrance. MaryAnn seemed genuinely glad to see him. She wore another sweater and tapered jeans with her personal flag, the purple-streaked hairstyle. Burns, ever the Western celebrity, wore a buckskin coat and the city-style cowboy hat. They showed IDs to the deputy behind the bulletproof glass and passed through the weapons detector here.

They found four officials in the conference room, a lot of government firepower because this meeting was about money. He recognized the local prosecutor, Bernard Ness, tall with a shaved head, specializing in outrage on behalf of White citizens. Ness wore an off-the-rack suit and necktie, same as in the trial. The strangers, two marshmallow guys also in suits and ties, introduced themselves as the state's top prosecutor and the governor's chief of staff. The fourth — yeah, Kurt Vandyke. Pale red hair and muscled, wearing a Sheriff's Department shirt and the Sheriff's badge, black jeans and heavy-looking boots, good for stomping people.

Burns drew everybody's attention by placing his hat upside-down on the table and spinning it like a top. "For months we've been going 'round and 'round," Burns said. "Your governor released my client from prison to reduce the odds that we'll sue for multimillion-dollar damages.

I've dealt with governors in eight other states in similar cases — either I force a settlement or I win in court. I don't abide cheapness."

The governor's rep fiddled with his tie and said, "I'm authorized to negotiate. Once we agree on a number, the governor will push for the money when the Legislature opens its session in two weeks."

"One month — that's your deadline," Burns went on. "If you don't settle within that time, we'll drag you into court and showcase every miserable detail. Not only did your state crime lab bungle the DNA evidence, your Sheriff's Department and the prosecutor's office were negligent and racist assuming a Black man was guilty, without looking for other suspects. We'll get on national TV again, to talk about you acting like the bigots in the Klan or White Pride. I'm the good guy trying to save you from all that."

"Burns, you need a bigger hat to fit your large opinion of yourself," Vandyke said. An angry cut.

His thoughts drifted back to when he'd met Vandyke five years ago.

~

"I didn't kill Nikki. I didn't kill her," he tells the deputies at the crime scene. "Go look for whoever did it. Do your job." They snap handcuffs on him anyway and read him his useless rights and seatbelt him into the cage in a Sheriff's Department ride. He's sick and dizzy and trying not to puke in his lap. The night stretches as they haul him down the Big

Sky road and through Bozeman to their Law and Justice Center. Around 4 a.m. they march him into a cinder-block dungeon that's painted white and so brightly lit he wishes for his sunglasses. They place him in a steel chair and change the cuffs around to lock his hands to the steel table in front of him. They leave him sitting in the dungeon by himself for a while.

The steel door bangs open and a cocky White guy in a plaid shirt and black jeans comes into the dungeon, badge on his belt, acting friendly. "Hey Dawson, how you doing?" A limited handshake, without undoing the cuffs, the guy introducing himself, "Kurt Vandyke, plainclothes detective with the Sheriff's Department. Hey bro, let's clear this up. You thirsty? Want coffee? Maybe a Coke?"

He almost tells this Vandyke guy, walk that "hey bro" shit off a cliff. Instead he asks for a Coke because it might settle the nausea in his gut.

Vandyke brings a Coke and begins the interrogation, only Vandyke calls it an interview. Vandyke seems to listen. "I get it, Dawson. The last time you saw Nikki, she was fine, both of you in that Big Sky condo, then you passed out and when you woke up you were shocked, seeing her dead body. But —" Vandyke pulls out something he'd tucked behind his back, a hand mirror — "look at yourself. See the scratches on your face? Fresh scratches. Like from fingernails clawing you. Some of the scratches leaked blood. How did your face get scratched so badly, Dawson?"

"I don't know."

"Looks like Nikki scratched your face. Maybe you got loaded at the party and you wanted sex, but she wasn't in the mood. Or maybe you wanted it rough."

"No. I didn't have much to drink. I think somebody at the party drugged me. A knockout drug. A roofie or whatever."

"Is that an alt-country song — Drugged in the End Zone Saloon?"

"Whoever drugged me, that's who killed Nikki after I passed out, and that's who scratched my face to make everybody think Nikki and I had a bad fight. Or maybe two or three people did it. I'm still sick from whatever drug it was. Draw a sample of my blood before the drug wears off, it'll tell you what happened."

"Hey good idea, I'm into collecting evidence. Including, we scraped under Nikki's fingernails and found shreds of skin and blood. I'm sending those scrapings to the Montana crime lab for DNA testing. If it's not you under her nails, you might be OK."

"When you draw my blood for the DNA, test for drugs too. That will tell you what somebody dosed me with."

"But Dawson, even if your blood has traces of a knockout drug, or several drugs, how can I be sure you didn't take the drugs intentionally? How can I be sure you passed out before Nikki was killed?"

More time grinds by in the dungeon and Vandyke still doesn't bring in a nurse to take a sample of his blood. Instead, a deputy who talks nonsense swabs his mouth for his DNA. "Words of wisdom, from me to you," the deputy says, "never vote in any election and never buy flowers for any woman." They never do test his blood for anything that might indicate he's not guilty. In the trial Vandyke presents the crime lab's conclusion that the flesh under Nikki's nails matches his DNA, a mistake that lasts five years.

~

When the governor's rep and Burns got around to talking about how much the settlement would be, Burns asked for the national average for five years of income, plus two million for what Burns called "Montana-induced pain and suffering. That includes the repeated violence against Dawson in prison, and the possibility that he could've earned a fortune playing pro football."

"That's a big number," the governor's rep said. "Maybe too big for the Montana taxpayers who'll have to cover it."

"Dawson, what do you think?" MaryAnn asked.

"They can start raising money by selling the governor's helicopter."

The governor's rep adjusted his tie again and said, "Did Burns tell you that he'll take half of any settlement? That's why Burns is jacking it up."

Which almost made him laugh.

"Burns deserves half," he said.

"And a public apology to Dawson," MaryAnn said.

Burns spun his hat again as they talked more, close to a deal. Then the politics shifted to apologies and handshakes, everybody using hand sanitizer, more of the worry about viruses. Vandyke hung back to do the last handshake.

He tried not to picture Vandyke with Rose, for a moment thinking peace might be possible. Vandyke weaponized the handshake grip and growled, "I'm an old-fashioned cop and I don't make mistakes doing it. I'm not backing off — I know you were involved in Nikki Fontaine's murder somehow, more than as a bystander. Better go back to Long Beach, out of my jurisdiction."

He snapped back at Vandyke, you want to prevent my talking to your wife?

He snapped that line silently. Out loud he laughed in Vandyke's face. A long time coming.

CHAPTER 12

Separating from the lawyers again, he drove to the address where Rose somehow tolerated Vandyke. The house was on the fringe of Bozeman, up Bear Canyon where pavement turned to icy gravel. The driveway disappeared in forest, but he found a spot on the road where he could see some of the house in a gap between trees. A Christmas wreath decorated the front door. He parked on the road and limped up the driveway and read the note on the door, beside the wreath:

LIZ – IF YOU'RE READING THIS, YOU DIDN'T CHECK YOUR PHONE MESSAGES. SORRY I CAN'T GO RIDING WITH YOU TODAY, A JOB CAME UP – ROSE

He pressed the doorbell and knocked. No response.

OK Rose, he thought, first thing tomorrow.

~

He returned to the Escape and called Burns, confirming his next move, "Still on track with Frank Meinhardt?"

"Damn straight," Burns said. "Meinhardt texted me, he'll be ready to talk at two-thirty. Come to my place and I'll introduce you to him, like you planned."

Burns's address was a suburban hilltop. On the way there, he noticed a blue SUV seemed to be tailing him now. He transferred one of his pistols from the glove compartment to his jacket. Thought about the bulletproof vest. When he pulled into Burns's driveway, the blue SUV passed him and disappeared.

Burns ushered him in, "Welcome to my cabin," even though the place was ten cabins big, made of designer logs and expanses of glass giving views of the whole valley. Burns only used it for his visits to Montana. The caretaker and Burns's personal assistant and a paralegal — all women, Burns was that kind of boss — hovered around. A blaze in the stone fireplace radiated heat. Paintings of fish in rivers — Montana art — decorated the walls, along with a stuffed animal head that had glassy eyes and gigantic antlers, maybe a mega deer or an elk.

"When Meinhardt calls, we'll put him on the big TV," Burns said. "Try this whiskey. It's from a micro-distillery in Bozeman. I'll grill us some elk burgers. Since I began coming here to push your appeal, I'm into Montana hunting and fishing and skiing — and micro-distilleries."

He noticed MaryAnn being quiet while Burns showed off the bamboo fishing pole that was hand-crafted by some artisan in Idaho, and the shotgun engraved with Burns's name, and five-thousand-dollar skis for powder runs. Burns went on, "Dawson, did you catch that *60 Minutes* story about me? You're the tenth convicted murderer I've saved. I'm making deals for a book and a movie — that's where the real money is. I'll connect you with my agent, you can do your own book and movie."

"I hate prison stories," he told Burns.

"If you do a movie deal it would also be good for MaryAnn and me, since we'd get a cut of it."

MaryAnn shook her head no. "I've made it clear," she said, "I'll be OK with the public defender salary, on top of what I make selling candles." Again her public-defender sense of humor. "Dawson can have my cut."

Burns's phone buzzed. Frank Meinhardt calling. Burns streamed the call to the cabin's Wi-Fi network so Meinhardt's face and voice linked to the big TV.

"Frank?" Burns said. "We've got Dawson with us."

This was his first glimpse of Meinhardt. He already knew Meinhardt's role in freeing him, because the lawyers had told him step-by-step while he was in prison — how Meinhardt had a low-paying career as a Montana crime lab tech, and how Meinhardt noticed Burns's standing offer on the Internet, a hundred-thousand-dollar reward to anybody who provided info that led to overturning a murder conviction, and how Meinhardt's deposition, handled by Burns and MaryAnn, exposed generally sloppy procedures at the crime lab, and that persuaded the judge to order the new analysis of the DNA in the flesh under Nikki's fingernails, the proof that the original DNA analysis was wrong. Burns had paid the first half of the reward, and Meinhardt had retired to Mexico, now it was time to pay the second half of the reward.

On the TV screen, Meinhardt was roly-poly and bald. The Mexican setting showed in Meinhardt's jungle-pattern shirt and a primitive statuette on a shelf behind Meinhardt — some Mayan or Aztec goddess with a green snake coiled on her head.

"I'll transfer the money after we talk," Burns told Meinhardt. "Dawson wanted this chance to ask you some questions about the evidence."

Meinhardt nodded. "Hello, Dawson."

"Thanks for stepping up for me, Frank."

"I'm no hero. I thought you deserved a re-do on analyzing the evidence."

The pleasantries continued for a while and then he asked Meinhardt, "The flesh under Nikki's fingernails, the flesh she scraped off the killer — any indication who it really belonged to?"

"No match to anybody in the DNA databases. Maybe there'll be a match in the future — say if somebody related to the killer provides DNA for an ancestry analysis, that might point to the killer. Relatives have similar DNA."

"Did the crime lab gather any other evidence that might help ID the killer?"

"I wish, but again, no — not that I'm aware of."

He tried angle after angle with Meinhardt, and Meinhardt kept trying to be helpful, but it didn't pan out.

Finally he asked Meinhardt, "Any advice for me?"

"Go back to Long Beach," Meinhardt said, similar to what the sheriff had said but with a friendly tone. "Long Beach has great weather and a handy ocean, right?"

"I might have more questions down the line. OK if I call you again?"

"Fine. Burns has my number."

"Where in Mexico are you?" Burns asked.

"A place I'm renting," Meinhardt said — meaning, *I'll keep it private for now.* Meinhardt focused on Burns and said, still pleasant, "I've enjoyed working with you on this case, Burns, but if you screw me on the second fifty grand, I'll go to the media and out you. Your tipline will dry up."

"Frank," Burns said, "I'd never cheat you."

Meinhardt shifted to Spanish, "*Hasta luego, Dawson, buena suerte,*" ending the video call.

"Well," MaryAnn said. "Meinhardt is still telling the truth — he's no hero."

"He's a mercenary," Burns said. "Nothing wrong with that."

CHAPTER 13

Too much comes down to money, Dawson thought — pretty soon there'll be a price for breathable air. He drifted to the edge of Burns's deck and pulled out his binoculars to study the guys in the blue SUV, where they'd reappeared, parked on a lower stretch of the hilltop road. Both of those guys were predictably White with the common knit hats and sunglasses. He'd check them out when he was done here.

Now he wanted to talk to MaryAnn, in a different way than when he'd been locked up. Burns was occupied in the steaming hot tub on the deck with two of his female employees. MaryAnn sat on the rim of the fireplace, open to him. She'd switched from the whiskey to white wine. Her fingers were graceful cradling the wine glass.

He told her, "Remember the first time we met? In the county jail before the trial? Your briefcase had a price tag on it, and your dress looked like your mother made it. I thought they'd assigned me a rookie."

"I bought that briefcase at a second-hand store," she said. "Same for the dress. My young idealist phase."

They laughed together remembering it.

~

During the trial MaryAnn stands up beside him every time the judge enters the courtroom. The first day, she's wearing a gray skirt and a gray blazer. The next day, a beige skirt and blazer. She alternates as the trial drags on, letting the judge and jury know she has only two outfits appropriate for courtrooms, and both are plain. When the prosecution presents witnesses, she grills them in her cross-examinations, pointing out that none of them witnessed the murder. She attacks any claims there were problems in his romance with Nikki. Most of all she attacks the crime lab's bogus finding that the bits of flesh under Nikki's nails match his DNA, which the prosecution presents as absolute proof Nikki fought him that night.

As MaryAnn strides back and forth in the courtroom, she unbuttons her blazer and uses a purple handkerchief — more of her favorite color — to blot sweat on her neck and face, even though she isn't sweating much, another show of working hard. She applies herself physically to the defense, her youthfulness an advantage at times.

Then it's MaryAnn's turn to present her witnesses, the full defense, beginning with a Census official who reports the basic fact, among all fifty states Montana ranks last for the percentage of residents identifying as Black. Then a campus cop talking about the incidents of White students harassing Black students before Nikki was murdered, and a town cop talking about White townies doing the same. The BRING BACK SLAVERY *scrawled in the elevator of the dorm where he and other Black players lived, the insults provoking fistfights, the windshield of a linebacker's car smashed overnight. Then a gay guy who organizes Bozeman's annual march against discrimination testifies about undercurrents of local racism.*

MaryAnn puts him on the witness stand, at his request, so he can tell the real story of him and Nikki and how the romance was healthy. To reinforce his testimony, she introduces the Bobcats football magazine that had him and Nikki on the cover and more photos on interior pages, showing Nikki cheerleading and him running the ball and Nikki and him hiking together and studying together and volunteering together at the food bank — the high-profile mixed-race couple.

Finally MaryAnn attacks the DNA evidence, calling witnesses who collected and transported and analyzed the bits of flesh under Nikki's nails and the swab from his own mouth, but not Frank Meinhardt because he wasn't a whistleblower yet. She presses them to admit they were also dealing with evidence from many other cases. They all testify, reluctantly, it might be possible for evidence to be mixed up or contaminated, but they insist it was highly unlikely. The only expert witness the public defender's office can afford is an ancient Harvard prof named Kingsman, flown in from Boston, who testifies that many state crime labs have problems. MaryAnn asks her expert, "What kinds of problems?"

"There's a pattern — state crime labs tend to be chronically underfunded and overworked."

"How about Montana's crime lab — what are the stats?"

"Montana's lab suffers below-average funding and staffing, calculated per thousand residents. And as I said, the average isn't good."

"What happens when a lab is short of money and staff?"

"Studies indicate, any lab with those problems is more prone to make mistakes in analyzing evidence."

MaryAnn takes off her blazer to present her closing argument in her plain white blouse. She tells the jury — the all-White jury of course — "We've shown you how the analysis of the DNA evidence isn't reliable, and how the Sheriff's Department never took a sample of Dawson's blood to test for traces of any knockout drug, even though we think the murderer, or a partner of the murderer, dosed Dawson with some drug. We've established reasonable doubt, and the Sheriff's Department's negligence. When you find Dawson not guilty, the Sheriff's Department can look for the real murderer — maybe some violent racist not identified in the rush to charge Dawson. Do any of you believe Montana has no violent racists?"

Trial rules let the prosecutor — the outraged Bernard Ness — maintain his advantage with a rebuttal to the defense's closing. Ness, his shaved head slick as a bullet, points out that a local school district employs a Black guy

— formerly a Bobcats basketball player. And voters in Montana's capital, Helena, elected a Black immigrant to be their mayor, even though less than one in a hundred of that town's residents are Black. As if that proved anything. "We don't see many Black people in Montana," Ness says, "but when we do, we're not framing them for murder."

The jury deliberates for seven hours of heavy minutes. Then the foreman, a carpenter named Houck, passes the written verdict to the bailiff, and the bailiff delivers it to the judge so it can be announced. In that hushed moment of suspense, MaryAnn's hands are strong clasping his.

~

MaryAnn had gained experience while he did time. She seemed seasoned. Now she's thirty, he thought, and I'm twenty-four. The difference in ages is less important than when I was eighteen. He watched her face as she sipped her transparent wine. She asked, "What's your plan? What are you going to do? Sometimes I have the feeling, you're concealing anger and want revenge."

"Justice is what I want. Justice for Nikki and me. You're an insider, can you give me any steering?"

She seemed to give it thought while she had another sip of wine, then she said, "I haven't heard any new angles either. I do wish you'd leave it alone. Did you call the escort service? That might take the edge off you."

"I didn't call the service." He touched her arm. "Let's go somewhere without Burns, the two of us."

She looked flustered and said, "Really? I've been

through this before. ... Men who are locked up often fixate on female lawyers ..." She dug into her purse, pulled out a photo of a brown-haired woman. "This is Nancy Perkins. Nancy runs a coffeeshop near the courthouse. Nancy and I have been living together for three years. We got married six months ago. She's my wife."

He paused, then clinked his whiskey glass against her wine glass. "To you and Nancy. I look forward to meeting her." He meant it.

~

After that, he drove down the hilltop road imagining he might ram the latest guys tailing him. But they were gone. Around eight he checked into a motel on an interstate exit, different place than last night — his plan to make it hard for anybody to locate him. His new room, on the second floor with no balcony, seemed more secure. He whipped through his pushups, his belly cuts complaining less, then he called the escort service. An hour later, a knocking. He opened the door with his usual caution, saw a redheaded woman facing him. She'd unzipped her parka to show him her body in a leopard-pattern bra and matching panties and super-high heels.

But as soon as she saw him, she said, "Uh uh, no way."

She turned around and tottered back to the elevator.

He called the number again and said, "Send another. This time, one who's willing to fuck a Black guy for money. Probably you have at least one."

And they did. She was reassured by his condom.

~

Very late, alone again, he took up his own whiskey, coarser than what Burns served. Looking out the window at the latest snowstorm, he noticed a huge guy in a parka standing on the sidewalk. Hard to make out the face. Definitely White.

The huge White guy seemed to be staring back.

He put on the bulletproof vest and his jacket and slipped both pistols into pockets. Went out of the room and down the stairs. Sneaking around the exterior of the building, he used the bushes for cover. If any cop happens to come by, he thought, I better not be waving a pistol, because a Black person with a gun is surely committing a crime. I want to win this round without getting dragged into court again.

When he got near where the huge White guy had been standing, he had his hands in his pockets gripping the pistols ready to fire through the fabric. Snowflakes filled his eyes making it harder to see. Seemed the huge White guy was gone.

"Sebastian! Perry Sebastian!" he yelled. Imagining opera music, Sebastian's soundtrack in prison. "Let's cap it off! Right now! Here I am!"

No answer.

Retreating, back in the motel room, again he assumed a defensive position, sitting on the floor with his back to the corner.

CHAPTER 14

The combat in prison rages. Sebastian and another 406er, with more of the boombox opera, take him by surprise in the cell, probably they bribed another guard. Nobody has his back because Billy has gone to the visitation room to be with family. The punches and counterpunches seem to go with the opera singing ...

~

Third day out of prison. Again he got up before dawn. He hit this motel's little gym, flicked on the lights and placed the pistols on a chair, covered by a towel. He stood at the chest-press machine and set the resistance to maximum, gripped the handles, imagined punching Sebastian — *push the left fist, the right fist, left fist, right fist.* The TV across from the machine showed the early news. Two more Asian-Americans had been assaulted by pandemic-blame-game racists, this time in Phoenix and Memphis. Sane people were marching for tolerance, and White Pride thugs attacked some of them with clubs.

His muscles heating up, he punched forty reps, paused, and forty more, then he showered and put on the bulletproof vest again, layered between his sweater and his jacket. Sunrise began to dispel the darkness as he drove back to the house Rose shared with Sheriff Vandyke. He parked in his spot on the road with the partial view of the house and waited for Rose to appear. A Sheriff's Department SUV occupied the driveway.

~

Rose, in the courtroom for the prosecution. He has to sit at the defense table as she's up there in the witness stand. She's trying to be calm, in the gray slacks and the blue Oxford shirt, probably medicated with tranquilizers. The prosecutor, Ness, begins her testimony by showing the jury photos of her with Nikki, so her appearance as an identical twin adds impact — it's like the victim herself is testifying.

The prosecutor asks Rose about discovering the crime scene in the Big Sky condo. Her face tightens. They play the recording of her 9-1-1 call, so everybody can hear her screaming, "I need an ambulance! My sister's not breathing, she's been hurt — beaten up! ... Oh god no no no!"

Rose almost breaks as the recording plays. She re-composes herself and stares past the prosecutor to focus on the defense table — focusing on him, pure negativity. Everybody understands, she thinks he's guilty.

Prosecutor: "And Dawson was lying on the floor, passed out beside Nikki?"

"Yes."

A while of that and the questions shift to the time Rose witnessed him and Nikki having an argument, a week before the murder, trying to make that important.

Prosecutor: "What were the circumstances of this argument your sister had with the defendant?"

"It was on a Sunday night. I was with Nikki and Dawson and about a dozen other cheerleaders and football players. We were shooting pool in the Student Union. Nikki … she got mad saying Dawson was flirting with another girl. She walked out. I went with her because she was upset."

Prodded, Rose details the pool hall incident, how the players and cheerleaders sneaked whiskey into Cokes while they hung out and shot pool, how things heated up. She's telling the truth but with her spin on it.

The judge, a crewcut ex-Marine named Jack Sterling enthroned next to the witness stand, leans forward as if he's pondering the testimony. Rumors about Sterling say, he might carry a pistol under his robe.

Prosecutor: "To skirt the prohibition on hearsay testimony, we've established that your sister had a history of dating football players, before Dawson. Did she talk about these dates in front of your friends in the pool hall?"

"Yes. She told everybody, 'I go for interesting guys' — that's how she put it."

"By 'interesting guys,' she meant Dawson?"

"Yes. And other Black players she dated before Dawson."

"Black players were interesting to her — why?"

"Various reasons. For both of us, sometimes 'interesting'

meant dangerous. The Black players tend to come from big cities that have lots of crime. She could imagine it was risky to date them."

MaryAnn: "Objection — imagining isn't evidence!"

Like that, Rose put her spin on Nikki's attitude toward Black players too, making him feel sick. Eventually, in the full cross-examination by MaryAnn, it's like swinging a pickaxe to dig up a sidewalk. MaryAnn has to pry each word out of Rose.

"Ms. Fontaine, in the pool hall, you also drank the whiskey and Coke?"

"... Yes."

"That was risky behavior — if anybody got caught for underage drinking, they could be suspended from football or cheerleading?"

"... Possibly."

"The boys sneaking booze to the underage girls — those boys were White?"

"... Yes."

"So the White-boys could also be dangerous?"

"Objection!" from the prosecutor, and so on, as MaryAnn gets Rose to admit, Nikki got drunk in the pool hall, and Nikki liked taking risks in general.

"So when your sister had too much booze and accused Dawson of flirting with another girl, did Dawson get mad?"

"He must've gotten mad at her, after she tore into him."

"How you phrased that, you're not sure how angry Dawson was, or even if he was angry — it wasn't obvious?"

"Dawson doesn't advertise what he's thinking or feeling."

"Did Dawson raise his voice, yell, shake his fist at her?"

"... No. Not that I saw anyway."

"Had Dawson flirted with another girl?"

"... I don't know. It can be subtle."

"Who did your sister think he'd been flirting with?"

"Lindsey Mason, a senior on the cheerleading squad."

"What was Lindsey Mason doing?"

"When Lindsey took off her coat, she was wearing a bandeau top, leaning over the pool table to shoot eight-ball. That probably got the attention of every guy there."

"What did Dawson say to your sister about it?"

"... He told her what you'd expect — he wasn't interested in any girl but her."

"Did Dawson ask your sister to quit the whiskey?"

"... Yes."

"Dawson staying cool, that made your sister angrier?"

"... Yes."

"Your sister imagined Dawson was dangerous, at least when she was drunk — did he ever manhandle her?"

"Not that I'm aware of. Until he killed her."

"Your honor, this witness already testified that she arrived at the crime scene after the murder, and she's not an expert in investigating murders, please advise her not to speculate about who committed the murder."

More lawyerly volleys, and MaryAnn asks Rose, "Did you ever see Dawson threaten anybody else?"

"The players on other teams, he'd run right over them."

"Off the field, you ever see Dawson threaten anybody?"

"... Not that I saw."

"So your sister making a scene in the pool hall, implying that sometimes Dawson seemed dangerous — wasn't all of that your sister's drama?"

"Objection!" from the prosecutor.

MaryAnn gets Rose to confirm, the morning after the pool hall argument, he and Nikki made up. But the damage Rose does with her testimony can't be undone. She's drawn her conclusion mostly based on discovering the crime scene, combined with the prosecution's strongest evidence — the scratch marks on his face linked to the bogus DNA analysis of the shreds of flesh lodged under Nikki's fingernails. All her testimony reinforces the prosecutor's tale — the defendant is a poor Black kid who couldn't handle what he got into. A tale told many times about many Black kids. The prosecutor calls a few more witnesses who describe a few more of the arguments he and Nikki fell into occasionally. No romance has an easy time in a courtroom.

~

And here he was, parked outside the house Rose shared with the sheriff, again looking at the Christmas wreath on the front door. Again with both pistols in his pockets. Again he decided to stash one pistol in the glove compartment to appear a bit more sane. He watched as the Christmas wreath swung with the door opening.

Rose came out with Vandyke.

CHAPTER 15

From where he'd parked, he could see Rose crowned by a beat-up cowboy hat and the faked blond hair, still cut to the most basic style, dangling straight down to her shoulders. Her puffy vest had been repaired with a few inches of duct tape, and under that she wore a khaki shirt, along with jeans and cowboy boots that had also been put to hard use.

She still looked athletic and light on her feet, the older cheerleader ready to spring. She walked with Vandyke, who towered over her and kept his hand to the small of her back. Vandyke looked splendid in his Sheriff's Department cap, tight jeans and a leather jacket draped open to reveal the badge — lawman bling-bling. They drove away in the Sheriff's Department SUV.

He followed them for several miles until they stopped at a supersize barn where people were doing things with horses. She climbed out of the Sheriff's SUV and walked to Vandyke's side and Vandyke buzzed open his window and she gave Vandyke a kiss on his cheek.

He watched Vandyke drive off without her and thought, that kiss wasn't much. She walked into the barn and led a horse out of the barn — a large horse that was a psychedelic color, pale orange with brownish tones and a black tail. She seemed expert loading the horse into a horse trailer. Then she climbed into the Toyota pickup hooked to the trailer and began driving. He followed her. About a mile from the barn, she stopped to make sure the horse and the trailer hitch were OK, then she pulled onto I-90 east and went up the forested Bozeman Pass where the snow was deeper and the four-lane had been plowed and sanded for traction. Beyond the pass he followed her south on a two-lane along the Yellowstone River, between mountain ranges that resembled icebergs. The river was broad and the sky roiled with gray and white clouds and gashes of blue. He saw wild herds, he guessed elk, grazing where last summer's grass poked through the snowcover, their hides the same tawny color as the dead stalks. An hour of this Montana extravaganza and he followed her onto a gravel road thinly covered with windblown snow, going to a large meadow where the snow was deeper — her destination.

A crew of guys had taken over the meadow with trucks and trailers, breaking the snow crust where they drove and walked. Some of the guys wore official jackets — Yellowstone Park and the Montana Department of Livestock and Montana's wildlife agency — and some seemed to be ranchers. They were assembling metal railings, forming a temporary corral and two fencelines that fanned outward. They heaved saddles onto their horses and readied all-terrain vehicles.

Again he parked and watched Rose. She led her big orangish horse out of her trailer. Some of the guys hailed her and she got into a discussion with them, something about recent storms that were unusually bad and that's why they were out here in December instead of later in winter. They were gesturing at a hill where more big animals were scattered, not horses or elk — bison, nicknamed buffalo, maybe a hundred or more. Now he understood what she was doing today.

~

Billy Redcherry and him, on the top bunk sipping prison moonshine and looking at National Geographic magazines another convict stole from the prison library. "Check out the photos of Yellowstone Park bison," Billy says, "not far from my tribe's reservation. Here's mama bison nursing her baby, and papa fighting off a rival bull — presented as if they're totally wild animals. It's propaganda. Yellowstone bison are counted and monitored, tracked by satellites and studied up close, horns to tail and interior organs. The park's bison have learned to stroll through tourist traffic jams. Their numbers are controlled by roundups and executions and other intrusive methods. Tribes adopt a few that are trucked to reservations, there's still great spirit in bison, but ..." Billy flings the magazine across the cell.

~

He didn't know if this meadow and hillside were part of Yellowstone Park or some other public land or a private ranch, but the bison here must've wandered across some invisible boundary they weren't supposed to cross. He watched Rose saddle her horse. She clipped a walkie-talkie radio to her belt and put on leather gloves and swung herself up to sit on the saddle.

Then she spotted him. He got out of his Escape to begin anew with her. As she rode to where he stood, her horse seemed to get bigger.

"Dawson?" she said. She rode so close she brushed him with her boot in the stirrup and the hooves almost trampled him. He felt the ground trembling but kept his cool enough to tell her, "Good to see you again, Rose."

She yanked the reins to back away and the horse reared up and issued horse complaints and spun around under her. She stuck to the saddle and regained control and rode close to him again, "You think we'll be friends again?" she said. "Like nothing has changed?"

"I saw you at the prison press conference," he said.

She leaned down from the saddle. "This is harassment — or worse. *Leave. Me. Alone.* If you're still here when I finish this job, I'll call 9-1-1 again." She reined around and rode up the hill toward the bison. Guys on the other horses and the ATVs rode up the hill too. They all began trying to coax the bison down toward the fencelines they'd established, which funneled into the corral. The bison had horns and weighed as much as a ton thundering around and the horses thundered around and the ATVs roared and the crew yelled.

"Hey hey you beast!"

"Git! Git!"

The weather changed again, a low black cloud flowing over the hill, hurling down rain that created mud. His jacket was almost good for it. As he watched her ride, she put on a poncho without dismounting and continued in rain turning to sleet. The cloud grew nastier as if the mud had been flung into the sky. A beautifully ugly day. Some of the bison cooperated and some didn't. The sleet became snow, then back to sleet, then more rain that came harder. She was the only woman here and seemed better on horseback than most of the men. One of the ATVs flipped on rocks and the other ATV ran out of gas, and when more gas was added to its tank, it wouldn't re-start. Mostly they did the roundup on horseback.

The damp cold made his bad leg worse. He tried to walk it off, slogging around the outside of the corral. The shank wound was a long-term problem. He stepped onto the lowest rail of the corral, hands on the top rail, and looked at the captured bison. They were obviously upset. One had blood matted in its fur.

Still she rode her big orange horse on the hill, where a big bull charged at a rider near her and then at her as she steered her horse to dodge the horns. Even from a distance he could see the bull slowing — some injury to one of its legs. Then the bull refused to move no matter what the riders did. He heard the crew talking about the broken leg. The storm paused as two guys with rifles approached the bull and the shots echoed across the valley – *boommmm boommmm*, the second for insurance. The bull seemed to accept the incoming fire, as if it preferred bullets over the corral. It dropped into the mud.

Eventually she rode down the hill and swung off her horse. She looked exhausted and sad but she took care of the horse instead of herself, pulling off the saddle and dishing out water and feed. Then she climbed onto the fence next to him, catching her breath. Which meant she'd thought it over and was willing to talk, then she'd decide whether to call 9-1-1 again.

"You've got five minutes," she said.

CHAPTER 16

The bison milled in the corral, slamming against the rails so he and Rose felt the shudders. He studied her up close. Her hat had slipped off while she rode and the chin strap kept it dangling on her back. Mud dappled her clothes. He could see a slight trembling in her, from the chill or stress or both. Still her face looked sharp. Along with changing her hair color to blond, somehow she'd changed her eyes from blue to brown.

"I found you beside my sister's body," she said, the trembling in her voice too. "Your face was scratched and there was blood on her fingernails. The first DNA test seemed to confirm you did it."

"I don't blame you for anything," he said.

She shook her head, strands of her wet hair sticking to her wet skin. "Don't give me that. Both of us can't be innocent. Either you're a murderer or I screwed up by testifying against you. Your hotshot Texas lawyer got a new test of the DNA evidence — does that really mean you didn't do it?"

"Yeah, that's what it means."

"My husband disagrees. You know who I married?"

"The guy who built the case against me with shaky evidence. He must've pressured you to testify the way you did. Then he used the publicity to get elected sheriff. Making a career out of his mistakes."

"He does a lot of good around here."

From her tone, he thought, she's suppressing some other emotion about Vandyke. He felt the clock ticking, her time for him dwindling. He'd brought a crime-scene photo — Nikki dead on the floor of the condo — thinking it might motivate her to join him. He pulled out the photo, but in that moment, he decided it was too much. She asked, "What's that?" and snatched it from his hand. She took a look and flung it away.

He told her, "The killer — whoever did that — he's the one I blame."

"*Whoever?*"

"I'll fill in the blank, doing my own investigation. I'm guessing the killer is still alive and free. I've learned that's how the world works."

"It's already been investigated, by professionals."

"Your husband? He fastened on me so quickly, he never looked for other suspects. My lawyers? My public defender had no budget for an investigation, then my Texas hotshot only focused on DNA. I'm here to ask you to help me investigate."

"You and me? Teaming up? Great. What a great idea."

Dawson doesn't show his feelings much. She'd described him in those terms in the trial. He thought, show her more. "My low point in prison," he said, "some of the convicts were hassling me bad — mad-dog racists. ... It seemed the only way I could beat them was to kill myself before they owned me. ... Then I realized, that's what they wanted. ... I started standing up for myself better. I put some of them in the prison hospital. ... From then on, I had something to look forward to — I promised myself, if I ever got released, I'd figure out who killed Nikki, and I'd settle it for Nikki, and for myself, and for you, Rose. You're damaged by it too. ... You're out here acting brave but deep down, you're scared."

She slapped his face. Hard. It stunned him. One of the guys across the corral yelled, "Rose, are you OK?"

"I'm OK, Dave," she yelled without looking over there.

His cheek stung from the slap. He told her, "You're scared of the fact that murder happens. You're so scared, you married a cop and changed your hair and your eyes. Now you see, if your husband and other cops were wrong about me, they can't protect you from anything."

He thought she might slap him again. Instead she stepped close to him again and said, "I don't need men to protect me. So I still wake up in the middle of the night thinking it's happening to Nikki right now — somebody is strangling her and I can't do anything about it. At least I'm not deluding myself by thinking I can fix it."

The bison in the corral made more noise as if they'd figured out what happened to the bull. Their huffing breaths sounded primitive.

"I'm scared too," he said. "But you and me, we've got to fix it. Nobody else cares as much as we do. And you know more about Nikki than I'll ever know. Was there any guy who was seriously angry at Nikki? Maybe some guy from her past? Did she ever mention anything like that?"

She didn't answer and he went on, "I bet you have some of Nikki's stuff stashed somewhere, stuff you're keeping to remember her by. Maybe Nikki's phone? Notebooks, photos? Let's go through Nikki's stuff with fresh eyes, you and me together, maybe we'll find a new angle on her murder."

How she reacted, her expression, he thought, yeah, she's got Nikki's stuff.

He told her, "And let's go back to Big Sky, the End Zone Saloon where we partied that night, and the condo where the murder came down. To help us remember. I think somebody in that party drugged me to clear a path to murdering Nikki. You can help make a list of who was at the party, help me contact everybody to ask about it."

She looked down at the mud, and off at the turmoil of clouds. "You're asking for a lot," she said. "After five years of me being sure you're guilty."

"What would Nikki want you to do? I'm driving to Big Sky, right now. Come with me."

Again he noticed her lips trembling. One of her front

teeth was slightly crooked, about the only thing that had distinguished her from Nikki before the murder.

She said, "Nope. I can't."

He watched her walk back to the others. He found the crime-scene photo in the mud and called to her, "How'd you turn your eyes brown? Contact lenses?"

He thought, give her time to think it over. He texted his phone number to her phone, inviting her to contact him anytime she wished. Then he got into his Escape and headed for the crime scene.

CHAPTER 17

More clouds, ominously dark, flowed over while he drove back along the Yellowstone River. He phoned ahead to Big Sky and verified that the End Zone Saloon — where he might've been dosed the night of the murder — was open now. Then he transferred to the resort's lodging and reserved the condo he'd shared with Nikki and Rose that night. Always watching for anybody tailing him, he passed through Bozeman and took a different two-lane up the Gallatin River's narrow canyon between dark cliffs. The clouds decided to drop more snow, a bombardment of thick flakes that coated the evergreen trees in whiteness.

It struck him again, how so much of Montana life was outdoors, prison was a special punishment. Ice covered some of this river and some stretches had visible flow. He watched the river flowing against the freeze.

A blare of gas stations and shops announced the edge of Big Sky. He turned at the stoplight to go up the resort's main road. The zig-zags got steeper. The ski village was crowded with the beautiful people. He saw the octopus of ski runs on Lone Mountain, the dominant peak. The sun's farewell flared between clouds and peak.

He parked by the End Zone Saloon and went in. The decor hadn't changed — TVs on the walls, slabs of wood for tables and the bar, flames performing in the fireplace. The TVs were showing highlights of football playoff games, and more players taking a knee during the national anthem, and another Minneapolis protest march about how police deal with Black suspects, the sports commentators linking the games to the streets. About fifty people he didn't recognize were enjoying drinks and food and talk. A young couple threw darts at things hanging on the dartboard — their castoff antivirus masks.

He claimed a barstool where he could stretch his bad leg. The bartender swung by with a menu. *Mountain Man Pizza, Downhill BLT.* He ordered a local draft beer but when the bartender brought the glassful, it reminded him, maybe somebody slipped a drug into his last glass of beer here. He took this glassful to the bathroom and dumped it, returned to his barstool and scanned the list of bottled beers. Spotted an import from LA — Smog City IPA, his favorite when he was underage using a fake ID in Long Beach. He told the bartender, "A bottle of Smog City with the cap on. I'll open it when I'm ready."

He sipped and searched his memory for scenes of the private football party here the night of the murder.

~

The band rocks, three guys and two gals beating on guitars and a keyboard and drums. The saloon is packed with Bobcats teammates and cheerleaders and their dates and the fans who paid a couple hundred bucks per ticket to get loose with the team. The waitresses mimic football refs, with the striped black-and-white shirts draping down to their pantyhosed thighs, whistles dangling around their necks. Whenever somebody gets too loose, the nearest waitress blows a whistle. One dancer is a big furry Bobcat — the mascot costume. Soft footballs made of foam zip around. Nikki dances in a wispy dress that reveals her shoulders and legs. She takes off the ankle boots she wore for the snow, beginning to dance barefoot. When the music is energetic, she does slithery dance moves without touching him, another parody, and when the music slows, she clings to him so tightly it's also a joke. This party is about being high on touchdowns and booster money and booze and the possibility of sex. He and Nikki are such a public Black-and-White couple, everybody knows she's with him bigtime.

~

Looking around the saloon, continuing to force his thoughts back to the night of the murder, he remembered guys checking out Nikki and every move she made.

~

Alonzo Davis, the star linebacker, over there at the bar. Bobby Holt, defensive safety, dancing without a partner. Tyrone Allen, ball-hiker for the offensive line, leaning against the wall. Those three especially. Alonzo dated Nikki until she broke it off, and Bobby and Tyrone had asked her out and got her instant no thanks.

~

He pulled out a notepad and a pen and wrote: *Alonzo Davis. Bobby Holt. Tyrone Allen.* When he'd gotten to know those three back then, Alonzo was a badass Black warrior roughing up Bobcats opponents, on his way to being drafted by the Seahawks. Bobby, a White guy, also had a temper. Tyrone was all mellow Blackness, so much that sometimes it seemed to be an act. Maybe one of them killed Nikki in a burst of jealousy. Alonzo in particular had a big ego, displayed most recently in Alonzo's reappearance in the Bobcats stadium two days ago.

A lot of guys had aimed their eyes at Nikki — it was hard to look away.

~

Rose is also dancing in a wispy dress — the identical twins doing their thing. The original Rose, with her natural shiny black hair and blue eyes. She hasn't brought the math prof she's dated, dancing with different guys and sometimes solo in a way that's also a deliberate parody of sexiness.

~

He refocused on his list of possible suspects at the party, and added more players who'd ogled Nikki more than average. *Kenny Dorn. JuJu Johnson. Lamar Owen.* Then he concentrated on what he'd consumed that night.

~

A glass of champagne. He's sipping it as the party gets into gear. A subtle buzz. Then he's dancing and enjoying Nikki and having a glass of beer that lasts. Then a second slow beer with a few bites of barbecue. Then the music seems too loud. The beat begins to hurt him. He stops dancing and stands unsteady getting bumped by other dancers. He shakes his head trying to dispel the dizziness. Grabs the back of a chair to keep his balance. The music pounds louder and louder.

"You almost fell down," Nikki says. She touches his neck. "You're sweating. But your skin feels chilled," she says. "Want some ginger ale? Maybe that'll settle you." The ginger ale doesn't help. His head, the room spin faster.

"Like somebody slipped me a roofie," he tells Nikki. He's dimly aware she's spreading the word that she's going to take him back to the condo. She's hugging people and kissing cheeks, her style of saying goodnight. She tells Rose, "Dawson is down. See you later at the condo." Then she takes his arm and guides him out of the saloon.

~

Propelled by the memories, he left his unfinished beer and walked from the saloon. He had one of his pistols in a pocket and the stiffness of the bulletproof vest around his gut and chest. Retracing the route he and Nikki walked that night, he crossed an icy parking lot and went up a brief street to the Alpenglow condo complex. Limping toward Condo 47.

The murder condo.

CHAPTER 18

Nikki, jacked up on her ankle boots, ski jacket over her dress, braces him up against the condo door and taps the numerical combination to open the lock.

~

At the condo door for the first time since the murder, he tapped the combination the current manager gave him on the phone. He went in, remembering more.

~

Nikki walks him as far as the couch where he collapses, like there's a wave crashing over him. ... He regains consciousness with Nikki leaning over him. Nikki's jacket is off and she's stroking his forehead, asking questions he can't hear. ... Another wave crashes over him ...

~

Again according to Rose's testimony, Rose walked from the party to the condo around 2 a.m., then she called 9-1-1. He hadn't heard Rose making that call, because he was unconscious at the time, but during his trial, her screams in the 9-1-1 recording were replayed again and again, "I need an ambulance! My sister's not breathing, she's been hurt — beaten up!" The responding deputies shook him awake around 2:30 a.m.

~

Somehow he's lying on the floor instead of the couch, looking up at the ceiling. Two deputies squat beside him, putting their hands on him, saying things to him, but his hearing still doesn't work. His thoughts are cloudy.
He notices Nikki lying next to him.
She's sprawled, limbs twisted, not moving at all.
Her face swollen. Her dress torn.
Damn Nikki, what happened to you?

~

He took out the muddy photo — the one Rose flung down at the bison corral a few hours ago. The photo of Nikki dead on the floor. He'd pieced together other fragments of memories, with some imagining of his own.

~

A shadowy presence, coming into the condo while he's passed out on the couch ... hands grabbing Nikki ... she's fighting ... the hands lock around her neck ... the cold arrangement of the crime scene, the hands rolling him from the couch to the floor beside Nikki, ripping his shirt, slapping and scratching his face to leave him looking like he'd fought with her and passed out.

~

He rubbed his face, remembering how the mysterious

scratches had been raw and painful. There were still traces of those scratches on his face a week after the murder, when Montana's crime lab made the original mistake claiming bits of his flesh were lodged under Nikki's nails.

Now he thought, fighting for her life that night, Nikki did scratch her murderer — and it was not me. That's why the re-analysis of the DNA in those bits of flesh under her nails freed me from prison. Thank you, Nikki. And thank you my lawyers and whistleblower Frank Meinhardt, for forcing the re-analysis.

He pulled out more photos of the crime scene and kept studying how the condo had looked then. The floor that night was exposed hardwood with a lavender rug and the walls were peach. Flecks of blood on the walls and the floor and the rug. Since then, somebody had tried to wipe out the bad history and impose a fresh start. Now the walls were motel beige and the rug was a florid Persian knockoff. The furniture and the art had also changed.

His thinking was a kaleidoscope of memories and what he dreamed or imagined and what was in the photos and what was here now.

Hard to know what was real anymore.

He hung out in the condo another hour, groping for more. He pulled out photos of Nikki alive, remembering good times with her. That time she perched on his shoulders as he walked the Peets Hill trail. The way she looked when she laughed, kind of bursting open with no shyness. She'd offered so much of herself, she'd opened him up some. He remembered the fragrances of her that last night, at the party, as she clung to him slow dancing — something cinnamon mixed with her natural peachiness. Always did like the scents of her.

The condo's walls closed in on him — a feeling he often had in prison. He took one more look at the crime scene, what remained of it after the redecorating, and walked out.

The cold Montana night and him, again.

He heard a whiff of music — is that *opera?* — and something came at him from the left too quickly just a blur and slammed his head. It triggered a red explosion behind his eyes. He staggered and dropped and rolled away on the snow and regained his footing and pulled out the pistol.

Four guys in winter clothes and the opera, such a low volume he couldn't tell where it originated. They rushed at him from all sides like tacklers on the field. He used football moves hard left and hard right to break free of some and it was obvious they wanted to disable or kill him so he shoved his pistol against one's gut and fired, the blast muffled with the barrel tight to the target, and something struck his forearm knocking his pistol loose. One of them drew a pistol and fired soft-sounding shots — must be a silencer on that pistol. He fell with the impacts to his chest and belly where he wore the concealed bulletproof vest or anyway the bullet-resistant vest and rolled again to his feet and knocked that quiet pistol from that guy's hand.

The one he'd shot was down and the one who'd dropped the quiet pistol had a little baseball bat now, and the third one also had a little bat — kids' bats they could swing quickly. The fourth he recognized — Perry Sebastian.

The 406ers. Grinning like they always did during prison fights.

Crouching in a football stance he rushed through the swinging bats to slam into Sebastian, a knockdown, riffing kicks to Sebastian's head and dodging away as bats struck his back and shoulder. In the melee something Sebastian had in his hand, a glass jar, spilled its contents on one of the batters. That one began screaming and giving off a strange fog. *Acid.* The other batter silenced the screamer with several swings. They wanted to do it quietly so they weren't using guns other than the silenced pistol that also seemed to be lost. He tried to yell but one of the blows had struck his neck and his voice didn't work. He dodged again, trying to find a gap so he could run to his vehicle, where he'd stashed his other pistol, maybe fifty yards away, half the length of a football field, that's all. The next swing of the bat caught his good knee and that nearly knocked him down again. Then Sebastian rose up and bear-hugged him and hurled him to the ground. As he tried to roll and scramble, the next swinging bat found his head. He went dark.

CHAPTER 19

*O*ne of his first mornings living with Aunt Cecie, she's in the kitchen dressed in her LA County dogcatcher uniform, and she offers, "How about you stick with me today? You can skip a day of second grade to ride in my Animal Control truck." So instead of doing subtraction problems in school, he's watching her deal with the devilish pitbull that's been biting people on West 27th Street. She captures that dog with a noose on a pole, smooth as Serena Williams chasing a tennis ball. A tennis ball that has teeth.

From then on, the ride-along in Cecie's truck becomes a routine, once or twice a month. Dogs, cats, reptiles, monkeys — Cecie shows him how to handle many creatures out of their assigned places. She also shows him how to handle angry pet owners. One time he watches a guy twice her size throw a punch at her and she grabs the guy's wrist and spins him down. That's when she first tells him her principle, "Whatever you do, do it right and do it strong."

CHAPTER 20

S ometimes he welcomed his own fear. He'd learned to do it in football and especially in prison. When they rush you, demanding you suffer injury or violent death, the fear can pump you up. Fear can make you stronger.

But now, surfacing from this knockout, he felt dazed. Disconnected. Breathing required effort. His vision was blurry. They'd strapped him into the front passenger seat of a vehicle. The Ford Escape he'd rented. Going somewhere in the night. Cold air rushed around him, but not directly at him, the rear windows must be open. He heard singing from the vehicle's speakers, a woman's voice with instruments backing her. He tested his ability to move with the seatbelt binding across his chest and waist. His hands were trapped behind his back. Maybe they'd used handcuffs. Or maybe not — his wrists seemed more tightly bound than handcuffs. Maybe a plastic ziptie.

He took inventory of his injuries. Sharp pain at the back of his head where wetness probably meant bleeding.

Different pain at the bind on his wrists, and his neck and other places where he'd been hit and kicked and shot.

The blurred numbers on the dashboard clock said 1:14 — the middle of the night. Some hulk rode beside him, dimly lit by the dashboard glow — Perry Sebastian in the driver's seat. And the inevitable opera music through the vehicle's speakers.

The good news, Sebastian likes to play with his prey.

"What are you grinning about, Mister Koloko?" Sebastian said with the same gentlemanly tone Sebastian often used for committing violence.

Don't answer, he ordered himself. Smile and stare ahead. Stare at what the headlights reveal beyond the clacking windshield wipers. A road assaulted by heavy windblown snow, the storm getting worse. A two-lane with curves. Hillside rising steep on the right, all the trees hooded with snow, the forest of ghosts again. Iced river on the left. No other traffic, not this late in this storm on this stretch of road. Except, visible in the side mirror, a set of headlights close behind the Escape.

Sebastian buzzed the rear windows shut. Without the rush of outside air, there was an awful smell — some pungent chemical and somebody's crapped pants.

"Smell *that?*" Sebastian said nicely. "That's two dead men in the back seat."

He tried to flex his hands, his fingers already numb along with the pain at his wrists. The bind would be tough to loosen or cut, especially with the seatbelt pinning him within Sebastian's reach.

"*You* killed those men," Sebastian said, "pulling out your gun and wasting Brock, and knocking my acid onto Simon's face. We were only going to pour that acid on your footballing knees, to slow you down. *Simon's face!*"

Don't flinch. Don't let Sebastian see any emotion. Except the smile.

"Mister Koloko, you might be happy to hear," Sebastian said, "your death will be slower."

He sat silent and unmoving as the opera singer soared on high notes, Italian or some other foreign language. Sebastian's right hand eased toward him. He couldn't prevent Sebastian's hand poking the bullet-holes in his jacket, the hand unzipping his jacket to expose the bulletproof vest. "My shooter, Harvey — he only acted in self-defense when you started blasting." The hand's knuckles tapped his cheek. "Good thing you wore the vest. So we can go ahead with taking you to a place where we can video your slow death. A snuff video. Then millions of White people can watch you die, over and over again. Very fun. Would you like to talk it over?"

Especially don't show Sebastian any desperation.

"You see that humungous pickup behind us? In your side-view mirror? Maybe that driver will rescue you? Oh, that's Harvey. So no hope there."

Stare ahead. The next curve goes left and there's a few inches of snow on the road and the flakes in the air seem slower so the wind might be letting up some.

The hand grabbed his neck and squeezed so hard he had trouble breathing. Then the hand let go. But a weird cloudiness appeared around the edges of his vision and grew toward the center and then he saw nothing, only blankness. *Struck blind?* He couldn't rub his eyes so he shook his head and blinked and blinked and thrashed against the restraints and more blinking and he regained his blurry view of the road ahead through the clacking wipers. Taking another curve too fast, Sebastian skidded past a blur of grave-style crosses — two or three small crosses beside this curve, marking where people had died in wrecks. Another cross at the next curve. So this might be the road continuing up the Gallatin River beyond Big Sky. No other road in Montana had so many crosses.

When the next cross appeared Sebastian ran over it. "Who cares about those crosses?" Sebastian said. "The Jesus in the Bible was a dark-skinned queer."

He couldn't prevent Sebastian explaining White supremacy in the Bible and how unstoppable it was. He thought he might be able to shift his hands to the left enough to undo the seatbelt buckle while Sebastian spewed the holy hate — if his fingers still worked despite the numbness, and if Sebastian didn't notice him making the effort. Once he got the seatbelt undone he might be able to shift his hands to the right to open the door and roll out. His ankles weren't bound and if he landed in the snowdrifted ditch, he might survive to run into the forest and hide until he figured out how to free his hands.

His vision faded again. He blinked and squinted and again cleared the fog. Directly in front of his knees was the glove compartment, where he'd stashed his second pistol before the ambush. He looked at the latch on the compartment — a simple latch. Maybe even with his hands bound behind his back, if he could turn sideways and reach that latch, maybe he could grab the pistol, aim generally and shoot.

As soon as the vehicle slows or stops, or if Sebastian gets distracted by anything, make the move. First the seatbelt buckle, then the pistol, then the door.

Sebastian's right hand reached for him again. Becoming a fist, punching once, twice — igniting more red explosions in his head and again total loss of vision.

"I'm really liking this, Mister Koloko. How about you? How's that grin doing?"

His vision came back but felt even more fragile.

Do something to distract Sebastian enough to make your move. Sebastian wants a declaration of weakness so keep giving Sebastian only silence and the smile, maybe Sebastian will spew out secrets or make a mistake that would be an opening.

Sebastian boasted like he did in prison, "You and your heroic investigation of a five-year-old killing. Since I'm a smart White man, I knew you'd get around to the condo where your girlfriend got choked off. I knew you'd walk into my trap." The hand grabbed his hair and yanked his head around. "When Harvey and I are done making your snuff video, we're not leaving you anywhere you'll be noticed — that would draw cops who might link your death to the old killing. You've got to disappear — you and your vehicle. Everybody in Montana will wonder, what happened to that Blackie from Long Beach? Except those who watch the video, they won't wonder." Sebastian waved at the back seat. "Simon and Brock, what's left of them, they've got to disappear too. Keep all this off the radar."

Silently he asked Sebastian, why are you talking about Nikki's murder and the chance I might solve it?

Sebastian positioned a phone in a bracket on the dash, starting to record the snuff video. Sebastian's fist lit him up again. Then Sebastian shifted to talking about opera, how he got into it when he was sixteen driving a stolen Cadillac to Florida, "That Cadillac's radio was broken, it only played CDs and all the CDs were opera. By the time I got to Florida, I was humming along." And how opera was powerful and classy but was also all about murder with swords and poison, and cheating on lovers and so on. "This opera we're listening to — it's *Carmen*, starring Maria Callas, the best soprano ever. Carmen is a gypsy girl who fucks whoever's handy, finally a guy stabs her to death. Such a tragedy."

Around another curve the headlights shined across an overlook, the hillsides dropping back, the drifted ground rolling down to a flatness that went on and on. He thought he recognized the flatness — Hebgen Lake. He and Nikki had rented a late-summer rowboat here. A large body of water, miles across. Extensive ice on it now.

Sebastian held up the phone to record the view ahead, and drove slower, turning off on a side road. Harvey's headlights followed. That gypsy gal kept singing.

Wait for it. Wait for Sebastian to make a mistake. This must be the road along the lakeshore. A narrow road, snowdrifted now but manageable in all-wheel-drive. Driveways went off to cabins, some of which were as big as houses. A few of the cabins wore Christmas lights on the rooflines and porches but all the interiors were dark. The lake was too remote and bad-weathered to have many winter residents or visitors.

He noticed Harvey still following, as Sebastian tried one driveway and apparently decided it didn't go close enough to the lake.

He was patient as Sebastian kept switching the phone's video view — recording what was ahead and the situation in the Escape. The gypsy gal was in a battle now, against a guy who was also singing big.

Keep waiting for a chance.

CHAPTER 21

He watched Sebastian trying another driveway that curved around a cabin and a garage, dead-ending at the lakeshore. Nobody home here either. The headlights showed lake ice out as far as the beams reached. The slanting snow-covered ground must be a boat ramp. Sebastian stopped the Escape on the ramp and turned down the opera to a murmur and slipped the tranny into PARK and yanked the lever for the emergency brake, and Harvey's truck pulled in close to the rear bumper.

"I better tell my wingman to ride with us now," Sebastian said to the phone recording the snuff video. "This lake ice can be iffy." Sebastian climbed out and left the driver's door open, the opera still a murmur, the engine idling to keep the windshield defrosted, the phone in the dash bracket recording more.

Now. He leaned forward as much as he could to use his bound hands to grope for the seatbelt buckle. But his hands were too numb and clumsy and he struggled with the buckle. He realized that Sebastian, instead of walking straight back to Harvey, was circling around to this side of the vehicle. All he could do when Sebastian opened the passenger door, just lean away and try to kick as Sebastian said, *"Ah-ah-ah!"* like a scolding. He couldn't prevent Sebastian grabbing his legs and whipping a cord around his ankles and a quick knot. "Nice and tight," Sebastian said. "Nobody cares if you undo the seatbelt now, you can't go anywhere with your drumsticks and wings tied up like a Christmas turkey. And your spare pistol hidden in the glove compartment? It's not there anymore."

He told Sebastian, "Fuck you," as Sebastian slammed the passenger door shut. Over the combined murmurs of opera and the engine he heard Sebastian's footsteps crunching on the snow as Sebastian walked behind the Escape to confer with Harvey back there. He struggled anew with his bound hands trying to get a hold on the seatbelt buckle with the phone on the dash recording him. His vision went bad again and he heard Sebastian and Harvey talking about the snuff video, something about somebody they were doing it for, somebody who wanted it done here on the frozen lake. He blinked and squinted and his vision came back and he struggled with the damn buckle as Sebastian and Harvey walked forward into the headlight beams. He watched them trudge through the snowdrift at the edge of the lake and they stepped onto the bare windswept ice, testing whether it would hold two men. The ice held. He saw more of the ice extending way out. He gave up on the buckle temporarily and told himself, in football terms, *Hail Mary Play*. He raised his bound legs sideways over the console between the seats and captured the transmission shifter between his knees and tried to shift from PARK into DRIVE. The shifter wouldn't move. He realized what else had to be done and kept the shifter between his knees while he found the brake pedal with both feet and pressed down on the pedal which activated the safety release on the shifter and then using his knees he shifted into DRIVE and turned sideways all he could and stomped the gas pedal. The engine revved but the Escape only crept forward because he couldn't release the emergency brake. The two guys out there noticed. He had no more options and could only remain where he was, tied up sprawled sideways with his legs over the console and both feet on the gas pedal and the seatbelt around him and his hands trapped under him and his head against the window of the passenger door. Through the glass he saw Sebastian scrambling to reach the passenger door again. There was a lock switch on the inside of the door. He applied his chin to it as Sebastian yanked on the outside handle. Sebastian yanked and yanked on the locked door and now Sebastian had to walk beside the door as the Escape crept forward maybe a little faster, Sebastian slamming the window trying to break in to grab him once and for all.

"The driver's door, Harvey — it's open!" Sebastian yelled. Already Harvey was at that door climbing onto the driver's seat.

He had to raise his bound feet off the gas pedal to kick at Harvey's hip and he kept kicking and knocked Harvey off the seat. The gas pedal needed more stomping so he lowered his feet to the pedal again and the vehicle gained speed onto the ice with louder shrieks of engine and tranny against the friction of the brake. Harvey still had a grip on the driver's door trying to climb in again but Harvey slipped on the ice and screamed as the advancing rear wheels ran over him. The Escape sped up as the brake surrendered to the engine and tranny and ...

Where is Sebastian?

He turned his head to the passenger window again and saw Sebastian still holding the outside handle a few inches from his eyes, Sebastian running to keep up and slamming the window again trying to shatter it but the tempered glass wouldn't shatter unless Sebastian used something like a tire iron which Sebastian didn't have within reach. Sebastian couldn't run fast enough and had to release the door handle and dropped back out of view.

He kept his feet on the gas pedal. The Escape raced out across the frozen lake. Not straight ahead but skidding to the right because he couldn't steer.

Do it right and do it strong.

He strained to keep his head high enough to see over the dashboard. The headlights showed no obstructions ahead. The driver's door flapped back and forth because Harvey hadn't closed it. The four attackers were down to one, only Sebastian. Maybe Sebastian was running across the ice trying to catch up or maybe Sebastian would run back to Harvey's pickup and use it for pursuit.

He started laughing — somehow driving himself no-handed across a frozen lake with a White monster in pursuit, opera music still murmuring, this would be a great snuff video. He let up on the gas pedal a little so he could lean forward against the seatbelt to establish a space behind him, trying to restore any faint feeling in his bound hands and ordering his fingers to claw the seatbelt buckle. His vision faded and came back several times in quick succession. He thought he heard Sebastian running behind him. He told himself, can't be Sebastian yet, but decided to stomp the gas pedal again just in case, sending the vehicle into another rightward skid. Searching his memories for anything he knew about this lake, not much. A lake formed by a dam on some river whose name he couldn't remember. The dam was to the right. The water would be deepest by the dam, so probably the weakest ice and any holes would also be there — to the right, the direction the Escape was going. He clawed at the seatbelt buckle willing to tear off his fingernails.

He was somewhere in the middle of the lake now, whiteness all around. Any holes in the ice would probably look black. He flung himself against the seatbelt again and again and tried the buckle again and again. He saw the blackness of open water ahead and thought he heard ice cracking. In the side mirror he spotted headlights approaching from behind, faster than he was driving. As the lights got closer he thought it must be Sebastian driving the pickup.

"Fuck you Sebastian fuck you fuck you."

If he stopped Sebastian would catch him for sure. He drove, still with no steering, into the patch of open water and found, yeah, it wasn't a hole yet, just a shallow pool over ice that probably grew thinner and thinner ahead. If he didn't change his situation, either he'd drive to an existing hole or he'd break through the thinning ice. The buckle sprung open, relaxing the seatbelt. He clawed the door handle and rolled out.

Now he found himself lying in the shallow frigid water atop the thin ice. His hands were still bound behind him and his ankles were still tied and knotted. He watched the red taillights of the Escape proceeding without him, heard the opera going on without him. Seeing everything in flickers now. The problem with his eyes getting worse. The sound of cracking ice grew and he saw the Escape sag forward, the headlights angling downward. The ice beneath the Escape gave way with a sickening *whoosh* and the Escape disappeared. No more opera. He didn't dare move anymore. He saw flickers of the pickup's headlights approaching him but the pickup stalled as the ice beneath it sagged too and Sebastian jumped out and the pickup dropped through and disappeared with another *whoosh*. Sebastian kept coming, Sebastian walking with a handheld light sweeping the ice, Sebastian calling out,

"Mister Koloko, dear Mister Koloko ... where you at? Did you sink with your car? Or are you out here on the ice waiting for me to find you? ... My phone must've sunk with your car, so I'm using Harvey's phone for this light and to shoot this much of your snuff video, the best part ... Mister Koloko, dear Mister Koloko, where you at?" Sebastian advancing slow and careful now, Sebastian had to be afraid that his own weight would break through and Sebastian yelled "Motherfucker!" as the ice beneath Sebastian sagged and with a quieter *whoosh* Sebastian and his light disappeared into the deep.

He listened to Sebastian resurface with no light, listened to Sebastian struggling in the water, Sebastian not yelling anymore only flailing for a hold on the ice. Those sounds gradually lessened as Sebastian couldn't get a hold. The sounds changed to Sebastian coughing and splashing and then Sebastian went under maybe surrendering to the cold and the water and there was silence.

Now he was as alone as it gets, lying in six inches of painfully cold Montana water over failing Montana ice. He struggled against the bindings and laughed and laughed. Only three days out of prison and here he was, looking up at flickers of the stars that could be bullet-holes in the sky. The storm clouds were gone. He spotted a glow near the horizon — a crescent moon. The stars and the moon flickered off and on more rapidly. Then his vision switched off maybe forever.

Instead he saw scenes from his childhood.

~

He's the boy strolling through the greenery of Inglewood Park Cemetery with his parents who are pointing out the graves of Ray Charles and Big Mama Thornton and Sugar Ray Robinson and other notable dead Black people ... the boy with his parents in front of the motorcycle-repair shop splashing in the flow from an open fire hydrant, so cool and refreshing ... and the crash he's imagined so many times it's like he witnessed it, his mother driving the big Harley-Davidson, his father riding tight against her back, she leans into the curves on the freeway and plays the bike like a seventy-miles-an-hour piano, she's riffing on the throttle grip and the hand and foot levers for the clutch and shifter and brakes, now the vehicles ahead flare their brake lights, some Porsche fool causing a pileup, her only option, she lays the bike and herself and her man down on the pavement ... the sunlight is good coming in the kitchen window in Aunt Cecie's house, Cecie making skillet cornbread with bacon fat, Cecie cracks a joke ...

~

Hell he couldn't remember Cecie's joke.

He yelled, "Dawson Koloko was here! Dawson Koloko was here!" and felt the ice beneath him give.

PART 2

ROSE

Her first consult with the marijuana M.D. in Bozeman, she thinks he appears to be stoned. On more than pot.

"What brings you here today, Rose?" he asks.

She's tempted to tell him, you advertise your services as Doctor Reefer, what do you think I'm here for? Out loud she says, "I'm applying for a medical marijuana card. I know marijuana is legal for recreational use here, but I don't need it for recreation. I have medical reasons. Severe anxiety." Not mentioning, I'm married to a cop and it would be best if I have the medical card justifying my drug of choice.

"What sort of anxiety?"

"My twin sister got strangled to death. I discovered her body. Then I testified against her boyfriend and helped convict him. I'm dealing with anxiety from that. Not the average anxiety."

"Symptoms?"

She taps the list she made on her phone preparing for

Doctor Reefer, specifics of what she experienced in the last week, and reads the list to him: "Talking to myself, in my head or out loud. Talking to my dead sister. Sometimes I get the shakes, flashing back to the murder. Sleep is difficult, nightmares ... imagining I'll die any second. I'm not a basket case, not as bad off as the soldiers who suffer battlefield PTSD. I think of it, I've got the Montana Blues. Otherwise I'm in good shape — a hundred-and-six pounds and I can run a mile in seven minutes. Or seven-and-a-half."

Doctor Reefer pauses, and says, "I see your hands are clenched even though we're talking in a nonconfrontational manner. I see an occasional trembling. Allright, medical marijuana for your Montana Blues."

~

Watching Dawson Koloko drive off at the end of the bison roundup, she felt some of her symptoms surging. On top of that, she was cold and soaked and tired from hassling the bison all day in bad weather. And her hand tingled from slapping Dawson's face. "Gummy time," she told herself out loud. She reached for the marijuana gummies in her saddlebag and nibbled one, cherry flavor.

Something Dawson had said kept echoing in her.

You're scared.

Dawson, convicted for the murder, had the gumption to track her down, to insist he'd been proved innocent. Un*fucking*believable that he'd asked her to go with him to investigate the real killer. But he was perceptive, seeing what Doctor Reefer had also seen in her.

You're scared.

She tried to block that echo as she loaded her horse into the trailer. The others in the crew were also leaving. She stood still for a moment to watch the late afternoon sun breaking through the clouds, the rays slanting across the landscape, spreading honey over everything.

You're scared.

She imagined the small dose of edible marijuana easing into her bloodstream. Shortly it would relieve a fraction of her anxiety with a mild high that wouldn't be incapacitating. She fired up her pickup and drove the same bumpy road as this morning. When she made it to the paved two-lane, she pulled over to check horse and trailer. Then she sped up along the Yellowstone River, heading back to Bozeman, the heater blasting and twilight fading. With her phone linked to the speakers in the cab, she tapped her playlist for Bob Dylan doing *A Hard Rain's A-Gonna Fall*. Buzzed down her windows so her music could reach her horse's ears too.

"Hear that, Bobby D? The singer I named you for?"

You're scared.

As darkness obscured the scenery, she noticed a red glow on the dashboard — a warning light, some electrical problem. "Great, just great." She almost enjoyed saying that when things went wrong. The pickup seemed to be running OK at the moment, but she knew, from growing up around oilfield machinery, the warning light probably meant a failing battery or alternator. She turned off the music and the heater fan to use less electricity.

The pickup didn't die while she took backroads to the Bozeman Equestrian Center. She decided to turn off the engine — less of a risk this close to town — and led Bobby D to his stall, fed and watered him fully, brushed him and thanked him. He was big for a buckskin quarterhorse, twelve-hundred pounds, his withers level with her eyes.

"Good boy," she told him. "Good *brave* boy, dodging that bison bull."

Bobby D blinked his horse eyes and slapped her with his tail. She liked his colors, the orange-brown trimmed with black mane and black tail and black legs. She also liked his can-do spirit. She gave him a goodbye pat, left the stable and unhooked the trailer from the pickup. When she tried the engine this time, it cranked slowly — the electrical problem getting worse — then it fired up with the warning light still red. She didn't know if it would start again without jumper cables or a repair.

She drove several more miles and up Bear Canyon to Sheriff Kurt's house. She thought of it as Kurt's house, because he owned it when she married him and he was fifteen years older than she was, set in his ways, not up for changing much. She pulled into the driveway that curved between the trees, and parked by the stack of bland political signs from his last campaign — SHERIFF KURT : PUBLIC SAFETY. She saw he was busy in the garage with a bay door raised, skinning animals he'd collected from his trapline, with his smart speaker playing Johnny Cash's smoky voice, *I fell into a burnin' ring of fire.*

Lately she saw Sheriff Kurt more clearly than when she'd fallen for him — a brawny intelligent man, ruddy-faced and ginger-haired, not quite a redneck. He must've taken time off work to check his trapline on his snowmobile. She paused and watched him using his skinning knife. He was tossing the pelts onto a tarp. Blood smeared his apron and gloves. She spotted several dead coyotes whose tongues lolled out and a dead fox with that fluffy tail. He'd sell the pelts to a broker and they'd be fashioned into expensive fur coats and fur wraps and fur hats and fur mittens and blankets and rugs for those who wanted remnants of animals.

Sheriff Kurt — he enjoyed her calling him that, even though sometimes she put a spin on it. He noticed her and said, "Hey, Babe," and came to her with his gloved hands wide apart so he wouldn't spread the blood onto her. She let him kiss her. "How'd your bison roundup work out?"

Again she heard the echo of Dawson accusing her. *You're scared.*

She knew Sheriff Kurt would go at Dawson again if she told him about Dawson stalking her. Sheriff Kurt wanted command of everything, including her.

She thought, what would me *not being scared* look like in this situation?

She told him, "The roundup went OK. But we had to shoot a stubborn bull."

CHAPTER 23

Sheriff Kurt didn't ask for more info about her day. She went on anyway, "My pickup has an electrical problem. I'll try cleaning the battery connections in the morning. If that doesn't work, I'll take it to a repair shop."

"I'll check it out when I finish these skins," he said, with the helpful tone he often used, regardless how many times she informed him she didn't need his help.

Again she told him, "I'll do it myself in the morning."

He began to drain one coyote's blood into a bucket, as if he wasn't listening to her. The Johnny Cash song ended and his smart speaker began playing Dolly Parton, *I will always love you-ooo!* He liked all that conventional country western — men singing about women doing them wrong, and women, poor darlings, singing about dependence on men. She noticed a beautiful patterned pelt and asked, "Was that a bobcat? I've told you many times, I wish you wouldn't trap any more bobcats."

"Nature needs harvesting, Babe. I only trap stupid

bobcats." Two of his sayings that she was also tired of, more than three years into the marriage.

"I've also told you," she said, "don't call me *Babe*."

He took off one bloody glove to have a swig from his beer can and put the can down on the workbench. "Did you have a bad day or something? You said it went great."

"I need to shower," she said. She went into the house and got a beer from the high-tech fridge he liked, and a glass from the high-tech dishwasher he liked, and poured the beer and sipped as she walked past the giant TV that played a gazillion satellite channels, which he also liked. To her, the civilized house in the suburban forest was boring — another trait she and Nikki shared, being allergic to boredom. She shed her damp muddy clothes in the bathroom and as she showered, she was thinking, all the news about White cops overdoing it against Black suspects coast-to-coast, it's affecting how I see him. She toweled off and put on clean jeans and a fleece top, and brushed her hair. In the mirror she noticed dark roots showing and made a mental note to visit her stylist. Then she studied the reflection of her eyes. The last thing Dawson had said, *how'd you turn your blue eyes brown?*

She retrieved her brown eyedrops from the medicine cabinet and treated both of her eyes. The drops were less hassle than colored contact lenses. Going brown-eyed and blond, she could look in the mirror without Nikki's face reflecting at her.

Now she noticed something unfamiliar on the

bathroom counter. A hair clip that looked like it was made of silver and gold. She grabbed it. A claw-style hair clip, opening when she squeezed it and spring-loaded to close. It was distinctive, probably very expensive, stamped with the French CHANEL logo. She'd never seen it before.

"Great," she said again. She grabbed a clean jacket and returned to the garage and made sure Sheriff Kurt saw her placing the hair clip on his beer can on the workbench. She told him in the sweetest voice she could summon, "Some woman left this in our master bathroom. Probably she's wondering where she left it. Would you like to return it to her?"

He began spinning his usual lies and she cut him off, "I am really tired of you screwing around."

As he came to her pulling off his other bloody glove, she brushed past him and walked out to her pickup. Trying the ignition key now, all she got was a click. He didn't dare try to help her as she fired up his Sheriff's Department Ford Explorer and used jumper cables to start her pickup. She made up something to tell him, "I'll spend the night at Liz Porter's place."

Sheriff Kurt raised a hand for a solemn goodbye as she got rolling again.

~

A few miles more and she laughed. If Nikki could be here with her, Nikki would be laughing too. A mix of anger and amusement. She pulled out her phone as she drove and placed it in the cradle and called Liz. "I told

Sheriff Kurt I'll be with you tonight. If he calls, cover for me. I've got something else in mind."

"Sure," Liz said. "Are you thinking separation again?"

"Thinking about it. He fucks any female who falls for his badge and gun."

"Who was it this time?"

"I don't know. I found her silver-and-gold hair clip in our master bathroom."

"He did it at your place?"

"Probably in our bed."

"He makes me puke."

"Liz, are you missing a five-hundred-dollar hair clip?"

"*Ewwww* — that's gross!" Liz said. "If you're not going to spend the night at my place, where are you headed?"

"I'll tell you later."

"Want to go riding tomorrow?"

"Maybe not — I was on Bobby D all day today. Bye."

The red light on the dash kept warning her about the electrical problem. She had no solution for that at the moment. She kept driving. To be less alone, she streamed today's news on her phone, not drawing electricity from the pickup's battery. The weather forecast called for more snow and wind, followed by more snow and wind. Then a report about Dawson, some journalist at the prison press conference asking, "Since you believe you were framed, can you comment on why any Montanan might want to do that?"

She listened to Dawson answer, "Maybe the color of

my skin had nothing to do with it. But how Montana is, most of you haven't spent much time around Black people. Most of you see me only skin-deep. Or if something goes wrong, you revert to seeing me only skin-deep. Of course some of you, or people you know, are racists on purpose, never seeing deeper than skin color — Montana seems above average for that. Whoever framed me figured that most of you wouldn't see who I really am."

She turned off the news, to think it over without distractions. "Nikki, what do you think?" she said. Talking to a ghost — another habit she'd adopted after the murder. "Is Dawson telling the truth?"

The Gallatin River's canyon drew her, like an archery target on a hay bale attracts an arrow. A road sign said thirty miles to Big Sky. Dawson had said he'd be in Big Sky right now, revisiting the scene of the murder, trying to reconstruct what happened. She clicked into the text Dawson had sent her, which provided his phone number. She called and he didn't answer. She left a message.

"This is Rose. I've decided to join your investigation ... because I owe you ... and for Nikki and myself, like you said. I'm on my way to Big Sky. See you soon."

CHAPTER 24

Slithering up the canyon road in the wintry night, she passed through brief squalls of new snowflakes slapping her windshield. She took the Big Sky turnoff and climbed the mountainside to the ski village. Ahead was the condo where, five years ago on a night like this, she'd discovered Nikki dead and an unconscious Dawson. She fought off the memories to concentrate on the driving as the roads got slicker. The dashboard warning light was still shrieking silently about her electrical problem. She parked a block from the condo and sat with the engine idling, reluctant to turn it off here because she'd need another jump-start to get going again.

She saw Dawson's Ford Escape parked in front of the condo. Hard to see details with the sparse lighting along the street. She thought the person-shape in the Escape's front passenger seat was Dawson. An obviously huge man was stuffing a couple of things into the back seat. Maybe those things were two more men. Maybe two injured men.

The huge man squeezed into the driver's seat and pulled out, with Dawson still in the passenger seat. She watched the Escape's taillights going away.

Once more she remembered Dawson saying to her, *you're scared.* And Dawson adding, *I am too.*

A snap decision, she pulled a U-turn and followed the Escape's taillights. More difficult than she expected, because another vehicle — a king-cab pickup much bigger than her pickup — slipped in close behind the Escape. She followed both vehicles down the mountainside to the intersection with the canyon road. She watched the Escape turn right, going up the canyon road instead of left to continue descending toward Bozeman. The big pickup also turned right. She followed both vehicles up the canyon, toward the Gallatin River's headwaters. Beyond the resort's developments, the roadsides reverted to continuous forest, and the passage tightened, cliffs rearing up on both sides, tons of snow everywhere.

She wondered out loud, "What are you up to, Dawson?" And, "Girl, are your headlights getting dimmer?" She guessed she had warning-light anxiety on top of her PTSD anxiety. If a vehicle's electrical system couldn't even run headlights, it must be on the verge of total failure. To reduce the load, again she turned off the heater fan and the wipers and even turned off her headlights, trying to drive with only the light of the quarter moon and the natural glow of the snow on the trees and the ground.

She could still see the road, more or less. "Damnit!"

She kept driving with no headlights, hanging back from the two vehicles ahead of her, partly because she couldn't see enough to drive with closer spacing, and partly because she had a teeny tiny feeling it would be smart to hang back. More snowflakes slapped her windshield. At least, with the heater off, the windshield was so cold the flakes didn't stick.

Mile by mile, she kept on. Then around another curve she spotted the lead vehicle — Dawson's Escape — far ahead turning onto a lesser road that went west along the shore of Hebgen Lake. She knew the lake from fooling around here over the years. The high-altitude water was cold even in summer. The big pickup also took the turnoff, confirming those two vehicles were together. She kept following them, still hanging back with her headlights off.

The lakeshore road hadn't been plowed recently. With her pickup's all-wheel-drive she slipped and slid as she drove several more miles, then she saw the vehicles ahead turning into a driveway for a cabin. She stopped on the road a ways from the driveway, kept her engine idling and her lights still off to remain as invisible as possible. She wanted to see what they would do next. The cabin was dark and they swung around it to get pretty close to the shore, then they drove back out to the road. She felt a rush imagining they were coming back to where she was, and she ducked down inside the cab, a game of hide-and-seek that felt serious. They turned the other way and continued on the lakeshore road. All the cabins along the shore seemed unoccupied tonight but a few were strung with Christmas lights that twinkled. She continued following, watching them check out more cabins, couldn't understand what they were looking for. Then they found whatever they wanted behind one cabin. They drove all the way down to the shore and paused there.

Then her engine sputtered and died. She tried the key again and again. Not even a click. Nothing.

So the electrical system was dead. The snowy road in front of her sloped downhill. She glided a few yards in NEUTRAL and pulled off as much as she could and parked. She couldn't see the shore behind that cabin from where she was now, due to the contours of the land and the drifts, couldn't see what they were doing down there.

She told herself, "From now on, never go anywhere without a horse."

She listened. The landscape was so quiet, faintly she heard their engines idling down there out of sight. She took out her phone to see if she could make a call if she needed to, saw she was out of range. Gut level, she felt she needed a weapon. Not sure why, but she was a woman alone, and all this might be about the murder. She pawed through what she had behind the seats. The jumper cables, worthless if no other friendly vehicle was around to give her a jump. An X-shaped spinner wrench for changing flat tires. An old blanket. A knit hat. She put on the hat and opened the glove compartment and found her

Leatherman — a bunch of little steel tools folded into a steel handle. She unfolded the knife blade, less than three inches long.

"Right," she said, scoffing at the little blade.

She closed the Leatherman to store it in her pocket and reached up to adjust the setting for the ceiling light so any residual electricity wouldn't trigger that light when she opened the door. Then she climbed out and stood for a count of sixty seconds, making sure they weren't coming back this way.

She felt very on her own in the boundless penetrating cold under the black sky with the barrage of stars and the moon's sly grin.

They were still down there in two vehicles behind the cabin they'd chosen.

She walked toward them, hands in her pockets, one hand holding the Leatherman. Walking in the ruts the men's tires had made in the snow. She wanted to see what Dawson was doing with whoever else was down there.

"Yes, Dawson, I am scared," she said.

Many movies she'd seen had this scene: The girl walks into trouble because she's curious. Her boots seemed louder in the snow, despite her effort to move quietly, or maybe it was her imagination. She wondered if she should cut across the snowy terrain to save some time and surprise anybody who might try to intercept her, but she worried about the depths of the snowdrifts. She continued in the ruts on the road. She reached the driveway and began walking down it. She heard voices now, along with the engines idling down there, and some kind of faint music. Couldn't make out the words being said but it sounded like two men who weren't Dawson. She reached the cabin and walked closely along the side, definitely sneaking toward them. She saw the red taillights on the big pickup and the red taillights on Dawson's Escape, the two vehicles lined up one behind the other at the edge of the frozen lake, the headlights shining out across the expanse of ice. The huge man and the other were standing on the ice in front of the Escape. The faint music was coming from the Escape and she was surprised, it was some opera. An engine roared from idle up to thousands of rpm. She realized it was the Escape's engine but the Escape was barely moving forward. The huge man yelled and ran to the nearest door of the Escape, the front passenger door, and he tried to get in that door but it was locked from the inside. Simultaneously the other man ran to the driver's door of the Escape and tried to climb in and got pushed or kicked out. She understood, Dawson must be driving the Escape now and he was trying to drive onto the ice and away from the others and they didn't want him to. As the Escape went a little faster, the man on the left slipped and fell and the rear wheels ran over him as he *screamed!* ... The Escape sped up and the huge man hanging onto the passenger door handle couldn't keep up with it anymore. The Escape went off across the ice, curving toward the right, heading generally away from shore. The huge man walked on the ice back toward her. She flattened herself against the cabin wall and tried to be invisible. But the huge man wasn't coming for her, he was dealing with the one who'd been crushed and was still screaming — lifting the screamer and dropping him like a sack of mulch into the bed of the big pickup. Then the huge man got into the cab of the big pickup and drove onto the ice and sped off after the Escape. The screams faded with distance.

She guessed Dawson was in real trouble. She took out her phone again and double-checked and saw she was still out of range of any tower. She could use the phone's flashlight but the phone's battery was down to thirty percent and anyway the light would attract attention that could be too dangerous. She put the phone back in her pocket and took out the Leatherman and opened the blade, holding it ready as she walked toward the lake and gingerly onto the ice. Testing to see if the ice would support her, even though it had already supported both vehicles ahead of her — maybe the weight of the vehicles had weakened it. "Ice be nice, don't you dare break." The ice held under her. She could see the taillights and headlights of both vehicles in motion way out on the ice. The ice was flat and probably there would be no obstacles on it. But this early in winter, she knew, almost certainly there would be gaps in the ice and weak places and open water. She walked faster — "Silly silly girl." — and then broke into a run, conscious of the open blade in her right hand. She ran after the two vehicles and the men. After a minute or two or three she felt it in her lungs, the icy air and the work of breathing hard. She slipped and nearly fell, gathered herself and kept running, slipped again and sprawled on the ice. She heard the opera music again ahead of her. She got up and kept running with the knife out. She gained on them and could see the Escape slowing and then it stopped maybe because it had reached a weakness of the ice. Then the Escape sagged forward and plunged through and disappeared, its lights gone now. The opera also gone.

She ran faster thinking Dawson was in the Escape headed for the bottom of the lake unless he'd managed to escape from the Escape. She laughed at that and understood she was getting winded and crazy. The big pickup was still ahead of her, then the big pickup also broke through the ice and disappeared. The huge man hadn't gone down with it. He was walking with a light, then he broke through and thrashed in the water with no light. She thought she might or might not try to rescue him and when she got to the edge of the hole he'd made, he'd sunk and didn't come up. Now there were no lights ahead of her, only the vastness of flat white ice under the beautiful Montana wilderness night sky. She ran as fast as she could, everything she had, and got near where the Escape had gone down and her boots splashed through cold water and she thought she was going down but the water was shallow and she understood it was a sign of weakness in the ice but the actual hole was still ahead of her. She stopped moving — yes too scared to take another step — and then ordered herself to keep going forward, slowly now, shuffling her feet through the shallow cold water. She heard a voice ahead of her sounding strangely victorious.

"Dawson Koloko was here! Dawson Koloko was here!"

She yelled, "Dawson, it's Rose! ... Where are you?"

She heard no answer, only him continuing to yell "Dawson Koloko was here!" over and over, so the sound he made filled his ears and he couldn't hear her. She splashed through the water on the weakening ice getting closer to where his sound was, and still she couldn't see him. Then she noticed a disturbance in the water ahead and realized, he was lying in the water as he yelled his refrain to the sky.

She could see the shape of him and yelled again, "Dawson! It's Rose!"

He heard her and said with a calmness that was eerie: "I'm tied up and I seem to be blind. The ice is breaking. Don't come any closer. Save yourself."

Then he disappeared into the total blackness of the water and she understood, the ice had broken under him. She paused for a moment, made the next decision and ran at where he'd disappeared, the splashing around her legs getting more difficult and then she broke through too. The water was the coldest thing, all around her trying to keep her down. It would be so easy to let it happen. She fought her way back to the surface, already losing the ability to move. There was splashing to her left and she swam two strokes over there and grabbed Dawson with her left hand. He was keeping his head above water some of the time but that was all. She tried to support him in the water feeling less and less of herself and what she was doing. She still had the Leatherman in her right hand with the blade out and she tried to find where his hands were tied. She groped him and found his hands and got the blade between his hands and applied pressure. She couldn't keep her head above water anymore and let herself slip under and then she powered back to the surface and sucked in another breath of the icy air. His hands were free now and he was flailing around but he was even colder and more numb than she was and he was going down again. She grabbed him again with her left hand keeping the blade in her right hand and swam herself and him a few more sheer willpower strokes to where there was an edge of the ice shelf still intact. She raised the blade over her head and plunged the point into the ice and the ice broke. She swam into the break to reach ice that hadn't broken yet and swung the blade again and more ice broke and then again and again with the blade and then some of the ice held under the blade. Using it like a rock climber uses an ice axe, she pulled herself slowly inch by inch from the grip of the water up onto the ice. Trying to drag Dawson up onto the ice with her left hand, trying to get him up with her, battling the panic because the combined weight might cause the ice in this place to break too. She didn't know if she had the strength to drag him up onto the ice one-handed and she told herself she did have the strength because she could do eight pullups lifting her hundred-and-six pounds and if he weighed one-ninety to two-hundred and the water provided buoyancy she could drag him up once. She realized that while she was calculating she'd dragged him up onto the ice. He seemed in worse shape than she was. She knew time had run out on her and him a while ago and somehow that was very funny and she heard herself laughing like she'd never laughed before. She found herself back on her feet, standing over him, trying to pull him to his feet, and she realized, his ankles were tied. The blade was still in her hand. She could figure that out by looking at her hand in the thin moonlight and starlight, not by feeling it in her grip. She cut the binding on his ankles, and then as she continued to try to pull him to his feet, he could help support himself a little bit anyway. She got him standing up, and grabbed one of his wrists and drew that arm over her shoulder and began walking him toward the distant shoreline. Walking, staggering, sliding, falling down and getting back up, she kept him and herself going forward.

CHAPTER 25

Her reserves running on empty, she wrangled him to the shore of the frozen lake where three cabins clustered together but there were no lights. Slowing nearly to a standstill, so numb that everything required much more effort. He kept collapsing. She had to kick through the drifts as she half-dragged him to the nearest cabin.

"Dawson! Dawson!" she kept shouting trying to bring him to consciousness. She'd lost her phone and began yelling louder, "Help! We need help!"

She ordered her frozen hands to try the front door. Locked. Her wet clothes were freezing solid to her and somewhere she'd lost her hat. She left him slumped in the snow, fully unconscious, and used her elbow to break the front window and tried to climb in, scraping over shards stuck in the frame. She lost her balance and fell forward onto the floor of the main room and yelled more.

"Help! Help us!"

She stood up again, no more difficult than climbing a

mountain, tried a light switch and found the electricity was disconnected. She unlocked the front door from the inside and dragged him in and left him on the floor and began searching the cabin with the only light coming from the stars and moon through the windows and the doorway. She found a flashlight in a kitchen drawer and managed to turn it on. It cast a weak glow on the floor as if its batteries were almost spent. She used it as she continued searching.

"OK, no furnace ... no hot-water heater ... just the wood stove." She could hear her shivering making her teeth chatter. A landline telephone was mounted on the wall and when she lifted the handset she heard the dial tone, "Yes!"

But the handset slipped from her grasp and dangled on the spiraling cord. She let it dangle and tried pressing the buttons on the phone's base to call 9-1-1 and kept misdialing. Her fingers seemed dead and her mind was foggy. The flashlight died. The dial tone changed to the screech signifying the handset was off the hook too long. She gave up on trying the phone and kept searching for anything that might save them.

In a kitchen cabinet she found a box of wooden matches. She fumbled with the box, got it open. She ordered her fingers to light a match. She dropped the first match and then dropped the second and remembering her favorite Jack London story about the Alaska man freezing to death as he tried to light a match — "Fuck you

Jack London!" — she dropped the third match and then the box slipped from her grasp. She couldn't do it with her hands so she tried stomping on the box on the floor. She stomped to split the box open and tried sliding her bootsole on the loose matches against the striker strip on the flattened box and then the whole box began flaring. Using her booted feet as her tools she slid a newspaper from the stack near the stove toward the flaming box of matches. She got the edge of the paper burning and began managing the precious flame on the floor and positioned her hands over it. Feeding the flame with another newspaper she warmed her hands and then she shoved both flaming newspapers into the stove, maybe burning her fingers as she did it, and added wood from the pile, kindling and then bigger pieces, the growing fire crackling in the stove.

The landline phone was still screeching off the hook but she had to concentrate on what was most important, propping him up so the back of his jacket was against the stove and then she added more wood to the fire.

"Dawson! Don't die!"

The stove got hot, warmth beginning to fill the room and reaching him through his frozen clothes. She grabbed his shoulders and shook him, getting the blood flowing a little better in him and herself, kept shaking him and yelling his name. His eyelids fluttered so maybe he was a few degrees more alive than dead but he remained unconscious. The screeching from the phone felt like the whole world screeching at her. She used two hands to hang up the handset and got a fresh dial tone and concentrated on her fingers and succeeded pressing 9-1-1.

She told the dispatcher her name. "That's right, the sheriff's wife." She didn't know the address of wherever she was, but the dispatcher could pin it down.

~

Feeling they might not last long enough to be rescued, she sat on the floor close to the stove and drew him to her, his back against her chest. She imagined blankets somewhere in the cabin and it might be wise to strip off the cold wet clothes but she had no energy or willpower left and she felt a flicker of shyness. Still sitting behind him she wrapped her arms and legs around him, trying to capture the stove's heat for both of them. Feeling delirious she began to sing softly — *Puff the Magic Dragon*, an old Peter Paul & Mary tune Jules had sung to her and Nikki as a lullaby.

"... *Puff the magic dragon ... lived by the sea ... and frolicked in the autumn mist ... in a land called Honaleehe.*"

She sang the verse over and over as time passed. She couldn't stop her shivering and then through the open door she saw red-and-blue lights strobing across the snow. The emergency lights on some vehicle. The vehicle got bogged down in the unplowed driveway and the driver trudged the rest of the way yelling "Sheriff's Department coming in!" and slammed through the front door. She recognized him from some of the Department's social events but only recalled his last name — Deputy Atkins. Probably he'd come from the Sheriff's substation in West Yellowstone. He rushed to her saying stuff like, "Rose! What's going on?"

Then Atkins recognized Dawson and acted more surprised by the fact that she and Dawson were together. Atkins, getting professional. She kept her hold on Dawson and kept singing softly and shook her head indicating to Atkins that she'd explain later. She barely heard Atkins using his radio. Atkins found blankets in the bedroom but when Atkins tried to separate her from Dawson she shook her head again and continued to hold him so Atkins draped her and him together. Atkins stoked the stove more and an ambulance showed up and paramedics wearing antivirus masks took charge. She let them pry her loose from Dawson and they began their routines. She'd never passed out in her life up to now, even that time she got thrown from a borrowed horse and broke her leg on a loner ride in the backcountry above Cooke City.

"So girl, you are not passing out now," she told herself.

She lay quietly concentrating on keeping alive and awake while they cut her clothes off and wrapped her in a special paramedic blanket and specific heat wraps on her hands and feet where they suspected frostbite. Then they started an IV in her left arm and loaded her into the ambulance and loaded Dawson too and began driving toward the hospital in Bozeman.

Stretched out riding in the ambulance, she saw

Dawson stretched out beside her, still unconscious. She heard the siren and felt the speed of the ambulance and the bumps and curves of the road. Then the ambulance braked to a stop somewhere short of the hospital and the back doors opened and Sheriff Kurt climbed in. She closed her eyes to avoid him, acting like she'd passed out.

~

Around dawn in the emergency wing of the Bozeman hospital, they placed her in a wheeled bed and she began to feel the pain of frostbite. A doctor wearing a mask said actually she'd suffered frostnip, not as serious as frostbite. A masked nurse dressed her in a backless hospital gown and bandaged her frostnipped ears, and the tip of her nose, and her fingertips and toes. Protecting her flesh from further damage. It seemed masks had become a habit for the medical people but few of the patients were masked. She felt ridiculous in the bandages, especially the one on her nose and the one that wrapped around her head to cover her ears.

She didn't have to explain much about the cause of her injuries yet, because the medical people didn't ask many questions, as if they already knew or they thought asking would upset her. They kept the IV going while they also gave her apple juice and toast and pushed her bed to a private room in the back of the emergency wing. Private room for the sheriff's wife.

Around nine in the morning Sheriff Kurt came into this room, his hair more ginger-red contrasted with the whiteness of the walls and the ceiling. He seemed relentless in his sheriff outfit with the Glock on his hip. He stood by the bed where she was on her back with the IV needle still in her forearm. He captured her free hand and leaned down to kiss her, finding her lips below the bandage on her nose.

"How you doing, Babe?" he asked.

She heard the worry in his voice, and the other good feelings he had for her. She didn't remind him not to call her Babe. She squeezed his hand, reciprocating that much but no more, and told him, "I'm OK."

"You're all bandaged up. Does the frostnip hurt?"

"A little."

He stroked her cheek with his knuckles. "I thought I might lose you."

He intended it to be an affectionate remark but she thought there was a hard truth behind it. If she were dying, he'd see it partly as himself suffering a loss. She knew he wasn't that bad, but she felt something deep inside her had soured on him, something more than she'd felt in the past in all the arguments and his affairs with other women. She didn't know if she could recover from this new feeling.

Maybe sensing her reaction, Sheriff Kurt pulled up a chair and sat beside the bed, lowering his profile. "This is so weird," he said. "You and Dawson Koloko?"

She used the bed's electric switch to prop herself up to nearly a sitting position, more able to deal with him. She thought he was being as fair with her as he could manage. She began, telling him how Dawson had approached her yesterday during the bison roundup. And how Dawson had tried to recruit her to go to Big Sky to help reconstruct the last night of Nikki's life. And how she'd told Dawson no, then reconsidered and went to Big Sky to join him. And how she'd interrupted men who seemed to be kidnapping Dawson, men she didn't know. And how she'd pulled Dawson from the icy water of Hebgen Lake as the attackers maybe drowned. Hard to talk about so much all at once — the trouble involving Dawson and the bad men, and indirectly, her marriage — but it felt related.

As she talked, Sheriff Kurt got out a notebook and jotted. He listened to her account, then stared at his notes instead of looking at her.

"Quite a story," he said, and even in those three words she could hear his doubt and his anger rising.

CHAPTER 26

"Ignore the bandages," she told him. "Don't hold back, lay it on me."

"What the hell, Rose?"

There was a time when she'd enjoyed his gray eyes and the ginger of his hair. Now his eyes seemed difficult to read and his hair seemed to advertise his temperament. She told him, "Some men tried to kill Dawson. You have no right to be mad at me. Yesterday you screwed some woman in the bedroom you and I share — the woman who left her silver-and-gold hair clip behind, your latest fling, who was that?" She hated having to say that. She went on, "Where's Dawson, what's his condition?"

"He's still unconscious. If he wakes up, I'll be interviewing him."

"*If* he wakes up?"

"His core temperature is so low, if he wasn't an athlete, he'd be dead already."

Hearing that, she felt lost. "What's going on, Kurt?

Other than you and me."

"I've got a team at the lake collecting evidence. With scuba divers equipped for winter. We located the vehicles that broke through the ice, on the bottom of the lake, deep underwater. We pulled up four bodies, all men that were in or near the vehicles. We've identified three so far — all associated with the prison gang that harassed Dawson."

She pressed him, "Have you called in the state cops, or the FBI?"

"I'm in charge of law enforcement in this county."

"You always prefer to be in charge," she said. "You made a mistake about Dawson killing Nikki. You haven't confessed to that yet. Now I'm involved in something new with Dawson. You've got a conflict of interest, you shouldn't handle any investigation of what your wife is doing."

He stood and fingered the badge clipped to his belt, one of his tells, indicating he was about to assert his authority. "You're not a suspect," he said. "The state cops and the feds are deferring to me, as a professional courtesy. This is simple — the 406ers prison gang kept targeting Dawson, by deploying gang members who weren't locked up." Again he leaned over the bed and took her hand. "I wish I could've been there to deal with those assholes."

"You sound like John Wayne in the old Westerns," she told him, "except John Wayne never acted the role of an unfaithful husband."

She saw she'd scored on him. He shoved his hands into his front pockets, to brace himself up or keep from punching the wall. "When you get this negative about me," he said, "some of it has to do with who you are — *your* problems. You never talk about the PTSD but sometimes when I touch you, you're so tight I think you're going to leap out the window."

"I guess that's why you chase other women?"

She could tell he was tempted to say yes.

His phone rang and he left the room to answer it. When he came back he had a tote bag of stuff for her — fresh clothes, a new phone to replace the one she'd lost in the lake, and her driver's license and a credit card retrieved from the jeans the paramedics cut off her. "I had your pickup towed to the repair shop," he said.

"Thank you."

"We've identified the fourth body from the lake — he was also a gangster."

She asked him, "Will you please get an update on Dawson's condition?"

He decided to keep being helpful. Ten minutes later he came back and said, "Still unconscious. They hooked him to a machine that's warming him slowly. They'll know more in an hour. ... Rose, you're a hell of a woman even when you're being difficult. I'm sorry I've disappointed you." It reminded her of all the other times he'd apologized without changing his behavior.

"I better go," he said. "Work."

She watched him leave again, and shook her head, telling herself, "Who ever needed such a macho man? Guess that was me." Drifting into sleep.

~

The path by the Gardner River is a good walk on an August evening, with the nighthawks taking off from the ground to feed on flying insects. Dozens of sharp-winged nighthawks, swooping back and forth so near her, she hears their wings rustling. She imagines, if I reach up I might catch one in my hands.

She's on the path with Kurt and the nighthawks. Six months after the trial. All the time they've spent together, sharing the goal of putting Dawson in prison, has grown into a closeness beyond what's official. She likes how they're both Montana born and raised, sharing a love for the land and the weather and the wildlife.

The walking beside the river seems to be the climax of their day trip to Yellowstone Park. They're talking about how the air is almost warm, rare for an August evening around Yellowstone. The river has spent the snowmelt but there's enough flow for the pleasing sounds of water sliding over the boulders. The path has sandy spots that are comfortable underfoot, and sagebrush and pines. The moment feels right. Been a while since she could say that.

Kurt must feel it too. He turns toward her and silently with his posture he asks, ready? His hands reach around her for the first time, touching her back, making her aware of the thinness of her shirt on her skin, a light touching but with authority. His hands find the tense muscles around her shoulder blades and her backbone groove, sliding under her shirt, and he begins easing her whole body closer to him. She raises her arms around his neck, nerves firing. Sheriff's Detective Kurt Vandyke, enforcing revenge on my sister's murderer, the champion of virtue amid the bleakness of murder, maybe I am ready.

The sunset fills the sky with orange and red. The historic Mammoth Hot Springs Hotel above the river has a room available due to a canceled reservation. In the room she stands facing him again, giving in to her fate, her general philosophy since the murder. She lets him unbutton her shirt and slip it off her. He kneels below her naked chest and she lets him lift her left foot to slip off her hiking shoe and sock, and then her right foot. She lets his hands undo her belt and zipper, lets him slide the jeans down, lets him remove the jeans one leg at a time. She lets him slide her panties down and off. He stands, still in his clothes, and pulls her firmly against him, her bare nipples touching the roughness of his wool shirt, her bare thighs touching his jeans, her groin barely touching him, a tickle.

She lets him proceed as his manhood emerges from his fly. He remains standing and lifts her by her thighs to straddle him and he's got her entirely off the ground as he drives himself inside her and he brings her along right with him. She hasn't been with a man since the murder and never with a man who seems this powerful. Her toes curl on the far side of him, all her muscles tensing and releasing and she actually sees stars inside her eyelids. She rests with him on the bed, briefly, then he removes his clothes and starts again. He's the realest thing for her since the murder, seeming to reconnect her with the world.

~

When the hospital crew graduated her from the emergency wing, early afternoon, they pushed her bed into an elevator that had a cardboard Santa Claus stuck to one wall. They delivered her to a private room on the second floor. This room had a window with a view of the Bridger Range, where sunlight made the fresh snow brilliant. The TV was on, news about a mentally-ill Black man dying kind of accidentally in police gunfire, this time in Seattle. She turned off the TV, so trashed that she nodded off again. She woke up when more people she didn't want to see came into the room.

Dawson's defense lawyers. She searched her memory for their names.

Langdon Burns and MaryAnn Meloy.

Burns was wearing one of his custom Texas suits and the little cowboy hat. MaryAnn Meloy had that lilac hair-streak and a leather vest over a corduroy shirt and jeans. They made her more aware of her bandages and her backless hospital gown under the bedcovers. These lawyers had been her adversaries when she'd aligned with the prosecution. Now they handed her their business cards and said nice things. *Good job pulling Dawson out of the lake ... Call me MaryAnn please ... Everybody calls me*

Burns, especially my friends. They asked her what happened last night, just as Sheriff Kurt had asked. She filled them in too, still didn't trust them.

"Dawson's version of the events last night jibes with yours," Burns said.

"Dawson woke up?"

"We made sure we were present," Burns said, "when the sheriff — your pissed-off husband — interviewed Dawson an hour ago."

"I need to talk with Dawson — what room is he in?"

Burns looked at MaryAnn, some silent messaging, and Burns said, "Dawson has been obsessed with investigating your sister's murder. As if that would heal the injustice he suffered. We advised him to drop it."

"I don't want him to drop it. I want to find who killed my sister and I'm going to help him investigate it."

She watched them getting more uncomfortable.

"Dawson is in no shape to investigate anything now," MaryAnn said. "He has internal bruises in a part of his brain that controls his vision. He has all his mental faculties except ... he's blind. They don't know how long it'll take for the brain swelling to diminish. He might or might not recover his eyesight."

She processed that. Last night on the ice Dawson yelled that he'd been blinded. Again she asked, "What room?"

"Probably he already left the hospital."

"He's blind and he already left?"

Burns took off his hat and ran his fingers through his hair, figuring out how much to say. "I phoned his Aunt Cecie in Long Beach as soon as I heard he'd been attacked, and Cecie took the first flight here — a ticket I paid for. She's taking him back to Long Beach and a paramedic is making the trip with them."

She unhooked her IV. *"What room?"*

They told her Dawson's room number, or former room number, and she climbed out of bed and tried walking, unsteady at first with the bandages on her toes. They said *take it easy!* and *whoa whoa whoa!* but she brushed them off and made her way along the hallway to Dawson's room.

Nobody in the room. She braced herself in the doorway and noticed the IV stub still taped to her arm. She made it to the elevator and down to the lobby, with the lawyers hovering around her.

Dawson wasn't in the lobby. She walked out the hospital's front door and the lawyers stopped at the hospital desk to snitch her off. She saw Dawson getting loaded into an ambulance. He wore bandages like hers, and sunglasses. A paramedic was doing the loading, assisted by a middle-aged Black woman who had one wrist bandaged. They didn't notice her as she walked toward them. They began to pull out.

She yelled, "Dawson! Hold on!" and tried running after the ambulance like she'd chased after him last night on the frozen lake, and found she hadn't recovered enough to run. She slowed and felt the solid cold of the pavement under her bare feet and a breeze chilled her spine and she realized, she was wearing only the hospital gown. She watched the ambulance disappear. The physical weakness overtook her and she had to sit her bare ass on the pavement. The lawyers rushed toward her followed by a male nurse with a wheelchair. They scooped her into the wheelchair and rolled her back to the hospital.

CHAPTER 27

T he hospital lunch on the bed tray had a bland taste intending not to offend any patient. She ate some of the sandwich — steamrollered turkey on air bread — spicing it with industrial mustard from the little packet. She realized she better get in touch with Jules, on the general principle that any daughter in a hospital should notify her father. Jules was probably at work, in the oilfield, running his drilling rig, where he was almost every day. She called his cellphone and left a message.

"Hi Jules. I was involved in an incident where some men were fighting. I'm OK but it'll be in the headlines and news stories. Call me when you can."

Jules phoned her back five minutes later. "What *incident?*" She filled him in briefly and he said, "I'll hop in my truck and see you for dinner. Does the hospital serve Jell-O?" She laughed, which meant he'd accomplished his immediate goal. She talked him out of coming to see her. "That fight is over, Jules. I'll explain later and if I need your help, I'll let you know. Maybe I'll come see you for Christmas." That eased his concerns a bit. With his considerate nature he didn't press her.

Late afternoon a doctor with a delicate touch removed the bandages on the frostnipped parts of her face and body. He seemed pleased — no blisters or infections, only prickles of pain. She got him to agree with ending her medical confinement. She changed into the clothes Sheriff Kurt had brought — sweatshirt and sweatpants, wool socks and sandals, all easy to slip on.

"Thank you, Sheriff Kurt," she said again, this time to herself, "you do a lot of things right, just not the things that are most important to me."

She took an Uber home and was relieved to see Sheriff Kurt wasn't around. Her pickup rested in the driveway, presumably repaired. She went into the bedroom where Sheriff Kurt had accomplished his latest fling, and packed bags of her stuff including medical marijuana gummies and the brown eyedrops. Careful with the frostnipped spots on her hands, she lugged the bags to her pickup.

Then she walked through each room of the house and claimed some things she'd hung on the walls during the years she lived here. The framed photo of her mother and father getting married on the shore of Yellowstone Lake, two years before her mother bled out giving birth to twins. The framed photo of herself with Nikki, junior year of high school, posing in that school's cheerleader outfits on the hood of the old Dodge Charger that was a present from Jules — two teenage girls sharing a manual-shift V8 engine. And the framed prints of Nikki's favorite paintings — the Matisse and the Van Gogh, reminders of Nikki's interest in art history.

She put the framed photos and art in her pickup and went into the house one more time to open the combination lock on the gun safe. From the clutter of Sheriff Kurt's guns she retrieved hers — the classic Winchester lever-action rifle and her little pistol, the Walther PPK automatic, .380 caliber. And ammo for both.

Because the violence might not be over.

Her pickup started with a roar, no warning light now. "OK," she told herself, fighting the feeling that she was on thin ice again. She had about seven thousand in her individual savings account, along with access to the joint accounts for now. Three paychecks coming in soon, for horseback jobs. And her credit cards. And the gummies.

She nibbled a third of a gummy and drove to a grocery store for apples and carrots, and on to the Bozeman Equestrian Center. In Bobby D's stall she fed him the snacks from her hands and told him some of what had happened. "Sorry, Bobby D, I can't ride you today, too sore." He huffed horse breath in her face and slapped her with his tail. Bobby D was always glad to see her.

She drove onward to a motel where maybe nobody would know her. Checked into a generic room that had two beds. Used her antivirus wipes to clean the light switches and other risky surfaces. Brought in her bags and her pistol and propped up the family photos and the Matisse and the Van Gogh on the dresser. Depleted, she flopped down on one of the unfamiliar beds.

"Dawson," she said, "how long will it take you and your aunt to travel back to Long Beach?" Probably too soon to call him. And if the blows to his head blinded him, could he even use his cellphone? Then she realized, probably he'd also lost his phone in the fight last night.

She called Sheriff Kurt with the new phone he'd brought her, and told him, "I moved out."

Sheriff Kurt said nothing for a few long seconds and in that silence she could hear his emotions. "Please ..." he said and paused again. "Don't give up on me. I'll go back to Ginny, to work on our issues more."

She pictured Ginny, their marriage counselor, in the slit skirt during the sessions. "I'm beginning to wonder," she said, "are you screwing Ginny too? Anyway your flings aren't the only issues between you and me." She steadied her voice. "I've said it all before. Your need to give orders, your need to help people, even those who don't want help — good traits for a sheriff, not so good in a marriage. And that trapline, how you treat animals, I can't stand it. And your flings with any female you fancy. You shrug off what I say. I wonder what we ever imagined we had for loving each other, other than Nikki's murder."

"You're the only one who sees me like that," he said.

"I'm also your only wife."

"I'll sleep on the couch and you can have the bed."

"I'm never using that bed again. I need time on my own. I'm sad about it too."

"Where are you?"

She named the motel because if she didn't, he might deploy deputies to find her. She told him, "Don't come here," and hung up.

She rested a few more minutes, thinking about her wedding in the amusing Vegas chapel, and further back, to the murder. Her position on the bed had her looking at the family photos on the dresser. That old Dodge Charger she and Nikki posed with, it was good for high school, then the Charger threw a rod that wasn't worth fixing and Jules replaced it with the Jeep she and Nikki loved to drive in college. After the murder, the Jeep seemed haunted, and Jules sold it. She reflected back to that April day when she and Nikki were ten years old living in Billings, the town that had small colleges and large oil refineries.

~

Nikki and her, the scrappy little Fontaine twins, preparing to take the bus to fifth grade in the Billings school, with no supervision, making a fashion statement in worn-out jeans and plaid flannel shirts. She's wearing mismatched shoes — a blue sneaker and a red sneaker — and Nikki is too. Nikki flashes her gonna-be-naughty grin and says, "We could skip the morning lessons. How about we do the cliff?"

The schoolbus passes by outside as they remove textbooks from their daypacks and load water bottles and apples from the wooden bowl on the kitchen counter. The walk to the rimrock cliff that borders the northern edge of Billings requires about a mile on sidewalks and cutting through vacant lots. At the base of the cliff, shading their eyes with their hands, they peer upward, can't see the top the way the cliff overhangs them. They scramble up through a crevice. Clawing the nearly vertical sandstone, stretching for holds, losing traction in places where the rock is rotten, they enjoy it — the exciting precarious feeling.

"I can't get past the overhang here," she yells to Nikki.

Nikki yells back, "Come this way."

When they earn the top of the cliff, they turn and perch on the edge, breathing hard, dangling their legs over the dropoff, clapping dust off their hands and chomping the apples. There's a view, gaping below and clear out to the horizon, but Nikki is examining her fingers. "I tore three nails on the way up," Nikki says.

"I tore a couple too," she tells Nikki. "They sell fake nails at the drugstore."

The idea gives them the giggles. They do the physics experiment, hurling apple cores off the cliff and watching them arc downward, and they open up to the view, overlooking the whole town and the meander of the Yellowstone River far below them. The cottonwoods that are dense along the river and scattered in the neighborhoods haven't leafed out yet after the long winter, the branches like skeletons. A storm front of clouds in the distance erases the Beartooth Range and the front comes toward them faster than they expect and the first raindrops reach them. Quickly they're soaked. The wind rips at them and they grab the rocky outcrop to keep from being blown over the edge. As the rain solidifies into hailstones that sting, they're grinning at each other. The world shrinks down to the storm versus them, the hailstones filling their shirt pockets and bouncing into the necks of their shirts and thawing against their skin. The storm might last forever but it passes abruptly as Montana storms often do and the sun breaks through and a double rainbow glows right in front of them.

"Montana!" Nikki yells. On the edge of the abyss.

~

Her buzzing phone coaxed her out of the past. Caller ID said it was Sheriff Kurt again. She let her phone take a message. This motel room felt even more impersonal than the hospital. A series of strangers had landed here briefly like birds on a budget migrating to different destinations. She got up and went to the motel's lobby where they had all-day coffee, poured a cup and came back to the room and sat in the generic chair and looked at Nikki's favorite paintings, thinking of how an oilfield girl had enjoyed them until a killer's hands closed around her neck. As she sipped the coffee, feeling a boost from it, she listened to the message, Sheriff Kurt's voice, "We found evidence that one of the prison gangsters killed your sister. It's ugly. If you want to take a look, I'm in my office."

She listened to the message again.

It's ugly.

She said to the walls, "You better not be making this

up, Kurt. Better not be your trick to save the marriage."

The sun slid into the western horizon as she drove to the fortress of concrete and bulletproof glass called the Law and Justice Center. This lobby had been designed by the government, with hard plastic chairs and a female deputy as the receptionist. The deputy recognized her and said "Howdy Missus Vandyke."

She forced a smile as she spoke, "Actually I have two family names — Faber and Fontaine. I never adopted Sheriff Kurt's family name."

The deputy pressed a button on the desk phone and said into the headset, "Your wife is here."

Sheriff Kurt appeared from the guts of the building and asked her, "You sure you're up for this?"

She went with him past more deputies and detectives who nodded terse greetings. His office had windows with views of snowy bushes. He closed his office door for privacy and offered a chair. She said, "I'd rather stay on my feet," and realized she was still wearing the sandals and wool socks over her frostnipped toes. He sat in his leather armchair behind the desk, turned on a desk lamp, opened an eight-by-ten envelope and took out some photos.

"We've checked these photos for fingerprints and other trace evidence," he said. "It's OK to touch them."

He stacked the photos on the desk and pushed them toward her.

CHAPTER 28

She felt clumsy holding the stack of photos with her sore fingertips. The first photo showed Nikki's battered body lying on the rug in the Big Sky condo. She looked more closely — Nikki's swollen face, Nikki obviously dead.

She fought tears. Sheriff Kurt pulled a whiskey bottle and a glass from a different drawer and poured her a ration. She drank some. Liquid burn. She looked at the photo again, concentrating on details. Dawson was lying next to Nikki, his eyes closed. Nikki's outflung left arm rested on him, indicating he'd been lying there when her arm dropped. There were no scratches on his face.

She'd never seen this photo before. It seemed to verify Dawson's claims that he was unconscious, drugged, at the time of the murder, and Nikki hadn't scratched his face fighting him. Maybe the killer shot this photo and then scratched Dawson's face to make it look like Dawson and Nikki had fought — Dawson's theory all along.

"Turn it over," Kurt said.

On the back of the photo there were words written with a red-marker, all caps: SHE BEGGED FOR MERCY.

The next photo was another angle on Nikki's body and Dawson, and on the back, STUCKUP BITCH SCREWED AN APE. The next, SHE CRIED IN PAIN. And so on, every photo showing Nikki dead and Dawson looking unconscious and innocent, every caption ugly too. The last, LET THE FOOTBALL NIGGER TAKE THE RAP.

She closed her eyes wishing everything would stop going bad. Imagining Nikki alive and smiling. Words crawled out of her. "Who —? Where did you —?"

"Basically, these photos came from one of the drowned guys we dragged out of the lake this morning. Perry Sebastian. We searched his home, a trailer west of town, found these photos in a plastic bag in his freezer."

She opened her eyes and said, "His *freezer?*"

"The freezer compartment in his fridge."

She paused and he laid it out, "Rose, you'd be amazed what criminals hide in freezers. Maybe they think nobody doing a quick search would check the freezer, and the cold preserves what they're hiding. ... With these photos and other new evidence, it's clear, Perry Sebastian killed your sister. He snapped these photos as souvenirs, and he wrote the notes on them, so he could review the murder anytime he wanted. ... Some murderers keep their victims' underwear, or jewelry, or photos like this."

"... Which man last night was Perry Sebastian?"

"The biggest. Boss of the 406ers gang, with a long criminal record that included assaults and suspicion of other murders." He pulled out a mug shot from the state police — the huge man, with strange tattoos around his neck. "It's also clear, Nikki was his primary target."

"Why would this man kill Nikki?"

Kurt tapped the photo of Nikki and Dawson captioned STUCKUP BITCH SCREWED AN APE. "The 406ers are White supremacists. Apparently Sebastian acted because Nikki was with a Black guy and their affair was as conspicuous as a billboard. Murdering her and framing Dawson, it sent a message to all White women — racial mixing is dangerous. A lot of people automatically believed Dawson did the murder."

"You believed it. I did too."

"Yeah, that's our fault. But now we can put together the timeline. A couple years after Nikki's murder, the state police nailed Sebastian for armed robbery and put him in the prison where Dawson was locked up. That's when Sebastian sicced the 406ers on Dawson — to finish off Dawson too. It's over, Rose. The crime is solved."

Some of the weight from losing Nikki should be lifting off her. But she didn't feel that. She finished the glass of whiskey and said, "Can you show me your report on Sebastian, whatever you've found out so far?"

Kurt handed her several pages of printout — he'd expected she'd ask for it. He said, "Sebastian was a hotshot among the local scumbags. In with meth dealers and cookers, assorted thugs and thieves. So popular, some of his pals are having a wake tonight in the Pussycat Bar."

That news knocked the breath from her. He came around the desk and tried to hug her. She turned sideways, avoiding most of the contact. As he walked her out to the parking lot, he squeezed her arm one more time and said, "If you want companionship tonight, let me know."

~

Instead of returning to the limbo of the motel, she drove out of town where the Montana scenery might reinforce her. As the twilight faded to dusk, the views lengthened to the horizon of a half-dozen mountain ranges surrounding the valley. She inhaled deeply as if she was inhaling the mountains. Fifteen minutes of that and the night veiled everything. She pulled over and switched on her pickup's ceiling light and read the report on Perry Sebastian. One tidbit — Sebastian's father was a successful hitman until he got incinerated by a Salt Lake City gang.

She read the report twice and thought more about the photos. Then she phoned Sheriff Kurt and said, "Those sick notes on the photos, about how Nikki broke down as she was getting choked? Nikki wouldn't cry and beg for her life. She would've fought him to the end. She would've understood, crying and begging only rewards him."

"Don't think about it. Most victims break down."

"Not Nikki."

"Maybe Sebastian only wished he'd broken her, and he wrote it on the photos as his final way of dominating her."

"Kurt, you're eager to close the case for good, I get that. It seems far-fetched to me — Sebastian wrote his *confession* on photos of his crime? ... When the state cops busted him, didn't they search his freezer?"

"They searched the house Sebastian lived in back then, in Madison County. Probably at that time he had the photos stashed somewhere else. Rose, criminals don't think like we do. Sebastian talked about Nikki's murder while he took Dawson to the lake. Dawson told me that at the hospital."

"So I should give you another chance in our marriage, because you've solved the murder? Is that what this is?"

She heard his silence — he was trying to be patient with her now but it wasn't easy. Then he said, "I'm not sure what you're accusing me of. My chief deputy, Bobby Nunn, found the photos in the freezer. You want to talk to Bobby, I'll order him to answer whatever you ask."

"Maybe Bobby will say whatever you order him to say. Or maybe being married to you is making me crazy."

"The offer stands, Babe. If you need a hug, phone me."

"You can never stop calling me Babe, can you? What you said to me at the hospital — you're right, I can be difficult. The world seems to demand that from me."

She hung up and ate another third of today's gummy. Then she skimmed the report to find Sebastian's recent address — rural. A twenty-minute drive west of where she was. She was always better in motion than standing still.

CHAPTER 29

The night took over. Her headlights stabbed the darkness. She found the gravel road leading to Perry Sebastian's place. The land in this corner of the valley was flat and sparsely settled. The road hadn't been maintained in a while. Her tires rattled over packed-down snow on washboard bumps. Almost no traffic. She refused to surrender to exhaustion. Reading the addresses on the mailboxes, she found Sebastian's. A yellow banner draped across the driveway warned CRIME SCENE ♦ DO NOT ENTER. A sign added SHERIFF'S DEPARTMENT ♦ NO TRESPASSING.

Probably nobody was here now. The only lights she could see were far away. She drove farther on the gravel road and parked on the shoulder, so it wouldn't be obvious what she was up to, and slipped her pistol into a jacket pocket. Using the flashlight on her phone she started walking across the snow. Still in the sandals and wool socks that cushioned her frostnipped toes. She crossed a field and through the rusted strands of Sebastian's barbed-wire fence. Sebastian's yard consisted of last summer's weeds poking through the snow, and piles of scrap wood and old tires and the bones of a cow. A trailer home squatted in the middle, poorly maintained, a monument to don't-give-a-shitness. She felt Nikki's ghost with her.

"Nikki, if your murderer lived here, you had bad taste in murderers."

The porch was old boards and loose nails, creaking under her sandals. More of Sheriff Kurt's CRIME SCENE ♦ DO NOT ENTER banner had been stapled across the front door. A new combination lock, on a new hasp, secured the door.

"Breaking and entering," she said. "Could be a whole new career, Nikki." Thinking of how she'd broken into the cabin beside the icy lake to save herself and Dawson. She stepped off the porch and walked around the exterior of the trailer home, checking every window and the back door, found no easy entry. The window spaces were covered by deteriorating plywood sheets secured by screws. She tried a screwdriver from her Leatherman but the heads of the screws were so rusted and stripped she couldn't get traction on them. One of the plywood sheets wasn't as tight as the others. She got ahold of the lower edge and yanked it toward her, an inch or two, again trying to use the parts of her hands that weren't frostnipped, as much as possible. She saw there was no window glass inside the plywood. She needed more leverage. She dragged an old tire from one of the piles and stood on it so she was on the same level as the plywood, and wedged a two-by-four in the gap to force the plywood's edge several more inches off the trailer. Tense, super tense, she slid one leg through the gap and squirmed in sideways until she straddled the windowsill with the plywood against her back, then used the leverage of her back to push the plywood more open, the screws ripping loose. "Nikki, here we are, still pulling capers." She kept squirming and pushing, making more noise kind of quietly, and got through the gap, both feet on the trailer floor. Still relying on her phone light, not trying the wall switches or lamps — less noticeable to anybody driving by — she walked through the trailer. It was a rectangle whose geometry had weakened into cockeyed angles, with two bedrooms and a bathroom and a kitchen/dining/living room, with shag carpet and walls clad in cheap paneling. Posters for opera performances were taped to the walls of the living room — Maria Callas singing Giacomo Puccini's *Tosca* in Italy and so on — reminding her that she'd heard opera music at the fight on the icy lake. Apparently Sebastian was an opera fan. The rest of the décor had a fascist theme — a giant swastika spray-painted on the wall over the couch. She waved her phone light over the vile symbol. It was taller than she was, and wider than her spread arms, and the paint was iridescent orange. She could smell the spray-paint faintly so the swastika was somewhat fresh.

"Great."

She was here to get more on who Sebastian was, without disturbing much of the evidence. She grabbed a paper towel for handling things, so she wouldn't leave her fingerprints or smear fingerprints left by others. The Sheriff's Department search had been thorough. The beds had been flipped up against the walls. Clothes had been pulled from the closets and the dresser and heaped on the floor. Some of the carpet had been pulled back from the nailer strips, and the covers of electrical outlets had been removed so those obscure spaces could be checked.

She became aware of her heartbeat fluttering. Again she could hear Dawson telling her, *you're scared*.

"Getting less scared, Dawson," she replied. "Ever since the lake."

She heard a rustling and drew her pistol and cocked it. Her phone light found a rat eating something on the kitchen floor. Maybe Sebastian had kept the rat as a pet, a warm body to cuddle with at night. The refrigerator waited for her touch. The photos of the dead version of Nikki had been found in the freezer half of it. Supposedly. She opened the freezer and saw tumors of frost and a lone bottle of beer that had cracked as it froze. "Nikki, why would he hide the photos here? Anything in this freezer would be found by anybody doing a thorough search."

She spotted a few photos scattered on the floor. Not photos of the murder — photos of Sebastian sitting on a snowmobile. A woman was with him, riding double on the snowmobile. Some pudgy baby-faced woman.

She slipped one of the snowmobiling photos into a pocket, thinking it might be useful.

Bright headlights appeared out on the road. She switched off her phone light and remained motionless in the dark. The headlights passed the end of the driveway and kept going. She squeezed out of the trailer the way she came in and walked back to her pickup.

She was thinking about something else Sheriff Kurt said about Sebastian's death: *Some of his pals are having a wake tonight in the Pussycat Bar.*

... Tonight — meaning right now.

CHAPTER 30

The Pussycat was a notorious topless joint in a sly location, conveniently off an interstate exit but far from any law enforcement office. The building was cinderblock with a few windows placed too high to see in. A sign on a tall pole announced what was for sale — red neon outlining a naked woman.

Mutant pickup trucks jammed the parking lot, some lugging snowmobiles in their beds. She ate the rest of today's marijuana gummy and walked to the front door, a slab of steel, and into a large barroom with red lighting and loud opera music, more of what she'd heard at the icy lake. Roughly seventy people were partying here, no masks, the air sour from damp winter clothes and sweat, men mostly in biker outfits, women mostly showing skin. Topless dancers not synced to the opera writhed on the stage, wearing Santa hats with their thongs and stiletto heels, and the waitresses wore similar outfits. On the walls there were more opera posters and Confederate flags and screens displaying a slide show of Sebastian from his toddler years to his mug shots, with folksy text, LOVED YA PERRY!! ... SANTA KNOWS WHOSE BEEN DOIN METH!!!

The music changed to heavy metal and people surged to the dance floor. Circulating, she found the pudgy baby-faced woman who'd posed with Sebastian in the snowmobiling photo. People were calling the woman Angel. Tonight Angel was wearing only a businessman's vest above bikini panties and sheepskin boots. Angel danced with no partner, yelling *Gonna miss my Perry!* and *Merry Fuckin' Christmas!* over and over. A tattoo on Angel's thigh — the numbers *4 0 6* — indicated Sebastian's gang owned her.

When the opportunity came, she cornered Angel in the hallway to the bathroom, where Angel was snorting whatever powder. She hugged Angel and yelled to her over the din, "I'm gonna miss Perry too!"

Angel nodded, and drew a half-smoked cigarette from a vest pocket, snapped a lighter and began breathing smoke, despite the NO SMOKING sign on the wall next to her. Powder residue clung to her nostrils. "Me and Perry," Angel said, "we had some *goood tiiimes.*"

She drew Angel deeper into the hallway, away from the din, and got Angel talking about living with Perry Sebastian and breaking up and getting back together and breaking up and so on. Then she asked Angel, "You hear what the cops are saying about Perry now?"

"Never believe cops! Sure Perry was out on the ice last

night to deal with that colored guy, but no way did Perry kill that White girl five years ago. Perry was nice to most White girls in order to get laid. You know how it is, honey."

"I certainly do."

"The lying cops asked me about it today," Angel went on, the way flamboyant druggies and drunks talk too much under the impression they're the center of the universe. "I told the cops, my Perry never hid no pictures of that murder in our freezer. And Perry never spray-painted no swastika on our wall. The cops blew me off. Maybe the cops theirselves are framing Perry."

"That swastika — aren't the 406ers into swastikas?"

Angel waved toward the dance floor. "Talk to T-Rex."

Imagining a gigantic prehistoric creature, she asked Angel, "Which one is T-Rex?"

Angel pointed. "The little guy."

T-Rex had a ragged beard and a ragged leather jacket. He was drunk and groping women who tried to squeeze by him. She tried to keep just out of his range until there was a break in the music, then she pressed him with questions, steering his talk to swastikas, and he said, "You get turned on by Nazis?" at which point he opened his collar to reveal swastikas tattooed on his upper chest.

"*Bee-yoo-ti-ful*," she lied. "But what was up with Perry and swastikas? I heard he didn't paint that swastika on his wall. That surprised me."

"It should surprise your tits off," T-Rex said. She tried to picture that, as he went on, "The whole time I knew

Perry, up until last month, Perry fucking *loved* everything Nazi. He had swastika decals on his snowmobile, and that poster of Hitler's stormtroopers marching, and videos of Hitler's greatest speeches with subtitles in English. Then last month he got a phone call from a cousin doing family history. He found out he had a grandfather who fought in the war against Hitler. His grandfather killed a nest of Nazi troops and got a medal for that. Perry was so proud, he threw out his stormtrooper poster and his Hitler videos and peeled the swastikas off his snowmobile. He dumped all that Nazi shit."

"You tell the cops that, T-Rex?"

"The cops didn't ask me," T-Rex roared, "and if they ever do, I'd tell them to shove it. Cops never did a damn thing for me except two stretches in Deer Lodge prison." She felt one of T-Rex's hands discovering the bulge of the pistol in her pocket. "You packing tonight?" he asked.

She slipped away from his grasp and, talking to more of them, she got more confirmation that lately Perry Sebastian wasn't into swastikas. One of the thonged waitresses wearing a Rudolph Reindeer nose said, "Last week Perry strong-armed a doctor to get me laser treatments for free, to erase my swastika tat," pointing to a vague swastika on her ankle. "It's already faded some from the first zapping."

The music and the celebrating got even louder, and an actual fight erupted across the room. Two men slamming each other. Another man jumped in swinging a pool cue and somebody fired a warning shot, fragments of the ceiling hailing down. The crowd surged for the exits and she got shoved and swept out the back door. The winter night exploded with sirens. A caravan of Sheriff's Department SUVs closed in — deputies who must've been staking out the Pussycat. They began capturing and cuffing some of the troublemakers.

She blended in with the dispersing crowd and spotted Sheriff Kurt knocking down the man armed with a pool cue. She made it to her pickup and drove off, wondering if she'd be followed by any gangster or her husband.

~

She felt it was time for a drink and stopped at a liquor store. While she looked for a pint of affordable brandy, another woman came in and browsed the aisles of wine. A Viking blonde, tall and fit with a skier's tan and the striking white-blond hair. Something about that blonde — the hairclip. It flashed silver-and-gold, the same unusual style of clip that showed up in the master bathroom of Sheriff Kurt's house, left there by his last lover.

She heard herself say, "You're kidding me."

She bought her pint and waited in her pickup. Imagining the Viking blonde entwined with Sheriff Kurt. She watched the woman come out with a wine bottle and drive off in a Lexus. She began following the Lexus. She imagined confronting the woman, *Nice hair clip. Thanks for leaving it at my house — it helped clarify issues with my marriage. I see my husband returned it to you.*

The Lexus turned off. Following it through a neighborhood of upscale condos, she got control of herself and let it disappear.

~

Back in the motel room she kept thinking about Perry Sebastian and the murder and Sheriff Kurt's fondness for good-looking women. She felt exposed to many threats. She had some brandy in a disposable motel cup and called Dawson, probably in Long Beach by now. She figured if Dawson had lost his phone in the icy lake, he might already have a new phone with the same number. The call clicked to a recording of Dawson, *please leave a message.* She felt a notch better hearing his voice. "Hi Dawson. This is Rose again. I hope your eyes are better. I've got an update on finding whoever killed Nikki. Please call me back." Then she got out the business cards Dawson's lawyers gave her in the hospital, and called MaryAnn Meloy.

"Hi MaryAnn, this is Rose Faber. Or Rose Fontaine. Is it too late to talk?"

"I'm awake, watching that old Christmas classic, *It's A Wonderful Life.* It always makes me cry — you called just in time. Are you out of the hospital?"

Apparently MaryAnn hadn't heard about the new evidence pointing to Sebastian as the murderer. "Yes, I've escaped from the hospital. I'm trying to reach Dawson. Have you heard from him? Is he reachable by phone?"

"His aunt got him a new phone, same number,"

MaryAnn confirmed. "But he's not answering my calls."

"His aunt — she's the one who moved him out of the hospital?"

"That's her. Cecie Koloko. I got to know her while he was in prison — every month Cecie sent me a new letter encouraging me to push appeals. I talked with Cecie today and she said Dawson is still blind from the head trauma. She's taking him to specialists around the LA area."

"Would you mind giving me Cecie Koloko's number?"

Then she called Cecie Koloko and reached her voice mail too, left a message, switched off the lights and mostly failed to sleep. In the morning her frostnipped spots seemed less sore. She sought coffee in the motel lobby, which was busy with Christmas music and customers having the corporate pour-your-own waffles. Listening to them chatter about their plans for the day, she realized, sheesh it's Christmas morning.

The crowd gobbled their waffles and left, better places to be on Christmas. She loitered at her table, drinking more caffeine. Sheriff Kurt walked in from the parking lot and said, "Merry Christmas, Babe."

"Same to you," she said and let him hug her.

He drew a coffee for himself and sat opposite her, both elbows on the table, both hands around the paper cup raising it to his lips. She could hardly look at him. He began talking about past Christmases with her. The extra-special Christmas when the two of them drove snowmobiles into Yellowstone Park, how the steam from geysers and hot pools created small snowstorms they motored through. She interrupted and told him, "I saw you at the Pussycat Bar."

"You were there? Crashing a party for the guy who murdered your sister? More reason to worry about you."

She watched him sip his coffee — he was close to getting mad again. "I had good reasons to be in the Pussycat," she said. "Why were you there?"

He crumpled his cup and said, "Spending Christmas Eve in my recliner, wishing my wife was home, didn't appeal to me. I had a team watching the Pussycat, to see who'd show up to celebrate the achievements of the late Perry Sebastian. Sebastian's friends are involved in more crimes. We made some arrests."

"Sebastian didn't kill Nikki," she said, as if that was a fact instead of a guess. She told him what she'd heard in the Pussycat. How Sebastian gave up swastikas recently, so he probably didn't paint the fresh swastika on his living-room wall. "Sebastian's girlfriend says there was no swastika on the wall, and no photos in the freezer, until after he died. Somebody is framing Sebastian. Probably the same person who framed Dawson."

"Some scumbags spun a story for you, and you have a feeling they're reliable? Look Rose, whether or not you believe it, Sebastian was the killer. We're running his DNA to see if it matches the flesh we scraped from under Nikki's nails. If it doesn't match, that only means Sebastian had help from his gang when he killed Nikki. Like I said, this case is over. You need it to be over."

She leaned toward him and tested the words in her mind, made her decision, told him, "Or is that what you need, Kurt? I know what's definitely over. I'm getting a divorce. And I'm going to identify the real killer. Please don't get in my way."

She sat with him a while longer and nothing more was said. He seemed to be receding from her, even though he wasn't physically moving. The Christmas tunes in the background began to sound twisted. Everything seemed so mixed-up, this Christmas morning somewhere between heaven and hell, for a moment she laughed. A brief laugh. Finally enough to cause Sheriff Kurt to leave her alone.

CHAPTER 31

"Merry Christmas, and all that," she said to Dawson's voice mail. "I'll keep on calling you, until you call me back." She hung up and gave Dawson a minute, called again and told his voice mail, "I'm thinking about how you wanted to examine Nikki's stuff. I'm up for it now." She waited another minute, called again. "I wish I hadn't testified against you." Called again, "I wish I'd done a lot of things differently since the murder. That's the Christmas card from Rose. You've got my number."

By sundown she was two hundred miles east, on Montana's hilly plains, towing her horse trailer on the gravel roads through one of Montana's oldest oilfields. Not much snow out here — the frequent wind swept the sagebrush after each blizzard. The oilfield was a scattering of old pumpjacks and wellheads that had flaming exhaust pipes, the natural-gas leakage getting burned off, and some active drilling rigs because this work went on day and night, every day of the year. She found Jules's rig outlined by Christmas lights. The cords of red and green bulbs twined around the framework that was more than a hundred feet tall. She parked in the dirt lot, got out and heard Christmas tunes blaring from outdoor speakers on the rig. Roughnecks in hardhats scrambled around the rig.

Horse people have priorities. She fed and watered Bobby D and let him roam. In the process she learned the roughnecks on the rig had a problem. They were yelling about it. The drill bit had broken off underground. She'd worked as a roughneck and knew they were scrambling to fix it, if they could.

She recognized Jules's voice bossing the others — it was his crew, his contract renting the multimillion-dollar rig from the owner, a faceless corporation in Oklahoma. Jules enjoyed the risk of making his living as a freelance driller, gambling that he'd drill more strikes than dry holes. The gambling, the risk-taking, were some of the traits he'd passed along to her and Nikki.

She walked across the bladed ground and grabbed an aluminum hardhat from a locker. The steel stairway led up past the stenciled lettering — SWEETIE PIE. The rig's name. Up on the main floor, open to the sky, she nodded to some roughnecks she recognized. She found Jules in the control room, where he was flicking switches and studying many computer screens that displayed conditions in the hole. He had a Frosty Snowman doll propped up at the back of the control board. The Christmas tunes on the outdoor speakers weren't as loud in here. Faintly she could hear Elvis, *I'll have-uh-uh blue-ue Christmas ... without youuu.*

"Be nice, Sweetie Pie," Jules said to the rig, his hands shifting to the joysticks and his eyes locked on the screens. While she waited for him to notice her, she assessed how he was aging. He'd survived a bad virus infection and still appeared to be a gray-haired dynamo, short and stocky with powerful arms. The SIERRA CLUB decal she'd stuck on his hardhat long ago was still in place — he shared her concerns about fossil fuels causing climate change but he'd keep drilling until people no longer needed it. She'd always admired his hands — such blunt fingers, battered by work accidents, yet a sensitive touch on the rig's controls.

"We'll go fishing, Sweetie Pie," Jules told the rig. His kind of fishing didn't require streams or lakes. He had the rig pushing a hook into the hole, hoping to retrieve the broken bit at the bottom. He spotted her. "Rose!"

She waved to him briefly, allowing him to refocus on the controls. One screen showed the bit had broken off eight-thousand-two-hundred-and-two feet underground. She heard loud noises and the whole rig shivered.

"Hook it now, Sweetie Pie," Jules told the rig.

Again and again Jules slammed the hook down on the broken bit with precise force trying to attach them. She'd come to understand, yes trout were tricky, but there were things in Montana more difficult to hook. "Reel it in now, Sweetie Pie." The rig shivered more, straining to hoist more than a mile of pipe and the bit. Everybody on the rig knew, last year a Wyoming rig collapsed, killing three roughnecks. She grabbed a railing to steady herself. There was a burst of noises and the rig smoothed out as it began to pull up the broken bit. This particular crisis was over.

"You eat yet?" Jules asked. "We've got Christmas dinner in the shack." Slang for the steel cargo container beside the rig, outfitted with a kitchen and a picnic table and bunk beds. Sitting at the table she told him, "I'm getting a divorce."

He took off his hardhat and reached across the table and gave her shoulders a reassuring squeeze. His steady look. Same as he'd been patient when she was a twenty-year-old marrying a man who was thirty-five. "Now I can say it. Rose, that guy is a jerk."

Which reminded her of Dawson saying the same.

She asked him, "OK for my horse and me to stay at your place for a while?" She didn't mean the house in Billings. Jules had a doublewide house trailer on five acres on the edge of this oilfield, more convenient than the house. She and Nikki had lived in the doublewide from the time they were infants until they moved to Billings for first grade, and from then on they stayed in the doublewide during the summers and other school breaks. Now she floated the question that had brought her here.

"Are you still keeping those boxes of Nikki's stuff in her bedroom?" She was thinking, the stuff that might lead to the killer?

CHAPTER 32

She left her hardhat in the locker at the rig and drove to Jules's doublewide, which was old but well maintained, and moved Bobby D into the barn, which was empty because Jules wasn't home enough to tend horses. Moved her own stuff into her old bedroom. She looked at herself in the bathroom mirror and decided to quit coloring her hair and her eyes.

"Getting back to where I started," she told her reflection.

She called Dawson and left another message, then slept restlessly on the narrow bed she'd used off and on her whole life. In the morning she made coffee and went into Nikki's old bedroom pulled Nikki's stuff from the storage boxes. She plugged in Nikki's phone and computer and began skimming digital records, including emails, photos and videos, some of which showed her with Nikki cheerleading at football games. And Nikki climbing in a gym, reaching for handholds on a practice wall. Nikki hiking with Dawson. Nikki and her celebrating that last shared birthday, eating cake without silverware shortly before they climbed that campus flagpole in the dark.

The surge of emotions shook her. She went outside and cooled off walking around and talking with Nikki. Then more hours looking through Nikki's clothes and other things that had been saved. She came across the medal twelve-year-old Nikki won in the youth sharp-shooter competition. And the wig Nikki wore the last semester of high school, so realistic because it was made with Nikki's own hair, buzzed off her head during a fund-raiser for a teacher who got cancer. Nikki's jewelry box, finely fitted cherrywood, *Nikki* inscribed on the lid. Jules had made it as a present for Nikki's thirteenth birthday.

And the art stuff. Colorful childish drawings Nikki did in kindergarten. The best watercolors Nikki painted in high school and college. The artsy wall calendars displaying a classic painting each month with a grid of the days, where Nikki jotted reminders of her college schedule. Flipping the pages of the calendar for freshman spring semester, she noticed Nikki's handwriting in the March 11 square, *Climbing gym w/Alonzo.* For September 18 Nikki had written, *Hike w/Dawson.*

As she examined Nikki's stuff, she kept on calling Dawson and leaving messages. The call she received was from Sheriff Kurt. He left a long message expressing his desire for the marriage to survive. She had to act on that front. She dedicated much of the next day to a drive to

Billings to meet with a divorce lawyer named Kaylee Nelson, who got good reviews on Yelp.

"Two hundred per hour," this lawyer said. "We'll file in the district court covering your current residence, your father's home — Big Horn County, out of Sheriff Kurt's jurisdiction. If you swear there's serious marital discord — that's the legal wording — and Kurt doesn't contest it, it'll only take ninety days."

"And if Kurt contests it?"

"He can't prevent it, only delay it. Montana is the last best place for divorce."

Lawyer humor.

~

On the third day of her investigation, she woke up with a feeling, something in Nikki's stuff whispering to her. Something in the piles of keepsakes and digital files. Only a whisper, no discernible shape yet. She thought a horse ride might bring it into focus.

The blizzard that was rattling the doublewide didn't intimidate her. She ate a gummy and put on long underwear and a wool sweater, Army surplus wool pants, wool socks and her riding boots. And of course her cowgirl hat. She wrapped a scarf around her face and up over her hat to keep it from blowing away.

She tested the intensity of the blizzard as she walked across the yard carrying her duster-style jean jacket and her gloves. It was a damn good blizzard.

Bobby D wanted to be ridden. His natural coat grew

long in winter, better insulation from the cold. She threw a pad and her saddle onto him, and because a steel bit might freeze to his tongue, she used a leather halter instead. Then she put on her jacket and gloves and swung up onto the saddle. Feeling the horse adjust to her, and the increasing awareness in her inner thighs and down to her bootheels notched in the stirrups, and up her backbone and through her shoulders and out through her wrists to her fingers on the reins, everything connected yet loose, the way a good rider feels it.

She donned sunglasses that would shield her eyes from the wind-driven snow and rode out of the barn. The flakes made the wind so solid it almost knocked her off the horse. Blowing away all distractions. She focused on the immediacies of the weather and horse and rider and landscape — her meditation, allowing her subconscious to operate with less supervision. The whisper from Nikki's stuff faded away and revived, faded and revived again and again as she rode into the wind.

CHAPTER 33

S he couldn't see far in the whiteout. Not many fences out here to complicate the ride — most of the land belonged to the Crow tribe or the White government. She rode among the fossil-fuel machinery and exhaust flames looming up. Bobby D plodded along under her, snow clumping in his eyelashes. She rode for an hour and kept going as what was whispering to her slowly emerged.

Climbing gym w/Alonzo.

Nikki had written the phrase — or a briefer *Climbing w/Alonzo* — on maybe a dozen days on the wall calendar for freshman spring semester, before Dawson showed up for the summer practices. *Alonzo* meant Alonzo Davis, a Bobcats linebacker from Denver, who was now a pro with the Seattle Seahawks.

She had vague memories of Nikki making remarks about climbing with Alonzo five years ago. A few remarks, not many. She'd also watched a video of Nikki climbing with Alonzo, as she went through Nikki's stuff.

She rode on, trying to remember more exactly Nikki climbing with Alonzo.

~

She's in the climbing gym with Nikki and Alonzo, watching Nikki go up the wall. Nikki seems to barely touch the holds, dressed in the thin climbing pants that tighten as she makes each move and the tank top revealing some of her back and her muscular arms. Alonzo is too heavy with football muscles to be a climber. She can see he's turned on by Nikki's moves ...

~

The blizzard got harder, the snow like shotgun pellets. Going through a draw she spooked a flock of grouse from the brush. The birds vanished in the whiteout.

~

Nikki and her, walking to class in a peaceful snowstorm that spring semester, no wind, the flakes soft. "How's it going with your math professor?" Nikki asks.

"Good," she tells Nikki. "I enjoy the tut-tutting. It's OK for me to date the prof, since I'm not in his classes, but we get the —" showing Nikki a disapproving look.

Nikki laughs. "I get those looks too, when I'm out with Black players."

They walk on, the flakes beginning to stick to their hats and jackets, and she asks Nikki, "How about Alonzo? Are you still climbing in the gym with him?"

"I climb, Alonzo stands on the mat staring up at my ass."

"When I watched you climb last weekend, you flew up

that wall."

"Alonzo gives me Addies for a boost," Nikki says. "A couple of Addies and I am flying up the wall." Addies, meaning Adderall pills — the stimulant popular among students, for studying all night and enhancing physical performance.

She's surprised Nikki is experimenting with uppers. She figures it's Alonzo's influence and asks, "Does Alonzo take Addies? Is that why he's so good at football? Doesn't the football program test his pee year-round?"

"Alonzo doesn't take Addies," Nikki says. "But he has Addies for me."

"Addies and sex go together, don't they?"

Nikki adjusts her scarf and smiles the way a woman smiles when asked about things like that. "Alonzo would like to," Nikki says. "I'm holding him off, so far. But when I'm on Addies I'm definitely tempted."

~

Nikki never mentioned Adderall pills before that walk in the peaceful snowstorm, and never mentioned the pills afterwards. Probably the pills were a brief experiment for Nikki. Toward the end of that spring semester Nikki broke up with Alonzo. Then Nikki got interested in Dawson and the whole story changed.

She nudged Bobby D's flanks with her bootheels to speed him up, heading back to the doublewide. To go through Nikki's stuff yet again.

Several hours later, she discovered a small drawer in

Nikki's jewelry box. Jules had made it so meticulously, the drawer was somewhat secret, no knob or pull on it — she got it open by slipping a fingertip into a subtle groove.

The drawer contained seven orange pills and three white pills.

An Internet search identified the pills as seven Addies and three Ambien.

Ambien — quick-acting sleeping pills.

~

Farther in that walk through the peaceful snowstorm.

"Nikki, when you take Addies for Sunday climbing with Alonzo, how do you get enough sleep to go to classes Monday morning?"

"Alonzo gives me a downer when I need sleep," Nikki says. "Or a couple of downers. Sometimes I don't wake up until noon Monday."

~

She could list her excuses even as she scoffed at them. She'd only heard Nikki mention Alonzo's pills on that walk, none of the other times they were together that semester. Then after she discovered Nikki's body, and the evidence pointed to Dawson, she was consumed by grief and rage toward Dawson. She especially wished she'd remembered Alonzo having downers, when Dawson claimed somebody slipped him a knockout drug the night of the murder.

~

Near the end of that spring semester, she's in the

apartment on a Saturday night — the math prof is out of town. Nikki comes in unexpectedly early from her date with Alonzo. Nikki isn't wearing the jacket she had on when she went out. Nikki's hair and shirt are messed up. Nikki says — toughly, the way she lived — "Break-up time. Alonzo got pushy, grabbing me all over. It was disgusting."

CHAPTER 34

Two simple words. *The murder.* That was her vocabulary for thinking about it. *The murder.* Sometimes in conversation with people she needed additional words to make sure they understood, such as *Nikki's murder,* or *my sister's murder,* or explaining it to a counselor, *my identical twin was strangled, she was the person I was closest to — it makes me lonely, in a way nobody else I know is.* In her internal dialogue it was just *the murder.* She never confused it with all the other murders in the news every day. It was so huge she couldn't block it out. It affected everything. It was the murder the way 9/11 was shorthand for so much horror.

She dug into the murder for another day-and-a-half at Jules's place, searching online and making calls, preparing for her next move. She wanted to tell Jules, but it had to be on a ride, a form of quality time in her family. The remnants of her family. Jules took time off work and borrowed an Appaloosa mare from a Crow family he was tight with. They rode cross-country, avoiding any drifts deeper than the horses' knees. When they reached the small town called Hardin they bought lunch to go and rode to the cemetery, where they brushed snow off the family gravestones:

ADELE FABER
BELOVED WIFE OF JULES FONTAINE
GAVE HER LIFE FOR THE TWINS

NICOLE 'NIKKI' FONTAINE
FOREVER WITH JULES & ADELE & ROSALETTE
A BOND UNBROKEN

Sitting on a tarp they spread beside the graves, they split the meals. A sandwich of rye bread and sharp cheddar and red onion, Adele's favorite. A bean burrito with green chilis, Nikki's favorite. Half of each meal for each of the living. They ate, and talked, and spoke to the dead in silent voices.

Over the years she'd often thought about how Jules raised her and Nikki. After his wife's sudden premature death, he'd thrown himself into drilling, allowing her and Nikki to grow up mostly unsupervised. Probably at first he was in shock. Then it became his philosophy of single-parenting in a world that drained the blood from a mother giving birth. He'd provided guardrails with allowance for being wild and free. Jules had a lot to do with her and

Nikki growing up independent, good at pushing boundaries. She and Jules always talked honestly.

"You've been going through everything Nikki left behind," Jules said. "We can talk about it here. Nikki and Adele won't be offended."

She filled him in about discovering the pills, uppers and downers, hidden in Nikki's jewelry box. How that awakened memories of Nikki getting pills from Alonzo Davis. As Jules listened, she saw hints of his suppressed grief over losing Nikki. He pulled out a red neckerchief and wiped his eyes and tucked it away neatly. His face crinkled into a smile and he said, "What's the plan?"

She told him, and he nodded. He'd back her play, even though he believed Sheriff Kurt's latest decree, pinning the murder on a racist Montana gangster named Perry Sebastian who conveniently drowned in the icy lake.

"Please take care of Bobby D while I'm gone," she said. "I'll call you if I need more than that." She knew how hard it was for him to agree with his surviving daughter taking chances.

"I hope you find some peace, Rose. And please, take care of yourself."

"I will."

"Liar." He smiled again.

~

She got to the Billings airport, on the sandstone rim above the oil refineries, for the early morning flight. At the airline desk she encountered a pack of men who handed in rifles as checked baggage. Their jackets had the insignia for White Pride, the racist nationwide movement based in Montana. They were headed to Washington, D.C. for a rally.

She flew to Salt Lake City and transferred to an LA flight, using Jules's frequent-flyer points. By noon California time the plane circled over LA and she marveled at the extent of the human imprint on the edge of the ocean. Walking through the LA airport, wearing her cowgirl hat, she saw Blacks and Asians and Latinos and Middle-Easterners and heard languages she didn't recognize. She felt White, something she never thought about in Montana. At the car rental counter she chose a massive Chevy pickup that had a chrome grill similar to a cowcatcher on the front of a locomotive. Good for surviving LA traffic. She took gnarly freeways to Long Beach, an extension of LA, and it was so sunny and warm, she buzzed open her windows and breathed exhaust fumes mixed with fragrances of exotic plants. Every palm tree was ridiculous and many of the flowers might've migrated from Venus.

She stopped at a grocery store for a couple of bottles of ginger kombucha. She drove on and parked at a vacant warehouse that had been rented for the day. The other vehicles in the lot, mostly specialized trucks, had logos saying LOS ANGELES COUNTY ♦ ANIMAL CONTROL. A sign taped to the warehouse's front door said TRAINING SESSION ENTER HERE. Inside, on vast concrete, workers in uniforms were busy with dogs. Looked like big German Shepherds or similar breeds, some on leashes, some in cages. Some of the people wore protective gear — thick gloves up to their elbows, pads strapped to their legs, full facemasks made of wire-grid. One of the women led a group of younger officers, training them in dogcatching techniques.

The trainer was the Black woman she'd glimpsed nearly a month ago spiriting Dawson away from the Bozeman hospital.

Dawson's aunt, Cecie Koloko.

CHAPTER 35

"*Rose, it's nice talking with you on the phone like this, good to hear you're OK in Montana, but I can't tell you where Dawson is. You're part of that whole mess he's trying to put behind him. You helped send him to prison.*"

"*But after I helped send him to prison, I pulled him out of the freezing lake. Cecie, I'm coming to Long Beach. Please meet with me face-to-face.*"

"*... Well, this week I'm training rookie dogcatchers. How about you bring me a bottle of kombucha, where I'm doing the training — ginger kombucha.*"

~

She watched Cecie in action now, thinking, this woman looks impressive — around fifty and solid in the Animal Control uniform, skin a cinnamon tone like Dawson's, accented by the shiny dogcatcher's badge and red lipstick and red nails. A Velcro wrap on one wrist. Only time she'd glimpsed Cecie before this, outside the Bozeman hospital, that wrist was bandaged.

Cecie was showing the trainees a dogcatcher's pole. "This here is your primary tool," Cecie told the trainees. "A telescoping metal pole with a grip for your hands and a loop on the other end that you tighten, like this." *Snap!*

Cecie signaled a man to release one of the big dogs. The dog charged, apparently intent on ripping out Cecie's throat but Cecie side-stepped and flipped the noose around the dog's neck and snapped it closed. The dog leaped and wrestled against the noose and pole trying to get free.

"Don't choke the animal," Cecie told the trainees. "Minimal force."

Cecie kept the dog at the far end of the pole, as the dog calmed and stood still, panting. Then Cecie walked the dog back into the cage and gave it a scratch on its head. Tail-wagging occurred. That dog was trained to train dog-catchers. "Minimal force," Cecie told the trainees again. "But get the job done."

Then Cecie took a break, walked over and said, "Rose? From Montana?"

Cecie held out a hand to accept one of the kombucha bottles, opened it and had a sip. "Hurray for ginger. Good for the gut too. But Rose, on the phone you didn't mention that you dress like you wandered off a Western movie set."

She showed Cecie a smile and opened the other bottle, tasting the ginger and the underlying kombuchaness. They walked out to Cecie's Animal Services truck and nursed their drinks as they leaned against the truck, getting comfortable with each other. "Like I said on the phone," Cecie said, "I'm not going to tell you where Dawson lives. He's breakable now, behaving messed up."

"I'd be messed up too, if I was struck blind and dropped in an icy lake."

"He could manage it better. He's lost his confidence. That was a big part of him — confidence in dealing with his parents dying, confidence in football, confidence in going to Montana and having your sister as his girlfriend, and getting through prison alive. I think he's got PTSD along with being blind."

"If he's got symptoms of trauma, that's another thing he and I share."

"You've got PTSD?"

"My sister and me, we were close. Losing her that way, I can't shake it off."

Cecie nodded. "I see it in combat vets. But a lot of people are tormented by a lot of things. It's up to each individual how to manage it."

"Those scars on your left arm, and the wrap on your other wrist — dog bites?"

"Mmm-mm. I got the bites on my left arm when I was a kid, dealing with a neighbor's pitbull."

"You're looking at me in person now, do I look like I'm going to bite Dawson?"

"You look exactly like your sister in the photos when she was alive. Except your hair is colored blond and your eyes are muddy blue instead of clear blue."

She took off her hat to show Cecie her hair had an inch of black roots now. "Letting my hair go natural, and no more brown eyedrops, I'll be back to who I am."

"Then you'll be back to identical to a dead person."

Cecie's frankness startled her. She paused, and said, "Actually my sister was one tooth better than me." She smiled again and tapped her crooked front tooth.

"Mmm-mm. And now you're taking on more trouble, still trying to make up for testifying against Dawson, coming here to give him a hug or something."

She felt her face blushing. She said, "Dawson thinks whoever killed my sister is still on the loose. He asked me to help him hunt the killer, then he got hurt. I'm going to tell him, I'll take the lead now, and I'll ask him to join me."

Cecie pulled out a wallet chained to her belt, extracted a business card and handed it over, except it wasn't a business card, only a few words printed on it: DO IT RIGHT AND DO IT STRONG. "I hand these out to people," Cecie said. "This is what I raised Dawson on. You could remind him. You could remind yourself too, if you do go hunting, do it right and do it strong, Rose."

"Maybe I'll shoot for fifty-one percent right."

"I'll tell you where Dawson probably is this time of day. Not where he lives. I wouldn't let him live with me — the more he has to do on his own, it might restore some confidence. And cowgirl, if you need to overnight in Long Beach, you'd be welcome at my house, long as you don't make a campfire on the rug."

~

She'd never been to any ocean.

She told herself, "Take a few minutes, girl." Checked her phone map and drove through downtown Long Beach and parked near the sand and wrestled herself in the cab of the pickup, changing into shorts and a halter top, walked barefoot across the sand and waded in. The saltwater made her toes tingle where the frostnip was healing. She lingered, looking at the ocean out to infinity and the people swimming and playing beach volleyball and flying kites. All of it looked like an advertisement. She splashed the saltwater on her face and ate half of a marijuana gummy to soothe her anxiety.

Then she walked back to her pickup and headed toward Dawson, or at least where she hoped he would be.

CHAPTER 36

The Long Beach Fitness & Garden Club occupied a one-story metal building that had been a car-repair shop, in Upper Westside, a poor neighborhood bordering the industrial complex for the Port of Long Beach. In the parking lot, a church's van was handing out free meals to people who looked like they needed it. The club sat at the back of the lot, with no garden she could see, no lawn, no landscaping. She noticed that the building's bay doors, where vehicles had pulled in for oil changes, had been replaced with glass panes, and over the glass, steel mesh for security. Graffiti artists had decorated the mesh with stylized lettering she couldn't read.

She felt like Little Bo-Peep Does Upper Westside.

She walked in and saw a cardboard sign warning NO STREET GANG SHIT ALLOWED IN THE CLUB. The tall skinny man working the desk — Cedric — spoke with a British accent and answered her questions: He was from Kenya and she could find Dawson *on dee roof*. She paid Cedric ten bucks for a guest pass and walked by people battling fitness machines and a boxing ring where two women slick with sweat pummeled each other. She climbed stairs to the roof, which was flat and had views of the ocean, and to the west, mechanical cranes unloading cargo ships. The roof felt solid, built to support the original car-engine hoists that had been attached to the underside of the roof.

This end of the roof was the garden — livestock troughs filled with dirt, people digging and tending plants. The other end was for weightlifting. She saw Dawson over there lying on one of the benches, pressing a barbell, doing reps. He was bare-chested in swim trunks and sunglasses and gloves for grasping the barbell. She walked to him and he seemed unaware of her. He was pressing maybe two hundred pounds, exhaling forcefully with each rep. The scar on his right thigh, from the prison stabbing, was obvious. A pink J-shaped scar — the attacker had shoved the blade in deep and jerked it down toward his knee.

She took a deep breath and tried to relax and said, "Howdy, Dawson."

He rested the barbell in the cradle at the head of his bench, sat up and aimed his sunglasses in her direction. "I can't see," he said. "Do I know you?"

"Here's a hint: I left forty-seven phone messages and you never responded."

His smile flickered on. "Rose Faber, the former Rose Fontaine?" He extended his right hand and she completed the connection, her bare palm clasping his gloved palm. "Thanks for hauling me out of that frozen lake," he said.

"I'm sorry I ever doubted you."

"Thanks also for saying that, if you mean it."

Having no eye-to-eye contact made it harder for her to figure out his emotions. She waited for him to say *glad you survived the lake too* ... or at least *glad you came here.*

Instead he asked politely, "How'd you find me?"

"Your public defender, MaryAnn Meloy, and then your Aunt Cecie."

"Did you bring the sheriff with you?"

"I moved out of his house and filed for a divorce."

His smile flickered again.

"Rose, you do have some moves."

An awkward moment. She told herself silently, do something amusing to remind him why we used to be friends. "Actually," she said, "I came here for weightlifting in the Long Beach sunshine." She watched his smile grow as she grabbed a barbell from a rack, loaded sixty pounds, and lay on a bench next to his. She began pressing her load up and down, weights clinking, exhaling loudly, so he could hear her. He laughed briefly and resumed pressing his barbell, probably thinking about how to deal with her. She felt the late afternoon sun on her exposed skin, which she had a lot of. Her arms and shoulders cranked up, and her core muscles. Dawson and her, side by side, sweat popping, like the old routines in the Bobcats weight room. She did ten reps and began another ten. His upthrusts looked like he'd smash the sky. He had a cane, thin as a willow branch, stashed under his bench. When he took a break, she did too.

"My eyes," he said. "That's what brought you here, right? Poor blind Dawson. I'll save you the effort of asking about it. Getting hit on the back of my head damaged the the part of my brain that runs my eyes. Nothing to worry about, because nothing can be done about it. Maybe the damage will heal, maybe not."

"Cecie told me that. Except the part where nobody should worry about it," she said. "Cecie thinks you've got PTSD, like combat vets. I've got a touch of it too."

"Rose, you and me, we're good now. But you don't belong in Long Beach, same as I don't belong in Montana. We can be long-distance friends."

She pulled out Cecie's card, read it aloud. "*Do it right and do it strong.* Cecie says she raised you on that." She could see the words touched him.

"Yeah, Cecie taught me that. But ..." He turned toward the sunset, probably feeling the day's end, the weakening sunlight and the change in temperature. "It's like when Cecie took me to the Rose Bowl when I was nine," he said. "UCLA won on the final play — a seventy-yard run by a guy who peaked at that moment. That's how life is, you never know when you're hitting your high point, until you look back on it. You and me on that frozen lake, that was the best play we'll ever make — four bad guys delivered to the bottom of the lake, including the one who killed Nikki.

What else do we need to do?"

She started to tell him about her investigating and he interrupted, "Perry Sebastian killed Nikki and paid the price. My lawyers told me that."

She looked at the sunset. Again he lay back on his bench and began more reps with the barbell. She said, "I think my husband — *my ex*, Sheriff Kurt — still isn't getting the murder right. I think somebody planted the new evidence to frame Sebastian. Probably the same person who framed you." He slammed his barbell into the cradle and sat up to face her. She told him, "I'm here because you asked me to join you in your investigation. You wanted me to go through Nikki's stuff looking for clues. I did go through her stuff, and now I have a lead."

She touched his upper arm, solid muscle, and told him, "The other weightlifters and the gardeners are staring at us as they leave. It'll be dark soon. How about we move our conversation to a private place with lighting? Do you live near here?"

CHAPTER 37

S he watched Dawson as he used his cane walking out of the club with her. He tap-tap-tapped, scouting where he'd step next, but he kept straying off course and correcting himself. Limping on his scarred leg. Not the Dawson who'd danced across football fields. "Maybe you should drop back a few paces," he said, "so when lightning hits me, you won't be caught in the blast. That's how things are going for me." He pulled out his new phone and said, "I got phone apps for the blind. The phone senses I'm walking outside and automatically looks for a driver." He told the phone, "No Uber. No Lyft."

She put a hand on his shoulder to guide him and said, "I'm parked over here, on your left. I rented the biggest pickup I could get. A big step up."

In the driver's seat she showed respect by following the directions he remembered, instead of using her phone map. "Take the Long Beach Freeway north," he said. "Then the exit that connects to the San Diego Freeway.

The ramp curves across the LA River, keep to the right on the frontage road, then I'll give you more directions. It's all Upper Westside."

Crossing the LA River on the elevated ramp, she looked down and thought, you poor river. Concrete riverbanks and a shallow flow. She kept following his directions on this side of the river, passing buildings that ranged from charming to abandoned. Wrought-iron bars on many windows and doors, iron fences. Most of Upper Westside was struggling. Streetlights switched on against the increasing darkness. A cop car zoomed by, lightbar flashing but no siren noise, maybe it wasn't an emergency. She heard a *pop-pop-pop* in the distance and asked, "Is that gunshots?" and he answered, "Fireworks. Gunshots are more of a sharp cracking sound, usually an irregular rhythm, later at night."

On West 34th she saw men and teens hanging out on a streetlighted corner and spilling onto the street as if they might stop the pickup. She described them to him, their tattoos and clothes and how they seemed ready to go off.

"Are they Latino? Probably the Longos. *Longos*, as in Long Beach."

As she tried to drive around them, one yelled Dawson's name and walked in front of the pickup. Then three more. "They're going to block us," she told him.

"Then stop. Be cool. Don't turn off the engine. Don't get out of the vehicle."

She'd been driving with the windows open and some

of the Longos leaned in. "Yo, Dawson, how's the blind thing going?" ... "Who's your lady in the cowboy hat?" ... "She's *hot*." Which made her wish she'd put on a shirt over her halter top and shorts. He recognized some of their voices and addressed them by name, slipping into their slang and extending his right fist so they could bump it. They came at her too. "What's your name, lady cowboy?" ... "Oh like the Rose Bowl Parade?" ... "Let me try on your hat." Snatch. "Now I'm a cowboy."

Eventually Dawson told them, "Rose and I have to go. Dinner with my aunt."

"Your Aunt Cecie? She still catching bad dogs? Plenty of bad dogs around here. Cecie better get her ass in gear."

They laughed genuinely and stepped back. The one who'd grabbed her hat handed it back to her without prompting. "Rose, you look better in this than I do." His grin twinkled, gems or fake gems embedded in his teeth.

She drove on, and Dawson said, "An aunt is still worth something in Upper Westside. Plus some of them have dogs and Cecie keeps order in the world of dogs."

On DeForest Avenue she parked in front of Long Beach Horizons, a three-story building where he lived. "Assisted living, all ages and conditions," he said. "Montana's government hasn't paid me the settlement yet, so I'm living on limited money my lawyers fronted me. Cecie placed me here, until my eyes improve or I get better at doing everything blind. The river is across the street, in the big ditch. I walk over there sometimes."

She put on a shirt and he led her into Long Beach Horizons, tap-tap-tapping across the lobby. The floor was old linoleum, mostly gray with other colors where repairs had been done. Cinder-block walls, painted yellow. She saw other Horizons residents who were blind or ailing, some in wheelchairs, one walking on a metal leg, as he gave her a tour, hallways lined with residential rooms and the entertainment room with the big TV. Many dispensers of hand sanitizer. The dining room was nearly empty because most Horizons residents dined early. She sat at a table with him, and a waiter — a man who spoke rough English, probably from Central America — served spaghetti and apple pie. She noticed Dawson having to push food around on his plate, his fingers assisting his silverware. She sampled her plate, similar to the hospital food she'd had in Bozeman.

"Good pie, isn't it?" he said.

She thought, nope. And said, "Delicious."

His room was on the second floor. The elevator seemed tired. He groped his key into the door of the room and led her in. A bare-bones room that he'd tuned to his liking, no conventional bed, no chair, only a sleeping pad folded over itself and stored in the corner, and a laminate countertop along one wall. Bathrooms down the hallway, shared by other residents. In the daytime his window would let in sunlight, a ration of physical and emotional warmth a blind person could appreciate. There were flowers in a vase on the counter, emitting a pleasant fragrance. Beside the flowers he had small clay sculptures and unshaped clay and wooden-handled sculpting tools. She remembered, during his few months in college he'd taken an art class that involved clay. Probably he stood at this counter to shape these sculptures — faces of animals and a torso of a naked woman, about nine inches tall, thighs to neck.

"You can sit on the counter," he said.

She watched his at-home routine. He lowered himself to sit on the folded sleeping pad, his back against the wall, his cane always within reach. Kept his sunglasses on. She perched on the countertop, her mostly bare legs dangling. The sculpted torso drew her. She took it into her hands quietly so he wouldn't hear.

"Every Sunday Cecie brings me flowers," he said.

"Nice," she told him. In her hands the torso had an interesting texture — dried hard but not glazed. The clay shoulders and dainty breasts and subtly rounded belly flowed down to the V-shaped groin. She put the torso back on the countertop in such a hurry it tipped over. *Clunk*. She prevented it from falling to the floor and said, "Sheesh, I knocked over one of your sculptures."

"I heard."

She righted the torso on the counter and told him, "It didn't break."

"The clay lady?" he said.

She nodded. Then said, "Yes."

"You wonder, how can I shape the clay without seeing

it?" He spread his fingers. "I been into clay since high school. Learned my best techniques in prison — an old sculptor came in to run a workshop for us. He had us wear blindfolds, teaching us to use our hands more than our eyes. Now I'm only going by touch." Then he said, "That torso, that's Nikki's shape."

"I thought so."

Also my shape, she was thinking, since we were nearly identical. Maybe he was thinking that too.

"I'll listen to your ideas about the killer," he said, "after you tell me, how come you're divorcing the sheriff?"

CHAPTER 38

She pulled the second half of today's anti-anxiety marijuana gummy from her shorts and downed it. "Lots of snags in my marriage," she told him. "Some have to do with Sheriff Kurt's new take on the murder. What have you heard about that?"

"My lawyers tell me, your husband —"

"Call him my *ex* — the divorce will be final soon."

He started over. "Your ex found new evidence in Perry Sebastian's place. Photos the killer probably shot, with notes written on them, all indicating that Sebastian was the killer. Maybe with help from his Whitey gang."

"The deputies found the photos in Sebastian's freezer," she said. "Is that a good hiding place? Or did somebody else put the photos in the freezer so the deputies would find them? I talked to Sebastian's girlfriend. She lived with him, at least part-time, and she never saw those photos."

"Sebastian's *girlfriend?* What do you expect her to say?"

She told him more of her findings, some of which she'd shared with Sheriff Kurt. "The big swastika spray-painted on Sebastian's wall, perfect art for a White supremacist? It also doesn't fit. A month ago Sebastian discovered that one of his grandfathers was in the Army fighting Hitler's Nazis. I verified it on military websites. Sebastian's grandfather earned a Bronze Star in the Battle of the Bulge, nineteen-forty-four, for destroying German tanks with grenades he took from German soldiers he shot. Sebastian was so proud of having that hero in his family, he got rid of all his swastikas — Nazi posters, Nazi videos, decals on his snowmobile. I think somebody else painted that swastika and put the photos in the freezer *after* Sebastian drowned in the lake. Probably the same person who killed Nikki and framed you five years ago. Or the same conspiracy."

Still he was reluctant — the loss of confidence Cecie described. "Sebastian and his gang fucked with me for years," he said. "He was into White power, whether or not he worshipped swastikas. Maybe one of Sebastian's friends thought Sebastian's wall was a good place to advertise White power with a new swastika."

She watched him thinking it over. His hair, the wiry curls, had acquired a rustier quality in prison. He asked what she wanted him to ask. "Who else you think did it?"

She pulled out her phone and streamed video highlights of Alonzo Davis in a Seahawks game last week. Aimed the phone's speaker at him. The analysts raved about Alonzo slamming the Saints. "Maybe Alonzo Davis," she told him. "He hurt people in college. All those penalties for roughing up opponents in Bobcats games. He shattered that Idaho player's knee. When Nikki broke up with him, I was glad."

He kept listening as she streamed a recent news segment about Alonzo punching a woman in a Seattle club where a security camera recorded it, and Alonzo grabbing a different woman in a Denver hotel elevator. She turned down the news and said, "We know Alonzo has a temper and a cruel streak, and he takes down women as well as men." She paused to let that sink in, and went on, "When I looked through Nikki's stuff last week, what you asked me to do, I found pills she hid in her jewelry box — uppers and downers. That helped me remember, when Nikki dated Alonzo, he gave her those pills. You think there's a chance Alonzo sneaked downers into one of your drinks during the party in the End Zone Saloon? And then Alonzo slipped into the condo while you were unconscious? He could've even rung the doorbell, Nikki might've let him in."

She watched him flex his hands like he was getting a hold on the possibility. "I went back to that End Zone Saloon," he said, "after I talked to you at the bison roundup and you wouldn't go with me. In the saloon I remembered more about the party and started a list of suspects. I put Alonzo on my list."

She told him, "I'm nodding in agreement. I got in

touch with Alonzo yesterday, by email through the Seahawks website, then he phoned me. He gets off on people thinking he's important, especially women he hasn't abused yet. I'm meeting him in Seattle, tomorrow night, after his New Year's Eve playoff game. Come with me."

"I'm blind, Rose."

"I watched you doing the bench presses. You're still Awesome Dawson."

He groped for his cane, stood and said with more force, *"I'm blind!"* and whipped his cane at the countertop, *whack whack,* knocking over the flowers and some of the sculptures, stumbling over her legs, knocking her off the counter as he fell to the floor taking her with him. She scrambled up off him. He reclaimed his cane and stood on his own. "Did I hurt you, Rose?"

"No. How about you?"

He seemed ruffled by the physical contact with her. "Time out," he said. He led her out to the gravel yard that had kind of fresh air, a mix of freeways and ocean. She stood with him and in a while he said, "Back in the day, I was as good at running the ball as Alonzo was at linebacker. I might've gone pro too."

"There are a few things about you I still like," she told him. "In the old days, you understood my sense of humor, that's important." She was relieved to see another flicker of his smile. She told him her plan for approaching Alonzo. He tapped his cane on the gravel as she talked, as if that helped him decide. When she finished, he tapped some more and then he said, "I did some wrestling in high school, along with football. Tomorrow morning I have wrestling practice at the club. Can you look for an afternoon flight?"

She hugged him briefly, maybe another mistake, said goodnight and returned to the pickup, started driving again. She imagined another lonely motel, and phoned Cecie instead and said, "I wound up hugging your nephew. He and I are flying to Seattle tomorrow. Are you still up for me crashing at your place tonight?"

"Come on over, cowgirl."

~

In the morning, when most people were gearing up for New Year's Eve festivities, she went back to the Long Beach Fitness & Garden Club and watched Dawson wrestle with a personal trainer who understood how blind people can do self-defense. Dawson seemed good at this sport too. As the wrestling went on, she took off her shoes and began working out on a big mat where they had equipment for gymnastics. She'd kept in shape at a private gym in Bozeman. Here she did stretches and whipped through handsprings and flips, only fell over a few times. Then she chalked her hands and jumped to grab the high bar. Only a bit of distress in her formerly frostnipped fingers. She began doing pullups, counting out loud. "One." ... "Two." ... "Three." ... "Four." ... "*Five.*" She had to pause, dangling from the bar, then raised her legs forming an L — lighting up her abs too — and continued, *"Six!"* ... *"Seven!"* ... *"Eight!"*

She couldn't do nine. She kept her grip on the bar, in the mood to try a flyaway dismount. Using her legs as a pendulum, she swung forward and backward, forward and backward, gaining momentum. At the maximum of a forward swing, she released and tucked into a back flip while gravity took her down. She landed it, bare feet slamming the mat. *"Yes!"* And fell over again.

She did more pullups and walked around on her hands and more flips and falling down, until Dawson finished wrestling. They swung by Long Beach Horizons and showered in separate bathrooms. He packed a bag and they went to say goodbye to Cecie, who had the New Year's Eve holiday off work. Instead of talking about the risks in Seattle, Cecie brought out new Hawaiian shirts for Dawson. "This is what we do, Rose, I'll sew a different number on each shirt, so Dawson can touch the number and tell which shirt it is. Numbers made of chenille yarn, like on letterman jackets." Cecie told Dawson, "Number seven on the palm tree shirt, eight on the fishes shirt, nine on the surfers. You'll be looking good."

To allow the Kolokos a private goodbye, she stepped out to the porch. Then she drove with Dawson to the airport's rental-car hub and turned in the pickup. At the security checkpoint he told the agents about his eyes. They ordered him to take off his sunglasses, maybe violating some law about respecting disabled people. She saw his eyes were unfocused, blank. Then the agents inspected his cane — different than the cane she'd seen him use before, capable of being telescoped down for traveling. She steered him onward, toward the gate for the Seattle flight. Special-needs travelers could board first. He qualified for that honor, and she did too, as his escort.

Part 3

Together

Walking the skybridge to board the jet, he told himself, take your time, man. Rose's hand on his shoulder was getting to be a habit. He used the cane with his right hand, tapping ahead and side-to-side to locate things. The skybridge slanted upward and he tapped objects on the right, probably luggage getting special handling. Approaching the doorway to the plane, he felt the airflow vented from the plane and knew where he was.

His blindness kept changing. He wasn't cloaked in constant darkness the way most people thought of being blind. Instead he saw frequent hallucinations the doctors said were not unusual with blindness. Flashes of color and shooting stars and random phantoms. Like a mild dose of LSD. When he wasn't hallucinating he saw nothing. Totally blank. As he tried to fit through the plane's doorway, Rose touched his head, "Low clearance."

The plane felt rickety under his feet and the air was cold and artificial, machined. He walked the narrow aisle between the seat rows and saw an explosion of red. Normal passengers — those who were intact and able — hadn't boarded yet. He bumped into a guy using crutches, then bumped a female flight attendant who turned sideways to squeeze by him, her slick polyester skirt brushing his hand. He kept tapping his cane and saying, "Excuse me." He'd learned to use a cane politely, in a Westside Community Center class. The instructor cautioned him, don't tap on anyone with the cane, because some White people might assume a Black guy was attacking them with a stick.

He groped farther through the aisle amid flickers of purple lightning until Rose said, "Our seats. Here." He sensed that she was scooting over to the window seat and he telescoped his cane down to its shortest length and took the aisle seat. Tight, his shoulder against hers. She patted his knee and said, "You're sitting on your seatbelt."

Much of what she was doing and saying reminded him of Nikki. He buckled his seatbelt and pulled out his phone and told it, "Turn on airplane mode."

"Understood," the phone's robot voice said.

The plane got crowded. The woman seated in front of him spoke a language that had a lot of crisp *ah* sounds, maybe Arabic. Across the aisle, a college-sounding guy smelled of pepperoni pizza. From Rose he got whiffs of lemony shampoo and mint mouthwash. He felt the plane lurch. Rolling to the takeoff, he sensed Rose getting tense. The thrust pressed him against the seat and the roar grew loud. The steep climb and the leveling off, then the engines quieted and he sensed her relaxing.

He was learning more of who she was now, her personality battered by tragedy. Her plan seemed pretty good and she'd prepared for it. But sometimes she caretaked him too much, like now, telling him about a book she was thumbing through. "It's a novel about a rancher trying to save the ranch from the bank."

"It's OK, Rose. Read to yourself, I'll do some thinking."

He'd given up listening to podcasts and music in public places — he needed to hear the world around him. If this thing with his eyes lasted, he'd learn Braille.

"Dawson, the eye doctors, what do they tell you?"

She'd become his partner so he filled her in. First the eye doc in the Bozeman hospital. Then the UCLA specialist in neurological trauma affecting vision. Then a different specialist who'd retired from a career treating combat vets.

"The docs taught me a language. PTVS — that's *post trauma vision syndrome.* They say it's unusual to lose vision in both eyes. Sebastian and his gangsters added to my concussions from football — *cumulative factors.*" He patted the back of his head. "The damage is here but it affects how both eyes work."

"Any treatment they can do?"

"A few years ago they would've tried surgery or drugs. Now they say give it time, if the damaged tissue heals on its own, I might regain full or partial vision."

"... What are the odds?"

He liked how she cut right to it. "They say about one in four that I'll ever have full vision again." He listened to her falling silent. "Rose, the way my life has gone up to now, one in four odds, that's pretty good."

He felt her tap his sunglasses. "Well, you look pretty good in these shades."

He remembered her face, her original deep blue eyes, same as Nikki's. "At the bison roundup," he said, "I asked you, how did you turn your eyes brown?"

"Eyedrops. After you brought it up, I quit using the drops. Also quit coloring my hair. Now I have two-tone hair, blond with black roots showing."

"Sounds good." He meant it, but he wanted to give her a break from dealing with him, so he added, "I didn't get much sleep the last five years."

"Me either," she said.

He closed his eyes, though it made no difference in what he saw. As he tried to retreat into dozing, he flashed to his medical journey.

~

Trapped in the cold beds of the MRI and CT scanners, one after another, with the buzzes and hammering noises as they penetrate his skull with mysterious rays. Outside the scanners, most of the doctors talk with a soft tone the medical schools must teach them. But Doctor Cordell, treating private patients after many years of dealing with soldiers who suffered battlefield injuries, lays it out:

"You're fucked, Dawson. But you're not fucked as badly as most of the patients I've treated. You have both your legs, both your feet, and all your toes. You have your arms and your hands and all your fingers. You have ears. You have a face. You have a dick and your balls. And your brain seems OK other than the visual cortex. You remember what a lot of things look like even though you can't see now."

~

He returned to thinking about Nikki's eyes.

And Rose's eyes.

"Rose, you're still gorgeous, I presume?" Alonzo Davis had said to her in their phone talk. "If you get to Seattle in time for the three-thirty kickoff, come to the Seahawks suite in the stadium and order the crab-and-caviar nachos. I'll try to swing by to greet you. Then we'll hang out after the game in my condo on the shore."

She hadn't mentioned she might bring Dawson with her. She rode with her big blind friend in a Lyft from the Seattle airport to the Seahawks stadium, through the city's notorious rain. The Seahawks suite was jammed with wealthy people and ass-kissers gobbling the fancy snacks. No sign of Alonzo. The suite's glass wall had been slid open so there was no separation from the field below. When the national anthem bellowed through the loudspeakers, she saw more players taking a knee on the field. Then she watched the game while Dawson listened to the play-by-play audio. They'd both burned out on football after the murder, but seventy thousand fans around them cheered madly and thanked god for touchdowns as the Seahawks and the Green Bay Packers crushed each other on the soggy plastic grass. Alonzo made some great plays on the field. Pointwise, the Seahawks scored thirty-eight, the Packers twenty-five, civilization zero.

After the game Alonzo still didn't show up in the Seahawks suite but he texted his home address. The rain obscured sunset as she guided Dawson from the stadium. They rode another Lyft splashing along the urban shore to the high-rise building topped by Alonzo's penthouse condo. The doorman checked her ID and confirmed she was an approved guest. There was a special elevator for the penthouse, and as it lifted her and Dawson, she told him, "The building is fourteen stories tall, modern, chrome steel and glass. The floors are rough wood planks, maybe for traction for wet shoes."

The elevator delivered them to a roofed porch atop the building. She peered over the railing, yes the sidewalk was more than a hundred feet below. The porch had hooks for hanging up the wet jackets and her hat, and a carved wooden door that was the penthouse entrance. When she took off her jacket she was chilly with only her cotton shirt above her jeans. She kept telling Dawson what she saw.

"Security camera over the door."

The camera must've alerted the man who opened the door. Not Alonzo — a medium-sized Blackish man wearing burgundy jeans and a gray t-shirt and a pistol exposed in a shoulder holster. She thought, Alonzo has a bodyguard. In burgundy jeans. "Hey Babe," the bodyguard said to her.

She told him, "Babe is not my name. I divorced a guy for the same mistake."

She saw his subtle hint of a smile. "Rose?" he asked. "Alonzo is expecting you. Who you got with you?"

Dawson said, "Another old friend. Dawson Koloko."

"I've heard of you," the bodyguard said. No remarks about Dawson's cane and sunglasses. "Welcome to Alonzo's nest. I'm Vernon Duke, I answer the door and do other things need doing."

She told Dawson, "Vernon has a pistol in a shoulder holster."

"Which shoulder?"

Vernon said, "The left. Nothing to worry about," and escorted them into the main room where floor-to-ceiling windows smeared with raindrops offered blurry views of city lights and the dark expanse of Puget Sound. It was a lot of interior space done in the same modern style as the lobby. Sleek leather sofas and chairs, glass tables, pole lamps casting a glow, the wood planks underfoot.

Alonzo Davis appeared from an inner doorway. Bigger than she remembered, must be at least two hundred and thirty pounds. He had his hair twisted into dreadlocks and wore a tank top and a gold neck chain, baggy shorts and flip-flops, showing off his veiny muscles. Ice packs were taped to both his knees.

"Montana girl!" Alonzo oozed. "You gone blond!"

She let him hug her too long. He slid his hands down to her butt and squeezed. With her face trapped against his chest, she noticed shiny things dangling from his deltoid muscles, near his armpits — acupuncture needles. When he released her, he turned to Dawson, "My man Awesome Dawson. Rose is full of surprises, including bringing you. Strange that you two are together now. What's with the cane? You gone blind?"

"I got injured," Dawson said. "Might be temporary."

"Damn, hope it clears up," Alonzo said. "Sorry you didn't see me play today." He boomed out a big laugh apparently thinking he'd made a joke.

Vernon directed her and Dawson to a sofa and handed out bottles of craft beer. Alonzo sat in a wide armchair facing them and drank and said, "I'm still sad about Nikki." Then Alonzo hijacked the talk to his injuries from today's game — bruises from tackling many Packers, the particular knee ligament he strained while intercepting a pass. "After every game I eat handfuls of Advil and CBD pills." He flicked one of the needles stuck in his chest, "Vernon does the acupuncture — he's a wizard for pain management. On top of protecting me from threats."

Alonzo raised his beer. "To old friends." He chugged the rest of the bottle and tossed the empty at Vernon, who snatched it from the air one-handed, good reflexes, and placed it on the counter. "Five years not being in touch, Rose," Alonzo said, "then you email asking for a phone talk, and on the phone you say you found something in Nikki's stuff you want to show me. You bring Dawson. It feels like you're setting me up for something."

She sipped her beer, kept the bottle in her hand. "You might not want Vernon to be in on this," she said.

"Vernon stays," Alonzo said. "Get to it, Rose."

"Rose and *me*," Dawson said. He stood and positioned himself beside Vernon, casual, not a confrontation yet. Vernon reacted with another hint of a smile.

She rested her bottle on the table, ready to throw it or use it for hitting, and pulled out Nikki's phone. "Alonzo, you might recognize this — Nikki's old iPhone with the artsy decal on the case. Last week I found videos stored on this phone. Videos Nikki shot when she was dating you, and a video you shot with this phone — you'll recognize your video too. I'll stream the videos to your TV, only twenty-three minutes in all. I bet you'll find it interesting."

She'd captured Alonzo's attention. So far, so good.

She got the TV linked to the phone and began with the video Alonzo shot when he dated Nikki. It showed Nikki on the climbing wall in a Bozeman gym. The soundtrack was mostly Alonzo's voice advising her about handholds, even though she didn't need his advice — "Up to your left, reach!" — and her responses, not as loud because she was far above him.

The climbing video lasted about three minutes and as it played she watched Alonzo getting antsy. She told Alonzo, "The rest of the videos are Nikki's diary — Nikki talking about her life, her feelings, her thoughts. She kept it secret — that's how diaries are. These are highlights from what she recorded about you, Alonzo."

Here was black-haired Nikki, starting her video diary in a bedroom lined with her art posters and artsy wall calendars, apparently her Bozeman apartment. Nikki saying "Dear Diary" to the phone and propping the phone on a shelf so it recorded video of her pacing the bedroom and talking about Alonzo being such an athlete. Cut to the next scene, Nikki in the same bedroom a week later, pacing and talking about how Alonzo treated her so nice trying to get into her pants. Cut to her talking about how Alonzo gave her pills — uppers for going up the climbing wall, downers for getting to sleep afterward. Nikki saying how fun it was, doing the pills and being with Alonzo. Cut to Nikki pacing the bedroom and talking about Alonzo getting pushy on dates, Alonzo starting to bother her. The final scene, Nikki at night outside, the phone jiggling as she walked with it in her hand, Nikki telling the phone that Alonzo had just pawed her. Nikki obviously upset, her clothes and hair messed up, talking about breaking up with Alonzo and how she felt threatened by him.

Rose watched Alonzo watching the videos.

She beamed a thought at him, *fall for it, Alonzo.*

He listened to Rose play the fake video diary that was her pretending to be her identical twin. He thought it sounded real, a pretty good performance. He could imagine the scenes too, because Rose had told him how she'd faked it. In Jules's doublewide where she'd had access to Nikki's stuff, she'd put on a black wig made of Nikki's hair over her own blond-colored hair, and she'd dressed in Nikki's clothes, several changes including the shirt and skirt Alonzo messed up on their last date. She'd also done a makeover on Nikki's bedroom in the doublewide so it resembled the Bozeman apartment five years ago. She'd even disguised her own crooked front tooth by slipping a clear mouthguard over it. Then she'd used Nikki's phone to record herself disguised as Nikki talking about Alonzo.

As he listened to the last diary scene streaming to Alonzo's TV, he tried to be ready for whatever Alonzo and Vernon might do. His hallucinations surged again like July Fourth fireworks as he listened to Rose turning off the TV and coughing once, her signal to him. He said, "Alonzo, we told my lawyers we're meeting with you." Then to her, "I guess Alonzo is sitting on a chair about four feet in front of where I'm standing? Vernon is standing to my left, just beyond the arm of the sofa?"

"Probably not for much longer," she said. "Alonzo is about to explode."

He aimed the word at Alonzo, "Don't."

"Shut up, blind man."

He shifted his blind focus from Alonzo to Vernon and said, "Keep your gun out of this." Vernon remained silent. Shifting back to Alonzo, he went on, "You didn't like it when Nikki took up with me. You came to the party in Big Sky's End Zone Saloon and got more angry watching Nikki with me. You're a walking pharmacy, pills for every occasion, so you must've slipped downers into my drinks at the party, and when Nikki walked me back to the condo, you killed her and framed me."

He heard her tell Alonzo, "You sick fuck," and then Alonzo exploded, "*Give me that phone!*" as if Alonzo had a gut reaction to destroy the videos. He sensed Alonzo jumping at her and heard the thud of her thrown to the floor and the clatter of furniture overturned. Then he got his hands on Alonzo, grappling and leveraging as a wrestler does — difficult but he thought he might be able to handle it, moves he'd practiced at the Long Beach Fitness & Garden Club. Time stretched as Alonzo began fighting him — Alonzo was strong but banged-up from the game and not a wrestler, only shoving and throwing punches that didn't work well in the clinch. He accepted the blows from Alonzo while he established an overhook hold on Alonzo, that was his priority. His effort powered wilder hallucinations, sped-up flashes of brighter colors. He felt the balance shifting, and sought more control to prevent Alonzo's punches and he called out, "Rose, are you OK?"

"Yes!"

"What's Vernon doing?"

"Spectating," she said.

He heard Vernon say, "A pro linebacker fighting a blind man — probably my only chance to see anything like this."

He bore down as Alonzo tried to pry and twist out of the holds. He felt blows to his legs and ankles, Alonzo trying to kick him off balance, and he used that to gain more leverage because every kick Alonzo had only one foot on the floor. He felt Alonzo stagger, an opportunity to establish a pinch grip tie hold on Alonzo.

He heard her coming close and she said, "I've got a lamp I can hit him with, if you want."

"Better not," he told her, "or Vernon might think it isn't a fair fight." Slow motion he forced Alonzo to the floor face-down as Alonzo yelled at Vernon, "You're my bodyguard, shoot this motherfucker! Get him off me!"

He tightened his holds more and heard Vernon say, "Dawson, I'm going to walk over and squat down beside you." Then Vernon walked and squatted and told Alonzo, "If this man attacks you, I'll defend you — that's a bodyguard's job. But this man didn't attack you. You attacked Rose, and Dawson is defending her."

He heard Vernon walking away, and Vernon doing something that sounded like opening a bottle that released carbonation, and Vernon smacked his lips loudly and said, "Wow, this IPA is hoppy."

She waited until Dawson said, "The handcuffs, please." Such a polite man. She retrieved the handcuffs from her coat and crouched down where Dawson held Alonzo face-down. Handcuffs she'd borrowed from Cecie in Long Beach. Why would a dogcatcher have handcuffs? You ever meet an irresponsible dog owner?

Alonzo began to yell more of the choice language he'd probably learned in the nice Denver suburb where he grew up. Once she and Dawson had Alonzo cuffed behind his back, they let him sit up on the floor. The acupuncture needles from his bare chest were strewn around the floor, along with the ice packs from his knees.

"That was dumb," she told Alonzo. "Even if you wiped out Dawson and me, the lawyers would get the cops to nail you for that alone."

"I lost my temper. I don't go around killing! Vernon, do your job now. Throw them out and take off these cuffs."

"I'd like to see the rest of their show," Vernon said.

She began to stream a real video clip to the TV — the news report about Alonzo having a lot of temporary girlfriends and abusing some in public. She paused it so she could tell Alonzo, "A short hop from *that* to murder."

"No!"

"Tell them the truth about your girlfriends," Vernon said. "Or I will."

Alonzo seemed to be having a panic attack, suddenly short of breath and popping sweat, "You're fired, Vernon."

Vernon said, "So, Rose and Dawson, the deal with the recent girlfriends ..."

"OK OK," Alonzo broke in. "Vernon is about to say I didn't hurt those particular girlfriends. I paid them to act like I was roughing them up. Vernon hired the last one for me. The one before, my agent hired."

She looked at Dawson, watched him shake his head expressing contempt. "You think that helps your image, Alonzo?" he said. "The big bad linebacker?"

"Something like that."

"Keep talking," Vernon told Alonzo, "or I won't have occasional sex with you anymore."

She and Dawson said at the same time, "You're gay?"

"... Yeah," Alonzo said. "I'm gay." Staring at the floor.

She paused thinking about it and went on, "You dated Nikki while you figured out you're gay? Or you were using Nikki for cover, pretending to want sex with her? You still need to persuade us that you didn't kill Nikki. Or we'll share Nikki's video diary with cops." More of her bluff.

"The diary proves that you shared pills and it makes you a suspect in the murder. The Seahawks skybox-ers would notice that."

"... Talk to Tyrone Allen, the Bobcats ball-hiker back then. Around the time Nikki was killed, me and Tyrone went to our room in Big Sky's Huntley Lodge. We shared the room. ... Tyrone will tell you that's my alibi. Tyrone is still in Montana, living on an Indian reservation — a Black dude gone Native."

Dawson said, "You had pills, you dosed my drinks."

"I never put pills in your drinks that night. I got my pills from Tyrone. He was my supplier."

She kept the pressure on, "Before that night, Nikki told me and Dawson, Tyrone had hit on her too. So you and Tyrone did the crime together?"

She watched Alonzo, who was still sitting on the floor handcuffed — Alonzo glancing around the room the way a bull elk looks for wolves. "You been watching too many crime shows," Alonzo said. "Tyrone didn't kill Nikki and I didn't kill Nikki."

She stepped between Alonzo's legs and pulled his neck chain to bring his face closer to hers, "If you're lying, Alonzo, we'll get back to you."

Vernon clapped briefly and walked with them to the elevator. "Probably Alonzo isn't lying now," Vernon said.

"Who are you, Vernon Duke?" she asked.

"Formerly Sergeant Duke. Eighty-second Airborne, three tours in Afghanistan. Quit the Army because of every reason you can imagine, to start earning more money in private security. Didn't quit my principles. If Alonzo does fire me, there are so many people hiring bodyguards, I'll find more of this work."

She gave Vernon the key to the handcuffs, "Please mail the cuffs back to me," and exchanged contact info. Then she and Dawson gave Vernon a fist-bump goodbye and rode the elevator to the lobby and walked through a block of rain to one of Seattle's gazillion coffeeshops. She bought two cups and they sat at a little table talking about what had just come down — and as usual, what to do next.

"Your plan worked," Dawson said.

"You handled Alonzo — now you're Awesome Dawson the wrestler."

He shrugged, "If I can get my hands on an opponent, I have a chance."

She thought, he's got his confidence back. "Are you OK?" she said. "You must have some fresh bruises."

"Not too bad. How about you? You're the one who got thrown down."

"I'm OK too," she said, not telling him about her scuffs and bruises.

She listened while he put his phone on speaker mode and called his favorite lawyer, MaryAnn Meloy in Bozeman. He told MaryAnn, "Rose can hear this. Our thing with Alonzo went OK."

He filled in MaryAnn, then MaryAnn updated them on events in Bozeman. "Sheriff Kurt closed the case for the second time. The new official conclusion is, Perry Sebastian murdered Nikki and framed you, Dawson. Did you come up with any proof the sheriff is wrong again?"

"Not yet. But we're making progress."

When Dawson ended that call, she used her phone to search for Tyrone Allen, "Like Alonzo said, Tyrone has a job in Indian country — on the Rocky Boy Reservation in northern Montana."

"And now you plan to ask Tyrone, were you having sex with Alonzo when the murder came down, or did you *do* the murder?"

"This is the thread we got ahold of," she said.

"Yeah. Alonzo might warn him that we're coming."

They headed for the airport in a Lyft driven by a woman from Syria, and got stuck in a traffic jam. A crowd yelling and carrying signs marched through the gridlock of vehicles. It was a protest against the Seattle cops who'd shot and killed a mentally-ill Black man having a breakdown. The marchers quickly got into it with cops in riot gear. Tear gas wafted around. The Lyft driver waved at the cops, "No rubber bullets in my country, only regular bullets," and eased through the melee.

At the airport they used more of Jules's frequent-flyer points, and took off through the abundance of raindrops, on tonight's last flight to Montana.

When the plane landed in Billings, he could imagine the town, because he'd seen it five years ago on a road trip with Bobcats teammates. It was Montana's biggest town, and it would fit in LA's back pocket. Now, walking through the Billings airport, he noticed how all the voices sounded White, overpronouncing words instead of riffing. He telescoped his traveling cane out to full length and resumed tapping the floor as he walked. He still had Rose helping him navigate but felt more independent and steady.

He listened to her say, "It's almost midnight here."

He heard the baggage carousel, and her unzipping a bag. She handed him his winter jacket. He put it on and walked with her toward the exit, heard the *whoosh* of the automatic doors. Outside the cold gripped him and she said, "They cleared the snow off the sidewalks and parking lots but it's slick. Be careful."

She guided him to where she'd parked her pickup

several days ago. He heard her placing the bags in the bed and unlocking the cab. He telescoped his cane shorter and climbed onto the passenger seat. She fired up the engine and he heard the tires crunching on the icy pavement. He was seeing the hallucinations, purple sparklers, as she drove in silence, then she pulled over and stopped. "This is a motel I've stayed in before," she said. "Not the Ritz but it's clean and quiet."

"Sounds good," he told her. He was saying that more often now. While she went into the motel office, he hung out in her pickup with the engine idling and the heater blowing, how Montanans spend a lot of their time. When she returned she said, "The motel is full. There's a high-school basketball tournament in town, busloads of teams from around Montana. The desk clerk called other motels and they're all full. We'll have to look for a motel along the road to the reservation."

He appreciated how she kept telling him what she was doing. She found a drive-through joint open late and got tacos and more coffee. Then she found the road heading north to where they might find Tyrone Allen.

He ate his meal by touch and heard the tires whine with the increased speed.

"How's the pavement?" he asked.

"Not bad," she said. "Decent two-lane, not much ice out here. Hardly any traffic. We're going through dark fields covered in snow, and I see a few pines."

"How far to the next town that'll have a motel?"

"About fifty miles. The town is called Roundup. Small ranching town."

"I would've guessed that," he said, "since they call it Roundup."

She laughed and said, "I'm sleepy. Can you help me stay awake?"

"Hmmm ..." He thought about what to say and settled on, "Did Nikki ever mention, she was my first girlfriend?"

He sensed her smiling. She said, "I always assumed you had lots of girls hitting on you, the big high-school football stud from Long Beach."

"Nikki was the only lover I've had. ... Your turn."

"Hmmm," she said, imitating him, "how about the time I pretended to be Nikki on a date with you?"

"You're making that up."

"Nope. You thought you were with Nikki, but Nikki got sick from bad egg salad. She asked me to fill in for her. We thought it would be fun, another risky caper. I pretended to be her, hanging out with you — like I faked Nikki's video diary to fool Alonzo. Any idea which date?"

He gave it thought and admitted, "I don't know."

"Figure it out," she told him. "How often did you hang out with Nikki — maybe thirty dates during your six months together? Forty dates? I'm not telling you what you and I did on the faked date."

"... I would've noticed your crooked tooth in person ... so the date must've been in some dark setting ... maybe Thursday night of Homecoming Week? When Nikki and

I agreed to meet at the bonfire near the stadium? It was dark there, other than the flames."

"... What did you do that night?" she said.

"You mean, what did you and me do that night? We hung out in the crowd, everybody whipping up Bobcats spirit for the Saturday game against Sacramento State. We kissed. You guarded your crooked tooth with your lips." He remembered the kissing. As that bonfire flamed high and hot, he'd explored her lips while she allowed him that much. He'd shifted to her neck and her ears and when he'd returned to her lips she'd kissed him back. No tongue but definitely two-way kissing. He'd slipped his hands inside her sweatshirt — Nikki's sweatshirt. Instantly she'd backed off. "I figure that's the date," he said, "because Nikki liked me touching her more than that."

She cleared her throat and said, "That was the date."

"The saucy twins."

"I didn't expect to kiss you." Silence for a while. He felt the road imitating a roller coaster. "We're going through a small mountain range," she said. Later she slowed and said, "We're crossing the Musselshell River." He heard the sound of the tires change on the bridge. She steered through another curve and slowed. "We're coming into Roundup. Population two thousand and nearly all of them asleep. Guess which street we're on now."

"Main Street."

"Correct. Guess which cafe we're passing now."

"The Bullshit Cafe."

"Close," she said. "The Pioneer Cafe. I see two motels, and both are old and basic. Sometimes it's good that you're blind." She parked and left him in her pickup as she scouted for rooms. She came back in a few minutes.

"Good news. Albert, the manager of the better-looking motel, was watching TV in his apartment behind the office. Only a few other customers tonight, so we can get two rooms, or we can share a room with two beds. I think sharing would be easier." What she meant, easier if he needed help navigating an unfamiliar room.

"Sharing a room sounds good," he said.

He walked with her into the warm motel office, her hand on his shoulder again. The floorboards creaked. Air freshener competed with mustiness. She used her credit card with Albert, who wanted to return to his TV. "Goodnight you two," Albert said. Then the sound of Albert retreating to his adjoining apartment.

He told her, "Probably not many blind Black cowboys around here."

"The expression on Albert's face made that clear. ... All of the rooms in this motel are ground floor, accessed from the long porch we're walking on," she said. She stopped him and he heard her fooling with a key. She got the door open and he heard her clicking the lights and the heater. She tugged him into the room. "The beds are on the left, kind of antiquey," she said. "There's a dresser on the right, and the bathroom is straight back. I'll get the bags."

Exploring with his cane and his hands, he selected a

bed. The bedspread had a bumpy knitted pattern he could feel. He took off his jacket and stretched out on the bed, suspended on springs that creaked. A wall heater blasted, already warming the room.

She invited him to do the bathroom routine first, then when she took her turn, brushing her teeth and so on, he stood beside his bed and stripped to his t-shirt and briefs. He folded his pants and his long-sleeved shirt and placed them on the dresser, running his fingers over the 3 sewn on the back of the shirt. Cecie had said this number three shirt was checkered, blue and white. He placed his shoes on the floor by the bed and tucked his socks into the shoes. Finally his cane, rested beside his shoes, everything where he could find it. He slid in between sheets that were coarse and smelled of bleach. He hadn't attempted to sleep in a bed since he got out of prison. This would be his first night not sitting on a floor in a corner.

He heard her emerge from the bathroom, probably in her undies — she didn't seem like a pajamas person. She did more clicking of switches. "The room is dark now," she said. "Can you tell?"

"No. But in my room at Long Beach Horizons, I turn off the lights at bedtime. Helps me feel sleepy."

"How can you tell when lights are off?"

"Click the wall switches down. Lamps are trickier. Classic lightbulbs cool off, but the newer LEDs don't change temperature so much."

He heard her bedsprings creak, then she said, "You're

getting better at ... Damn! I forgot something in my pickup." Then the sounds of her turning on a lamp and slipping on her jacket and boots. She opened the door to the porch and clomped outside, sounded like she hadn't laced up the boots. He imagined her clomping around in her jacket over her undies. She came back and he heard a *thump* indicating she'd put something on her nightstand.

"What did you fetch this time?" he asked.

"Oh. A flashlight."

"I imagined a pistol. Doesn't Montana require guns in every vehicle?"

"Just about," she said. "Now the pistol is on the nightstand between us. If the killer is anywhere we're headed, or near us now, we might be in danger again."

"What kind of pistol?"

"A three-eighty Walther PPK."

"A lady's pistol," he said. "Small, the rounded shape."

"You know guns too?"

"Cecie taught me. Are you pretty good with it?"

"Good enough," she said. "My father taught me to shoot when I was ten, and when I married Kurt, Kurt insisted on teaching me all over again."

"What's happening with your divorce?"

"... Kurt isn't fighting me over it. The paperwork will be wrapped up in a few weeks. I'm free of him, Dawson."

He thought he could hear some piece of her heart still loyal to Sheriff Kurt, and her mind and the rest of her heart were trying to pull away. He respected her for that.

He told her, "Goodnight, Rose."

Later he was still awake, and it felt like she was too. For a long time he'd dedicated himself to surviving and getting justice. Right now he wanted her above all else. He lay on his back staring up at the nothingness and more fireworks that weren't real. Thinking of her like this, and all the different ways he could fail with her, he felt his pulse racing. He whispered, "Rose?"

"... I'm awake."

"It's early New Year's Day. We never celebrated New Year's Eve."

"I'm thinking the same thing."

He got up and went to her bed and slid under her covers, within range of the heat radiating from her body. "I'd like to touch your face," he told her.

She drew his hands to her face, similar to how Nikki guided his hands his first time with Nikki. He used his fingertips to explore the curves of her lips and her cheeks and around to the curves of her little ears.

Her fingers found him, only the small rounded tips of her fingers and the fine edges of her nails. Her lightest touch on the tip of him.

She said, "Are you up for this? Oh, I guess you are."

He tasted her breath and felt the smoothness of her skin down her curves and disappeared into all of her.

She barely cried while she let him sleep. Only a few tears trickling. Because the lovemaking — after all she'd been through, and the mistakes she'd made about him, and all he'd been through — was too nice. She expected anything nice wouldn't last. In the morning she initiated more and again he was gentle allowing her to set the terms. Then she rested on top of him in the saggy bed, her palms on his chest, with the early sunlight brightening the window, and told him, "Dawson, let's enjoy this for what it is — a jump-start for both of us."

"I hear you," he said.

He slipped away to take a shower and she wondered, sheesh, why did I have to say that — *a jump-start?* As if we're vehicles with dead batteries? Probably I offended him. She collected her stuff in her bag. When she opened the door to the porch, something dangled in front of her face. A hangman's noose.

She stared at it. The rope was thick, heavy, roughened

by use. Cowboy rope, tied to a porch rafter. She glanced around, nobody on the shared porch, nobody in the nearly empty parking lot. The noose must've been rigged while she and Dawson were jump-starting each other. She slapped the noose aside but it swung back in front of her, an evil pendulum. She heard Dawson in the room behind her tapping with his cane, packing his bag. She used her Leatherman blade to cut the rope as high above the noose as she could reach. He tapped onto the porch and she kissed his cheek and didn't mention she had a noose in her hand. Then she realized she owed him the honesty he wanted, and she gave him the noose so he could feel it.

He asked, "You see anybody who might've done it?"

"I'll scout around." She clipped her holster to her belt and docked the pistol in the holster. "Dawson, I'm carrying my pistol today." She scouted the motel grounds and saw nothing else suspicious. "Let's get out of here."

She drove to the gas station store that was the happening place in Roundup, gassed up and bought yogurts and coffees to go. Ranchers, both genders in mud-splattered pickups, were getting gas or diesel fuel and coffees and donuts.

"Fucking cowboys," he said.

She told him, "Whoever rigged that noose is giving cowboys a bad name."

~

For his sake she narrated more of what she saw as she drove north from Roundup, starting with, "Today we'll be on some of Montana's lonesomest roads." The snow-covered plains rolled on and on, with the look of poor soil and chronic drought. Occasionally there were isolated houses, some of them decaying, occupied by more ghosts. Low mountains barely supported pine forests. The dots in the distance were cattle feeding on old hay the ranchers spread on the snow. Calving season, so the mother cows would be delivering on this winter range, timing she'd always considered unfortunate.

She drove a couple of hours and they passed through only a few towns, none larger than a few hundred people. Cutting across the Missouri Breaks, through the badlands of steep arroyos and scraggly plants, she took the bridge over the big river.

They found Tyrone Allen in the piney hills of the Chippewa-Cree Rocky Boys Reservation, fifty miles short of the Canadian border. They had decided on a friendly approach, with hostility in reserve if they needed it. Even though it was New Year's Day, Tyrone was on duty in the tribal medical clinic, a basic building that might've been sawed from the pines.

She knew Tyrone earned his nursing degree when he played center for the Bobcats football team, but she hadn't seen him since the murder. He was an enormous Black man, maybe two hundred and eighty pounds of muscle and fat. His arms and neck bulged from his medical scrubs. He put forth a friendly manner too, "Awesome Dawson. Not guilty! With Rose!" They holed up in the break room intended for clinic staff, sitting on metal benches bracketed to a metal picnic table. "When the virus spiked here," Tyrone said, "we started to keep the clinic open on holidays. Now we're keeping the expanded hours because of the virus's long-term effects and we're doing a study."

Every time Tyrone shifted his position, the whole table-and-benches structure trembled under them. Tyrone asked about Dawson's blindness and Dawson explained about the prison gangsters ambushing him outside prison. "Allow me to get medical," Tyrone said. "Can your eyes distinguish light from dark?"

"Not really. Sometimes I see hallucinations," Dawson said. "Bursts of color and lightning and twinkling stars."

She thought, that's interesting, Dawson. When were you going to get around to telling me about your hallucinations?

"Things can change," Tyrone said. "A positive attitude is part of healing."

Tyrone's character seemed unchanged, tolerant and mellow. What Tyrone was showing them, anyway. Tyrone said he'd taken the rez job to get credits applied to his college loans and he grew to like working here. And he'd come out as openly gay, living with a Chippewa carpenter named Edgar Windy Boy.

"I'm a gay Black dude from Detroit," Tyrone said. "This community welcomed me. Mostly good people here, even with half the rez unemployed and the high rates of diabetes and kidney disease, meth and booze addiction. People here pull together to help each other."

"The best cellmate I had in prison, he's a member of the Northern Cheyenne Tribe," Dawson said. "Billy Redcherry. He talked about problems on reservations."

"Redcherry? Some of that family live on our rez," Tyrone said. "We got members of a lot of tribes here."

She helped steer the talk to the five-year-old murder, adding her perspective as the victim's sister. Tyrone said yeah, he had been fooling around with Alonzo Davis in the Huntley Lodge when Nikki got killed a few blocks away. And Tyrone had supplied pills to Alonzo. Verifying the story Alonzo told them in Seattle.

"Tyrone," Dawson said, "I'm going to try a run up the middle, no dodging around. Just before Nikki got killed, you were in the End Zone Saloon with us and the others. Did you or Alonzo slip pills into one of my drinks?"

"Nah. We dosed ourselves — Addies before the saloon party, then downers later on. Football season was over, very little chance we'd have to piss in a cup for a drug test. Does this have anything to do with you wearing a gun on your hip today, Rose? I heard the sheriff in Bozeman just solved the murder properly."

She didn't answer, hoping that Dawson would keep handling Tyrone and regaining confidence, and Dawson told Tyrone, "We don't believe it's solved. We're doing our own investigation. Considering you're gay, why'd you ask Nikki out, months before the murder?"

"I was immature," Tyrone said. "Didn't know myself."

"Did you supply anybody else with pills?"

"Nah. I'd buy a few pills from a real dealer and split them up with Alonzo. And I stopped doing that before I graduated. It was another phase that ended."

"Who was the real dealer?"

"A White girl. Barbie Connor. At the time she was in college part-time while she worked as a bartender and a waitress. She knew a doctor who traded her hundreds of pills for sex. She sold the pills for extra income."

"Was Barbie Connor in the party in the saloon?"

"Nah. I mean Barbie wasn't partying. She was there working as a waitress, serving drinks and munchies."

She looked at Dawson grinning. He went on asking Tyrone, "Was Barbie Connor or anybody else in the saloon acting suspicious? You notice anything like that?"

"Nah. I didn't notice much, I was partying." Tyrone raised a sausage-sized finger and twirled it.

"Where's Barbie Connor lately?" Dawson asked.

"I lost track of her."

She saw that Dawson believed Tyrone. She did too, for now. She patted Dawson's arm, "Anything else?"

Dawson said, "Nah," and Tyrone laughed.

When Tyrone stood up, the table-and-benches sighed with relief. Back in the lobby Tyrone introduced them to Edgar Windy Boy, who wore a tool-belt and was building shelves by the front desk. "My partner," Tyrone said.

Edgar smiled and said, "Tyrone and I need a better

word for what we got going. Dawson, Rose, nice to meet you." His fist bump was sawdusty.

~

She began driving toward Bozeman and Big Sky, the bull's-eye of all their trouble. It was night and vague clouds were releasing specks of snow. The specks didn't accumulate on the windshield as she drove.

"Finally a *White* suspect," Dawson said. "An End Zone Saloon waitress who dealt pills." He told his phone, "Search for Barbie Connor in Montana."

The phone's robot voice said, "No Barbicon found."

"Not Barbicon," he told the phone. "Bar-bie Con-nor."

The phone worked some more and said, "Barbie Connor in Montana married Randon Yates," adding the date of the marriage, a year-and-a-half after the murder. "Barbie Connor lives with Randon Yates in Gallatin County, Montana."

They rode in silence for a moment, hurtling through the specks of snow.

Then they talked it over:

"Randon Yates?"

"Randon Yates!"

"Randon*fucking*Yates!"

CHAPTER 45 / DAWSON

Too many people knew about Randon Yates, from too many news stories and too much TV coverage and too much Internet. They talked about it more as he felt and heard her drive over a stretch of potholes, *brrupp brrupp brrupp.*

"White Pride — that's Randon Yates's brand," he said.

He listened to her say, "Recently, yes. But that wasn't Randon Yates's brand five years ago. Nobody investigating the murder would've seen any obvious connection to Randon Yates. And there was no reason to be suspicious about his girlfriend slinging drinks in the saloon party."

The noise of the tires became a hum, another change in the pavement materials. They both knew, Randon Yates began as an ordinary Big Sky real-estate developer, and then roughly a year after the murder, he went into politics, getting elected to the Montana Legislature as an ordinary self-righteous Christian rightwinger in bed with industry. Then Yates abandoned ordinaryhood and started the

White Pride movement, based in Montana and spreading nationwide, climbing to the top of the White-power dung heap, way more influential than the 406ers prison gang.

"Don't you love how Randon Yates spins it," she said. "Protecting the purity of the White Christian race — with assault rifles."

"Blaming every problem on Black people," he said.

"Blaming Jews and Muslims too."

"And scientists and journalists and anybody else who doesn't kiss his White Pride ass," he said. "If Randon Yates has an overdue library book, he probably blames Obama."

He heard another nervous laugh from her and she steered through a curve that changed the air flow along the car somehow causing a thin whine — *eeeeee* — probably outside air coming in a gap, or a mosquito flying around in a miniature parka. He buzzed up his window up a fraction of an inch for a better seal, took care of it.

"Some of the White Pride race-baiters were in the insurrection at the U.S. Capitol," she said. "And last week, when I flew to LA to start giving you a jump-start, I saw some White Priders in military gear in the Billings airport. They were flying to another rally in Washington, D.C. Did you hear about Yates whipping up the crowd at that rally? It was near the Lincoln Memorial, and hundreds of them were cheering."

"Yeah, like, *up yours, Emancipation Proclamation.*"

He rode with her onward through the immense Montana night he could sense but not see, talking about

Randon Yates's hate speeches echoing around the world, and how Yates's followers vandalized Black-owned businesses and turned Black Lives Matter marches into brawls. He used his phone to find audio and video of Yates leading rallies. With her help linking his phone to the pickup's media system, he began streaming a speech Yates delivered at a shut-down Ohio coal mine, and she described the scene to him, glancing at the dashboard screen as she drove — Randon Yates using a bullhorn to yell at another crowd, some of them carrying guns, some waving flags that displayed the White Pride logo, a white fist in front of a Nazi eagle. "The *propaganda* from the *whining liberals*," Randon Yates yelled, "and the godless communists and big-government socialists, the *N-double-A-C-P* and the *Jews* and *wine-sipping professors* and *New York Times* fake news, all of that propaganda tells you that all people, all races and all ethnicities are equal. They want you to think the obvious differences don't exist! *Think for yourself, friends!*" The crowd yelling, "*Whiiiiite Pride!*" and Yates continuing with the bullhorn, "It's not White people's fault we're superior. *Not our fault! Never apologize for being who you are!*" More of the crowd chanting, "*White Pride! White Pride! White Pride!*"

Again it was after midnight when she found a place to sleep, this time a hotel in Big Sky's ski village. She said she'd unwind with a marijuana gummy. She offered him one. It took the edge off the flashes in his head.

~

The next day they tried to spend time in the Big Sky condo where Nikki was strangled, but it was too much for Rose. They went on to the End Zone Saloon, where the Bobcats football party roared the night of the murder, and where a waitress named Barbie Connor might've served him a drink laced with a drug. They spent hours in the saloon trying to remember more of the party and thinking about the clues they'd squeezed out of Nikki's calendar and jewelry box and Alonzo Davis in Seattle and Tyrone Allen on the reservation.

In the saloon they began making a complete list of the partyers — not only the jerks — because anybody in that party might've seen something that didn't seem important back then but would be important now, given what they knew about Randon Yates and Barbie Connor.

The day of working the new angles flowed into more days based in the Big Sky hotel room. She searched online and found photos of Barbie Connor and described her to him, so he could imagine her. They began calling the partyers. Even blind he could do his share, talking to his phone for calls and surfing the Internet more, and going with her for in-person talks with some partyers who still lived in the area. They developed a script for the talks.

"We're reconstructing Nikki's last night, up to the murder. Yeah, five years ago, that's a long time to remember things, but it was a memorable night, wasn't it? We think the cops still haven't solved it — mostly cops concentrate on fresher cases. You were in the party in the

End Zone Saloon, did you notice anything suspicious? Anybody acting strange? Especially regarding Nikki? Who else did you see at the party? How can we contact them? How about bartenders and waitresses, you notice anything unusual with serving the drinks? Especially one of the waitresses, Barbie Connor, she looked something like Taylor Swift with chestnut hair, did you notice her? How about Randon Yates? Yeah, the White Pride guy, was he at the party? Did you take any snapshots during the party? Videos? We'd like to have copies of everything."

They talked to more than fifty people in a week, including waitresses who weren't Barbie Connor, and collected more than three hundred snapshots and some video clips. Some of the photos and videos showed Barbie Connor slinging drinks, but none showed her drugging a drink or acting suspicious. Nobody remembered seeing Randon Yates at the party, and nobody had images of Yates from that night.

They kept working it, talking to more people.

Late in their nights, while the marijuana helped her sleep, he worked on another sculpture, standing at the table in the dark hotel room he couldn't see. Sculpting a face that was her and Nikki. As he massaged and shaped the clay, his thoughts drifted into new worrying.

Sooner or later our investigation will alert the killer. Or the killers, if there was more than one. Isn't it inevitable? How will they come for us?

CHAPTER 46 / ROSE

She looked out the window of the Big Sky hotel room and got a charge from the morning sun and the sparkling snow. "We need another angle," she told Dawson. "We're hunting Randon Yates and Barbie Connor, but we have no hard evidence they were involved in the murder. If I had my horse here, I'd go for a ride, always good for thinking."

He said what she would've thought next, "Why don't you go for a run?"

She put on her winter running outfit — tights under gym shorts, and a long-sleeved t-shirt, ear band instead of a hat, running shoes with traction soles, and her belt pack with pockets for a water bottle, her phone and the hotel key card. She was doing stretches when he went off to the hotel's gym. Then she slipped her pistol into the pack.

She left the hotel and jogged out to the sunny cold. Landing each stride precisely, she tried to choose sidewalks and pavement that had been cleared of snow and sanded, watching for icy spots. The weight of her pistol in the pack in the small of her back nagged her. Loosening up, generating sweat, she ran faster along the base of the ski lifts, which were already filled with customers wearing poofy jackets and the Frankenstein boots. She passed shops and cafes and the morning's batch of customers, all the ways the resort made a profit by selling a lifestyle for the top ten percent. She ran between more hotels, through a parking lot filled with Range Rovers and other expensive snow-capable vehicles, and reached her goal, the End Zone Saloon. This early the saloon wasn't open. She just wanted another look at it.

She slowed to a jogging pace again, doing a thoughtful lap around the exterior of the saloon, a one-story building between a ski shop and a coffeehouse. She wondered if she and Dawson were right — had the murder begun with Barbie Connor drugging his drink in there? Jogging another lap around the saloon she saw something that stopped her. Above the back door, between the spotlights, there was a small discreetly placed security camera. Was the cam there five years ago?

"Ah-*hah!*" she said aloud. She ran back to the hotel to tell Dawson. He was in the hotel gym doing the exercises for his bad leg. Such a sensitive hunk, looking good in the sunglasses he wore indoors and outdoors. "Dawson, I ran by the End Zone Saloon and noticed, they've got a security camera over the back door. Probably shooting video of who comes and goes back there."

He told his phone to call MaryAnn Meloy, and he told MaryAnn, "Rose is still with me. Now we wonder, did the Sheriff's Department collect video from a security cam at the back door of the End Zone Saloon, after the murder?"

"How are you two doing?" MaryAnn asked. They detoured into some chatting and then they nudged MaryAnn back on track. "I don't remember any security cam video in the prosecution's evidence," MaryAnn said. "I'll check my files, in storage. I'll make some calls if I have to. Give me a few minutes."

Shortly MaryAnn called back and said, "The morning after the murder, deputies collected about sixty hours of video, total, from twelve outdoor security cams more or less near the condo. None of the cams had a view of the condo — that would be too easy. Sheriff Kurt watched about half the hours of video, concentrating on the cams closest to the crime scene, and found nothing suspicious. He didn't watch the twenty-three hours of video from cams at the saloon and neighboring shops, because those buildings aren't as close to the condo, and the murder didn't occur in those buildings, and Sheriff Kurt and the prosecutor thought they'd caught the murderer — a certain Black football player from Long Beach."

MaryAnn slipped into a refrain, criticizing her own handling of the case and the starvation budget of the public defender's office, again wishing she'd had money to hire an investigator. "During the trial, the prosecutor didn't bring up the video from the security cams. It was on the list of evidence they collected, but it was low on the list and it was described as worthless. I should've watched the video myself —"

"Sixty hours of video that didn't show the condo where the murder came down?" Dawson said. "Don't beat yourself up over it."

"I'll get a copy of all sixty hours," MaryAnn said, "on an external hard drive by lunchtime. Rose, you can have it anytime from noon on. I'm dealing with the clerk for Sheriff's Department records, not Sheriff Kurt."

Two hotel showers later, she and Dawson climbed into her pickup and she clicked the tranny into DRIVE. She was waiting for Dawson to ask, and he did.

"Rose, what'll you do if we run into your ex? We'll be back in his kingdom."

"I'll say hi," she said, "and you and I will go about our business. We have a right to review all the official records of the case. What'll you do if we run into him?"

"I don't know."

She told him, "I'd like to avoid Sheriff Kurt until the divorce is final."

~

She drove from the ski village down the mountainside and turned onto the Gallatin Canyon two-lane heading down to Bozeman. Hardly any four-lanes in Montana. She increased her speed to the limit, forty-five, and began these downhill curves, Montana's most-dangerous road according to little white crosses marking the sad locations where people had died in crashes.

Bzzzz.

What's that? she wondered. A new noise, not loud, close in front of her.

She kept driving, this curve to the left, this curve to the right. The new noise continued. "Sheesh."

"Sheesh *what?*" Dawson asked.

"I hear a buzzing noise. From under the hood. Maybe something broke."

"I hear it too," he said.

She felt the engine accelerating even though she wasn't giving it more gas. She moved her foot off the pedal. The engine kept revving.

"Something is wrong," she told him.

She glanced at the dashboard, several warning lights glowing, and the speedometer increasing to sixty. She tapped the brake pedal and saw the next curve ahead, not a good place to be speeding. She tapped the brakes again and again. She saw a semi-truck coming up in the other lane — there were always big semis on this road, along with skiers and workers going to and from Big Sky.

She kept braking even though the pedal seemed to have a limited effect, and got the speed below sixty, made the curve OK and re-applied her foot to the gas pedal, stomped and let off and stomped and let off to see if that would reestablish control. Nope. The gas pedal seemed disconnected from the fuel flow.

Sixty-three. Sixty-five.

As the next curve took over she stomped the brake pedal and forced the steering wheel to stay in the right-hand lane because now a line of vehicles was coming toward her in the other lane. Her pickup leaned and out of the corner of her eye she saw Dawson bracing himself on the dash as a car heading toward them *whooshed* by. She saw more vehicles coming toward them on a brief straightaway. She used the few seconds of straightaway to yank the emergency-brake handle. She felt some slowing effect and shifted the transmission lever from DRIVE to NEUTRAL. The shifter felt sloppy and the tranny still propelled the wheels as if it wasn't in NEUTRAL. She refocused on the road while she flicked the shifter again and again. No clicks distinguishing one gear from another. In her side-view mirrors she saw smoke coming from the rear wheels where the emergency brake was causing the rear pads to burn. The speed crept up again.

Sixty-seven.

"What's wrong?" Dawson asked again.

"The engine's going faster and faster, I can't control it. The tranny is stuck in DRIVE, I can't shift to NEUTRAL. We're going too fast for this road. Hang on."

She stomped the brake pedal harder going into the next curve because if the pedal fucking worked it should engage the brakes on the front wheels too. The brake pedal had no effect and she might lose it in this curve, the tires skidding sideways.

"Turn off the engine," he said.

In the next straightaway she kept her eyes on the approaching traffic, a semi straying inches into her lane as she groped for the key in the ignition switch and turned it toward the OFF position. The key wouldn't turn that far because the tranny was in gear, and nothing changed. Still the engine accelerated, road speed increasing. She swerved to the right shoulder to miss the trespassing semi. Then swerved left to reclaim her proper position in her lane. She told him, "I can't turn it off. Something's wrong with the computer or whatever controls the engine and tranny and maybe the brakes." Hearing her own voice beginning to fracture.

On her right, nearly continuous guardrails and the upward mountainside. In a break in the guardrail, a pair of crosses marked the site of a double-fatality. Zooming past the crosses. No vehicles in her lane but the other lane was full of traffic coming head-on. On the far side of that lane, more segments of guardrail and the dropoff to the river, ten or fifteen feet down to the shallow flow through ice and exposed boulders. She'd driven this canyon road often and she searched her memory for any stretch ahead where they might be able to crash without dying.

She made the next curve, barely, almost against the right-hand guardrail. The brake pedal was like stepping on a rock. Seventy. She glanced to make sure her seatbelt was fastened, and his too. Coming into the next curve she couldn't keep it off the guardrail, the right side of the pickup grinding against the rail, an awful noise and friction sparks shooting up, then they were through the curve in another straightaway that wouldn't last long. Somehow the side impact had cracked the windshield and she peered through the web of cracks.

Going so fast, they gained on a driver in their lane. A little car. She could see two people in the front seats of the car. The passenger was small, probably a kid. She rode the brakes still no effect and when her front bumper was about to ram the rear of the car she yelled, *"Here we go — we're crashing."* She made her final move with the steering wheel and skidded across the other lane between two vehicles coming head-on and through a gap in the guardrail and shot off the road where the river meandered away. For a moment she felt weightless as the pickup flew through the air and down and then she landed it, a two-ton belly flop in the snowy meadow she'd aimed for. She tried to keep steering but things got rougher, too much happening too quickly, her pickup hurtling forward through deep snow, the snow up over the hood knocking the windshield into her lap and the airbag exploded in her face.

CHAPTER 47 / DAWSON

*B*illy Redcherry, whose safecracking experience includes defeating high-tech vaults and security systems, is walking the prison yard with him on a sunny June afternoon, in between rainstorms. Some of the other convicts are pumping iron, and some are playing catch with a Wiffle ball — the only type of ball allowed, because the warden mistakenly believes a Wiffle ball can't be used as a weapon. Buster is talking about weaknesses in the prison's security system, for the millionth time. "Dawson, stand over here," Billy says, shifting a few inches to the left. "That camera on top of the wall, it can't see us here. We're in a blind spot. If I had my electronics gear, I could hack the prison's computer network and turn off all the cams. I could hack the warden's phone, or hack the warden's car and cause him to crash."

"Hack a car?" he tells Billy. "That's Batman shit."

"For real. Carmakers don't talk about it, but a modern car is a computer network with a unique Internet address *and electronic control units running the engine, trans-mission, brakes, pretty much every aspect of the car. The car's network communicates using Bluetooth, Wi-Fi, cellular and satellite signals, and radio signals linking to the key that unlocks the car. You can hack those things remotely, or attach a hacking module to the OBD-2 Port under the dash, to take full control of the car, and malware will erase any evidence after a crash. The new self-driving cars offer more opportunities. We're living Batman sci-fi now."*

~

Riding Rose's pickup through the air and getting a faceful of airbag, he found himself right-side-up and still in the passenger seat when the crash ended. He pushed the deflated airbag away from his face. He had the windshield in his lap, still in one piece but so fractured it was flexible, along with snow trapping his legs. He heard her struggling next to him and saw red fireworks.

"Dawson!" she yelled. "Dawson!"

"I'm OK, I think," he said. "How about you?"

"I'm OK too, I think."

Dialogue he'd heard before. He pushed the windshield forward to clear space for them to move in, heard the windshield flop onto the hood, and dug into the snow with his hands, unsnapped his seatbelt and worked on digging out his legs enough to try the passenger door. The snow outside the door prevented him from opening the door even when he applied his shoulder. He heard her doing the same on her side.

"Climb out the front!" she yelled. "Quick! Wrecks burn!"

He groped for his cane and sunglasses and she helped him climb out over the hood. Once they were standing next to her pickup, she described how the deep snow absorbed their momentum with minimal damage. Her driving skills and good luck had combined for a survivable landing. He heard a *poof* and smelled smoke and felt heat from the fire. She yanked him away through knee-deep snow. People in other vehicles had stopped and some made noise scrambling down the roadbank. She yelled at them, "Get back!" and guided him up the bank that was rocky and icy, difficult to assess with his cane. *Kaboom* — that was the gas tank exploding. The good samaritans tried to help, saying, "Are you hurt?" ... "Oh, you're blind?" ... "We called 9-1-1 for you." ... "Here's the guardrail, you can sit on it."

He heard her making a brief phone call but didn't listen because his mind was still hurtling and crashing. She hung up and said, "I called Sheriff Kurt and told him we don't need an ambulance. I hung up while he was getting mad again. He'll come here, and firefighters will too. We should leave now. We can hitch a ride to Bozeman. We haven't caused damage except to ourselves."

"Avoiding Sheriff Kurt, that still sounds good," he said.

He smelled more smoke from her pickup burning, as she recruited a good samaritan guy named Sandy to give them a ride to Bozeman. Sandy thought they wanted to avoid a bust for drunk driving.

"I've had two DUIs," Sandy said. "I know how it goes."

They squeezed into Sandy's van, Rose with him on the bench seat behind Sandy in the driver's seat. Sandy started down the canyon.

"You're Dawson Koloko, aren't you?" Sandy asked.

"No, but people say I look like him."

A siren passed them heading toward the wreck. She kept apologizing. "Sorry about the crash, Dawson. My pickup's electrical system died the night I pulled you out of the lake. I had it repaired and there were no problems with it until now."

He told her, "I think somebody rigged the crash trying to get rid of us." He began to relay what Billy said about hacking cars but she seemed distracted. He heard her talking to herself as she checked her tablet computer, salvaged from the wreck, "Seems to be working," and her hip holster, where she'd kept her pistol after her early morning run, "Still got my gun." He heard her unsnapping the strap that secured the pistol in the holster and sliding the pistol out and back into the holster, making sure she could pull it quickly if she needed to.

She was aware the wreck made her hyper, as if all her nerves had been strummed. In Bozeman she called to have her wrecked pickup towed to the junkyard where Dawson had gotten guns and intel. She rented a Subaru and an Airbnb condo where she and Dawson could hide out. And she called their Big Sky hotel to persuade the manager to put their stuff on one of the shuttle vans to Bozeman. When her phone kept buzzing with Sheriff Kurt's calls and texts, she turned it off and stored it in the Airbnb's microwave so Kurt couldn't locate her by its GPS.

Other than her nerves, she was generally sore from getting slammed by the airbag and had cuts on her face from the glass layers of the broken windshield. Dawson, the same. They stripped to assess any hidden damage, and soaked their aches and pains in the outdoor hot tub, naked except for his sunglasses, mulling over the crash.

Immersed to her shoulders in the hot water, she still felt her internal trembling. She ate a marijuana gummy and said to him through six feet of steam, "The more I think about the wreck, and what your safecracker friend said about hacking cars, the more I think somebody did hack my pickup."

"Billy Redcherry, he knows a lot of tech stuff. Safecrackers have to know a lot. Remind me to transfer more money to his prison account. I'll visit him in prison after we take care of all this."

She had her computer on a bench beside the tub. With her chin on the tub's rim and her arms exposed to the cold air, she did a quick search for info on hacking cars, and reported, "Billy's right. I see techies doing research papers and bloggers and YouTubers explaining how they can hack cars they aren't riding in."

"You did great driving almost out of control," he said.

She patted the top of her head, yes as she suspected, her hair was frozen stiff. She dunked herself to thaw her hair and warm her arms, resurfaced and told him, "If somebody is trying to kill us, we could back off. Or we could pretend to back off and restart a month from now."

"When you were driving so fast and scraping guardrails," he said, "I was flashing how my parents died. Rose, I'm not backing off."

She did a slow breast stroke toward him, placed her hands on his shoulders and gave him a floating kiss.

"That's what I'm talking about," he said.

She kept her hands on his shoulders and glided more around him, her legs brushing him underwater. "It feels more dangerous now," she told him.

"Because it is more dangerous."

"I've got my pistol on the bench. To your right."

"So if they sneak up and start drowning you, I'll be the blind guy grabbing the pistol and shooting in every direction?"

"Grab whoever's causing trouble," she said, "then shoot what you grabbed. Other than me." She patted his head and told him some Montana folklore, "Your hair is frozen and if you don't thaw it, it'll break off," and slowly applied pressure with both her hands on the top of his head and dunked him. When he resurfaced, she kept nudging him with her body underwater.

"You're also dangerous," he said.

"Dawson, when you're with me, how much are you thinking of Nikki?"

She saw nuance in his smile.

"Rose, I'm totally with you."

She thought he meant, when he was with her he tried not to think of Nikki. "The sweet man who attracted Nikki and me five years ago," she told him. "Nikki was on the rebound from Alonzo, so I gave her first dibs on you."

His smile grew.

"Can you detect any differences between Nikki and me now?" she asked.

"You're more amused by everything than Nikki was."

Her hands still resting on his shoulders, and with no coupling below, only nice friction, she eased herself and him to a shared climax, playing mermaid.

~

They showered together and re-dressed in their crashed clothes. Wary of any new trouble, she drove them to the office of the shuttle vans and retrieved the stuff from the Big Sky hotel, then to lawyer MaryAnn's office for the computer hard drive that had all video recorded by security cams the night of the murder. Back in the Airbnb, she began to review the video, informing him scene by scene.

There was a lot of video to review — the sixty total hours on the night of the murder, including the twenty-three hours from the cams over the back doors of the End Zone Saloon and the adjacent ski shop and coffeeshop. Quickly it was boring — soundless black-and-white video of people going in and out of buildings that weren't the crime scene, with long stretches when nobody went in or out. She began fast-forwarding the empty minutes. The chore stretched into a second day. Tired of pizza and Chinese take-out, they bought ingredients for bison burgers and Bloody Marys. Back at the computer they continued where they'd left off — more video from the camera over the saloon's back door — as they chomped the fatless burgers and sipped the red cocktails. She noticed something, and rewound a couple minutes, replayed those minutes, and replayed again. She told him, "Got a hit."

"Randon Yates at the saloon's back door?"

"Nope. Barbie Connor walking out the saloon's back door at 9:04 p.m. — about four hours before the murder."

"What's she doing?"

"She must be taking a break. She's wearing the saloon's waitress outfit — the long referee shirt over pantyhose and heels. No jacket even though it's a bitter winter night. She must be thinking it'll be a brief break, getting some fresh air or going to smoke a cigarette or reefer. She walks south, out of view."

"Let's check the video from the back doors of the buildings around the saloon. Maybe those cameras show Barbie doing more."

Already on it, she clicked over to the video from the back door of the ski shop, immediately south of the saloon, fast-forwarded to 9 p.m., slowed to real time.

"Got her," she told him. "At 9:06 she's walking into the view of the cam over the back door of the ski shop. The shop isn't open this late. She ..."

"She *what?*"

"... She's meeting three men who are hanging around behind the ski shop, somewhat concealed by a trash bin. Jesus." She rewound a few seconds, replayed, rewound and replayed, and zoomed in, studied the faces. "Maybe this is it, Dawson."

"And *it* is *what?*"

"The men she's meeting? I think one is Randon Yates."

"Goddamn."

"... and I think one is Perry Sebastian ..."

"Sebastian too?"

"I think so, in a parka. The third man is on crutches and he's wearing one of those plastic boots for an ankle injury. Like he hurt himself skiing. Maybe —" She took a bigger sip of her Bloody Mary and clicked out of the video and searched the Internet, another sip, remembering the news stories from several months ago, another sip, she found stories with photos, confirmation. "Frank Meinhardt," she told him.

"The whistleblower at the state crime lab?"

"I think it's him. I'm relying on news photos and news video of Meinhardt when he helped your lawyers with the appeal."

"Meinhardt wanted the reward Burns offered."

"If I'm identifying them correctly, they knew each other five years ago," she said. "Frank Meinhardt, Perry Sebastian, Randon Yates, Barbie Connor. They had a conversation behind the ski shop, a few hours before the murder, near the location of the murder. Like they had a plan, or were forming a plan on the fly."

"Yeah, maybe this is *it*. What do you see them doing?"

She clicked PLAY and concentrated on the screen and told him, "Since there's no audio, I'm making assumptions based on body language and gestures. It's an angry conversation — mainly Barbie Connor and Randon Yates going at it. Yates grabs her, getting up in her face. She's upset. Sebastian is nursing a whiskey bottle. Meinhardt is hanging around on his crutches. Oh, Barbie Connor is leaving — at 9:38, she walks out of view." She clicked back to the video from the saloon's back door. "At 9:40 she walks back into the saloon. Hugging herself, she's cold."

She clicked back to the ski shop's back door. "The men are drifting away. Going, going, *gone* — out of view of the cam there."

She pulled out her bag of gummies and told him, "It appears Yates pressured Barbie Connor to dose your drink. I'm having a gummy now." He held out his hand. She placed a gummy on his palm and he downed it as she downed hers.

He couldn't sit still thinking about their break-through. He asked her, "How about walking and talking? Bring your pistol." Outside, he used his cane walking with her around the snowy condo complex.

"They killed Nikki," she said. He heard her kick something that skittered off. Maybe a chunk of ice.

"The four of them — a conspiracy," he said. "And they laid the bad rap on me."

They walked on and another kick and skittering.

"So evil," she said. "People are really like this."

His cane wasn't good for distinguishing whether the ground ahead was dry or icy. He negotiated an icy patch and said, "What tied them together? At that time, Sebastian was already a White supremacist, bossing the 406ers as he went in and out of prison several times. Yates must've been getting into it privately, before he went public launching White Pride."

"Maybe Sebastian worked for Yates as an intimidator

in real-estate moves," she said. "Just standing behind Yates in a meeting, Sebastian would be like King Kong."

"Meth might've been another shared interest," he told her. "Sebastian was into dealing that drug, and Yates sounds hopped up in his speeches. And Meinhardt, he must've been into White supremacy privately."

"Maybe they had a plan," she said, "and Barbie Connor wasn't so much into those things and that's why Yates had to pressure her. She was probably dating Yates then, because they married a year or so later."

He told her, "A lot of maybes. If we're right, it was a political murder, a racist murder. They thought Nikki had degraded the White race by dating me. We still don't know exactly who did exactly what."

They played another couple hours of the video from security cams, found no more clues in that. Then they lay in bed together not sleeping much, imagining the murder in more detail with faces on the conspirators. In the morning they ramped up on coffee and began the rest of the video. They finished around midnight. Only those thirty-six minutes behind the ski shop and the saloon seemed significant.

The next day they shifted to angles the thirty-six minutes suggested.

He initiated calls to his lawyers, MaryAnn and Burns, filled them in some, and asked each of them, "Do you have access to facial-recognition software? We need to verify some suspicions we have now." Burns had a consultant who had the software, so they went online to transfer the video excerpt to the consultant to check whether the conspirators' faces matched any faces in the databases. The lawyers also agreed to search court records for anything involving the lesser-knowns, Barbie Connor and Frank Meinhardt.

Off and on, he heard her pulling her phone out of the microwave and calling people, including a friend on the Big Sky ski patrol who verified, yes Frank Meinhardt fractured that ankle skiing on the day of the murder.

They stretched their minds by driving out in the countryside. Up the Bridger Canyon road, which had traffic for smaller ski areas, she said, "We can make good guesses to fill in some of the blanks. Meinhardt was the crime-scene expert, I bet he was there to rig the crime scene to frame you. But he hurt his ankle a few hours before the murder and couldn't do much on crutches. I bet Nikki scratched ..."

She slowed down as if she was seeing Nikki fighting them. He heard a car passing them from behind. And another. She sped up, emerging from her imagination, and she said, "I bet Nikki scratched one or two of them, and Meinhardt realized they should scratch your face. Then Meinhardt finished rigging the evidence when it got to the crime lab."

On the Kelly Canyon road, where he felt the hills and curves as she drove, he said, "When Meinhardt went for Burns's reward for tipsters, maybe it was because

Meinhardt got crossways with Yates and the rise of White Pride. Or maybe Meinhardt had a tiny guilty conscience. Or maybe Meinhardt only wanted money."

On Dry Creek Road, which felt flatter with occasional curves, they checked what Randon Yates was up to lately, streaming a White Pride rally staged two days ago in a vacated Kmart in Idaho, Yates preaching to more of his followers about how White Christians were victims when Jewish bankers shut down Kmart and White was best and everybody else was second tier with Jews the worst. More crowd roars.

The next day the lawyers called back confirming the identities of the faces in the important thirty-six minutes of video, and reporting discoveries about Barbie Connor. After that phone talk, he rode with Rose out to Headwaters State Park, where three rivers came together to begin the big Missouri River. He'd been here with Nikki and now as he walked beside the water with Rose, they began putting together a new plan.

"We need backup," he told her. "Like when we faced Alonzo, we told MaryAnn before we did it, in case it went bad. I think we're at the point, we need Montana cops for backup — not interfering with us, just in case."

"I don't trust Sheriff Kurt," she said, not the first time.

"Me too. I can't forget that he never had my blood tested for traces of being drugged the night of the murder. But the security cam video, he handled that logically, concentrating on the cams closest to the condo. The thirty-six minutes from the cam behind the ski shop wouldn't have meant much back then. Sebastian was a minor criminal wearing winter clothes over his tattoos. Yates was a developer in Big Sky. Barbie Connor was working at the party. Meinhardt had been skiing."

"Are you standing up for Sheriff Kurt?" she asked.

"Don't know if I am."

"I agree, we do need backup here, somehow."

The evening news led with two Seattle cops getting ambushed, their car riddled with bullets, apparently a misguided retaliation for a different cop's mistake ending the life of a mentally-ill Black man. "It's chaos," she said.

He asked her, "Do you know any FBI agents? From your spending time around the justice system? How about, you contact Sheriff Kurt to fill him in, give him the chance to fuck up again, don't tell him you're also contacting the FBI."

She liked that idea. She used the speakerphone feature so he could listen to her calling Sheriff Kurt. "Meet me tomorrow," she told Sheriff Kurt. "To talk about the murder and who really did it." She explained when and where she wanted the meeting. Sheriff Kurt asked, "Where?" and she repeated the location and hung up.

Then he listened to her phone talk with Ron Jaworski, a Bozeman FBI agent she knew through the horse community — Jaworski kept two mustangs at the stable where she boarded her horse. She told Jaworski, "I'm with Dawson Koloko and we need to meet with you tomorrow.

We think Sheriff Kurt has made more mistakes on his second investigation of the murder. We have evidence that's been ignored until now, and we need to get the feds involved." She didn't mention that Sheriff Kurt would also be in the meeting, just as she hadn't told Sheriff Kurt that the FBI would be in the meeting.

"Repeat that," Jaworski said. "Meet *where?*"

Eight in the morning, an hour-and-a-half before the meeting time, she drove the rented Subaru and Dawson toward the meeting place, up Gallatin Canyon. She stopped at a pullout along the paved highway to arrange some things and drove ahead to a turnoff that became a one-lane bridge to the other side of the river, and crossed and doubled back on a graveled forest road. She told Dawson everything she did and described each place, "I like to come up here for cross-country skiing. County snowplows keep this forest road open so skiers can access trailheads. I'll park here, where the road hugs the riverbank."

They sat in the parked Subie, engine idling, windows closed to contain the heat. "The river is about eight feet from us," she told him. "Flowing between the icy banks. There's nobody else on this side of the river, not on a weekday. On the other side of the river there's traffic on the highway. We're directly across from where I stopped on the way here — the highway pullout for people who like to read the historical markers."

A half hour before the meeting time she said, "Cops like to arrive early. Ron's SUV, an FBI vehicle with no markings, just appeared over there on the highway. Ron parked at the meeting place." A few minutes later she said, "Sheriff Kurt's SUV just parked next to Ron. We might as well start the meeting early."

She got out and he did too. "They haven't noticed us yet," she told him. "I'll honk the horn." She reopened the driver's door and reached in and honked the horn repeatedly, louder than the river. "They notice us now," she said. "They're getting out of their vehicles, standing together on that side of the river."

Cliffs blocked cellphone signals in this stretch of the canyon. She yelled across the river, "Radio! Use the handheld radio!" and lowered her voice to say, "Dawson, I'm waving our little radio so they can see what I mean. Sheriff Kurt just found the radio I left over there, near a guardrail post."

She keyed her radio, the attention-getting squawk, and said into it, "Hello Kurt! Hello Kurt!"

Sheriff Kurt's voice, crackling with typical radio static, "Rose, what is this? You need a river between us?"

"Can you both hear me?" she said into her radio.

Ron's staticky voice, "Rose, when you get a divorce, you really go for it."

"At the base of the same guardrail post," she said into

her radio, "I left two briefcases, covered by snow. One for each of you. You'll find printouts of what Dawson and I figured out, and thumb drives that have copies of thirty-six minutes of video from the night of the murder. And photos extracted from the video."

As they retrieved the briefcases, she kept Dawson informed and continued to talk on her radio, "Dawson and I figured out, Randon Yates was involved in the murder. Mister White Pride. It was a conspiracy of at least four people — Yates, Perry Sebastian, and Frank Mein-hardt from the state crime lab, and Barbie Connor, who's Yates's wife now. Barbie Connor waitressed at the football party the night of the murder, and she had downers, probably she slipped some of those pills into Dawson's drinks. Then one or more of them strangled Nikki, and all of them framed Dawson. Apparently it was a warning against Blacks and Whites hooking up."

She told them about Alonzo Davis and Tyrone Allen getting uppers and downers from Barbie Connor. "You can get Alonzo and Tyrone to verify that she had pills." And how, probably Yates planted the murder photos and the swastika in Sebastian's place, after Sebastian drowned in the lake. "Probably Yates or somebody working for him sabotaged my pickup last week," she told them, "trying to kill me and Dawson. You can work those angles and collect Meinhardt — he's somewhere in Mexico."

Sheriff Kurt tried to cut in but she went on, pressing the talk button continuously so Kurt couldn't interrupt her, "Can you listen to me, for once? Dawson and I got this far, this is our investigation. From here, we're going to meet Barbie Connor at the White Pride Ranch — we think Barbie is the weak link. We have credentials that you lack. We were targeted by the conspiracy, we might be able to get Barbie to confirm what we suspect. We'll try to record the conversation. If Barbie gives us permission to record her, you can use it in court, and if she refuses, we'll record her secretly and circulate it to journalists. We're timing this to bypass Yates — this week he's off the ranch, staging maneuvers with some of his militia up by Kalispell, and flying his helicopter along the Canadian border, spreading his paranoia about migrants on that border. We're filling you in, so you can follow up if things go badly for us at the ranch. Please don't fuck this up again."

She turned off her radio and Sheriff Kurt and Ron started yelling over there, yelling her name, yelling versions of *don't*. "They're waving at us," she told Dawson.

"You run a good meeting," Dawson said. "But my feet are cold."

"Who knew you could be so delicate? I'll get the heat going in the Subie, you thin-blooded Long Beacher."

She and Dawson, what a team, got back into the Subie.

She said, "The White Pride Ranch," and put it in gear.

CHAPTER 51 / DAWSON

He rode beside her and felt the Subie going steeply uphill around the millionth slippery curve Montana presented. "Rose, we are *rockin'*," he told her.

"Another mile to the gate," she said. "I'll admit, they have a pretty road here, curving through sagebrush and pines with heaps of snow along the sides."

The Subie surged and slid, surged and slid, as the all-wheel-drive sought traction. He thought about Barbie Connor forted up on many acres at the end of this road. The fucking White Pride Ranch.

"Still don't know if I like your plan," he said.

"My plan?"

"OK now it's our plan."

Both of them, unarmed, because they expected they'd be searched. "We're coming up to the gate," she said. "A heavy-duty gate made of steel pipe with spearheads along the top and wrought-iron curlicues. On the right side they've got a huge boulder engraved with the words they love — *White Pride*. On the left there's a guard shack and a man in White Pride winter camo. He's got a pistol in a holster."

He asked, "What's a curlicue?"

"Your hair," she said, "is entirely curlicues."

He saw lightning bolts as she stopped. He heard her buzz down her window and she told the guard, "Rose Faber and Dawson Koloko, coming to meet with Barbie Connor."

"Beat it," the guard said.

"We have an appointment," she told the guard. "Check with Barbie Connor."

He heard the guard making a call and some phone talk. Then the guard issued more orders to them, "Stay on the road to ranch headquarters. If you attempt any side roads, our security forces will intercept you. And tune your vehicle's radio to White Pride's local station, eighty-eight-point-one FM, for important announcements."

He heard the gate click. The hum must be a motor opening the gate. The Subie began rolling again. He heard Rose fool with the radio and she said, "What type of announcements does a ranch have?" and then Randon Yates's voice boomed from the radio's speakers, another recorded speech by the beloved leader to another crowd, the preacher-like cadence: "*Human beings* — you mind if I call you that? (Laughter from the crowd.) Human beings *evolved* — you mind if I use that word? (Laughter and jeers, some in the crowd yelling *Fake science! Fuck science!*) We evolved as *independent families* — one family over here, including grandma and babies and weird uncles and cousins, and a different family over there, and each family was *self-sufficient*, each family doing *everything required* to stay alive — hunting and gathering food, sheltering, raising the young and *defending the family from threats*. Then we formed larger groups that were more powerful. *Tribes!*"

She turned it off and said, "There's a Hummer coming down the road with a man and a woman in it. They're also wearing White Pride camo. Militia goons on patrol. Oh, they turned around to follow us. It's what we expected, not many of them here today — most of them must be up north securing our border with Canada."

"They're losers," he said. "But losers can be dangerous too. Sometimes losers win."

"Wow, the road is going up a ridge and the pines dropped away so there's a view of the peaks. Beautiful."

"You're a real Montanan, Rose."

"Thank you," she said. "The *Last Best Place* — that's Montana's nickname, but White Pride wants to change it to *Last Best Hate*. We've reached the ranch headquarters. It's a modern castle made of peeled logs and stones, two stories tall with a tower going higher. There's another goon on the porch, looks like a body-builder. The man from the Hummer is joining the one on the porch. Both have pistols. Stick with the plan?"

He touched his new sunglasses. "Right," he said.

He eased out of the Subie as she did the same on her side. He heard her walking around to him and then felt her hand on his shoulder again. He used his cane as she walked with him across the driveway that had been cleared of snow, onto the first step of the porch, which didn't creak, and up four more steps to the porch itself. A solid wooden porch under his shoes. He heard one of the goons shift his stance on the porch, pictured the goon's hand on a pistol. Whose plan was this?

The goon said, "Stand with your arms out." The high-pitched whine was probably a bug detector in the goon's hand. The other goon patted them all over. An arrogant frisking, not thorough, checking for concealed weapons and confiscating both of their phones. That one took his sunglasses for a moment, then returned the sunglasses. Most people don't want to see a blind-person's eyes. Part of the plan.

The two goons escorted them into the house, where the floor was slightly uneven, probably stone tiles. They sat him on a wooden bench in what was probably a hallway, and sat her next to him on the bench, and one said, "Wait here." That one went deeper into the house while the other stood next to the bench. The same Randon Yates speech spewed from speakers in the hallway.

"... We're *always competing* with other tribes for limited resources. *It's natural* to be suspicious of those in the other tribes, *natural* to cooperate with those in our own tribe. You see it everywhere today. *Blacks hanging out with*

Blacks. And *Mexican-Americans* — that's what we're supposed to call them (some laughter and jeers from the crowd) — hanging out with *Mexxy-caan-Amerry-caaans.* (Some yelling *Go back to where you came from, Pancho!*) Muslims (prolonged jeers) hanging out with *Muhhh-slims.* (Some yelling *Go back to Mecca! Camel fuckers!*) And *Whites with Whites!* (Prolonged cheers.) *Look in the mirror!* That's who you are, and that's who your people are! Discrimination is natural — *we should celebrate it!* (Prolonged cheers becoming a chant, *Whites with Whites! Whites with Whites! Whites with Whites!*)."

He felt her hand settling on his thigh, an encouraging squeeze, and he covered her hand with his and gave her the same. So far they were successful bringing in his sunglasses and her belt buckle, which they'd bought yesterday through Amazon same-day delivery. The sunglasses and buckle had tiny audio recorders embedded in them — recorders that most bug-detectors couldn't detect because the recorders didn't transmit signals, only recorded.

Do it right and do it strong, he was telling himself, we're going to get confirmation of who the killers were, that's why we're here, we'll finally solve it.

"They didn't confiscate *this*," she said. She tapped him with the envelope that contained one of the eight-by-ten photos she'd made from the murder-night video.

He heard footsteps deeper in the house and the goon who'd gone that way came back and said, "Both of you, follow me."

He did what he was told, for now. Followed this goon through the tiled hallway with her hand on his shoulder again, and a right turn onto a staircase made of substantial wood that also didn't give under his shoes. His cane located the banister. He counted twenty-one stairs up to a landing, turned and counted another twelve stairs up to the second floor. A tall second story too. He followed her and the goon through a long hallway, twenty-four paces to a sliding door that opened onto a deck exposed to winter sunlight he felt on his face. Four paces onto the deck, the goon sat them on an outdoor couch, weatherproof cushions, metal frame.

He smelled whiffs of a campfire somewhere close and thought, a campfire on a second-floor deck? He heard the wood crackling, felt the assertive warmth of the flames. He realized the campfire was burning in the center of the deck, probably nested in some kind of metal bowl.

Again she gave his thigh a squeeze and he covered her hand with his, the strength of two together.

He heard some new voice, a woman, saying, "You really can't see?"

"Right," he said again. "Barbie Connor?"

"I prefer Barbie." Rough voice.

"Thanks for agreeing to meet us, Barbie," he said, because the plan called for being nice to Barbie. "We've been looking forward to this," which was true.

"*Dawson Koloko, starting at halfback!*" Barbie said as if

announcing a game. "*In the number twenty-seven jersey!* I went to all your games in the Bobcats stadium. You were damn hard to knock down." Barbie sounded like she chainsmoked and drank too much and talked too much. Traits that go together. "Too bad, what's happened to you since then," Barbie said.

He paused to allow Rose to introduce herself and then he occupied Barbie with more talk about the good ol' days at Bobcats stadium. As he talked, he drifted off the couch and went tap-tap-tapping around to learn the layout of the deck, beginning with the campfire, yeah, in a metal bowl supported by metal legs, which dinged when he tapped there. Beyond the campfire, he tapped to locate Barbie in a metal-legged chair that probably matched the couch. He made more comments about playing football as he found the edges of the deck, defined by a waist-high wooden railing. He sensed the dropoff beyond the railing. He found several big posts made of logs supporting an extension of the house's roof, and tapping up there, he found the roof covered only half the deck. And where the deck attached to the house, he found the goon positioned by the sliding door, the goon silent and observing.

The campfire smoke kept finding him. He suppressed a cough and returned to the outdoor couch and sat beside Rose again, so he wouldn't loom over Barbie.

"Figuring out where things are," Barbie said, slurring the s, "you do that wherever you go?"

He said, "If I can," and thought, yeah, she's pretty

drunk right now. Also part of the plan. They knew Barbie had a drinking problem, thanks to his lawyers discovering her three DUIs that added up to forfeiting her driver's license, and two wrongful termination lawsuits — housekeepers she'd fired claimed that most days she got drunk by lunchtime. She'd never given a White Pride speech or been spotted at a White Pride rally, never appeared with her husband in news interviews, didn't even venture off the White Pride Ranch much anymore.

"I like it up here on the deck," Barbie said. "Much as I like anything, which isn't much. My parents put *Barbara* on my birth certificate. But they raised me as Barbie, making jokes about the doll. When I was three —"

He interrupted to say, "We're recording our talk." Because a statement was less confrontational than asking, "OK if we record you?" and didn't require Barbie to say yes or no. If Barbie said, "Turn off your mic," or anything along those lines, they'd pretend to cooperate while recording anyway.

"When I was a kid, I had a Barbie hairdo," Barbie went on, sounding drunk, no comment about recording her. "I was the flesh-and-blood Barbie doll on a dryland ranch in the Sweet Grass Hills, driving an old tractor to cut hay, poisoning weeds, shoveling horse turds from the barn. My parents kept telling me, sooner or later I'd marry any guy named Ken. They went bankrupt with jokes like that and the drought ruining the topsoil. Mom and Dad, belly up."

He asked himself silently, does anybody imagine a

woman living with Randon Yates would be a happy soul? He heard Barbie take a drink of something that involved ice cubes clinking in a glass.

"You've got balls, showing up here," Barbie said.

He complimented her, "Talking with us, Barbie, you've got balls too."

Barbie's laugh was harsh and self-aware. The fire crackled louder and there was the sound of Barbie shoving another piece of wood into it. "All that White Pride rigamarole?" Barbie said. "That's Randon's thing."

He heard the goon going back into the house, probably to contact Yates to report that the drunken wife was saying too much. If Yates stuck to his schedule, he was flying along the Canadian border, and it would take him hours to fly back here.

"When I started with Randon," Barbie said, "he was a run-of-the-mill bigot raking in money on shady land deals and making speeches at Rotary breakfasts and the Legislature," slurring especially *Lesh-ish-lay-shure*.

He sensed Barbie taking another drink and Barbie asked nobody in particular, "What girl from a disappeared ranch, getting by on saloon work, wouldn't have hooked up with Randon at that time? Who knew that Randon would start a *goddamn movement* claiming to be *smarter* than everybody else?"

He heard her poking the fire more aggressively.

"All the sex between me and Randon?" Barbie said. "I avoid getting pregnant. If we had a kid, Randon would march the kid around like the Hitler Youth."

He felt Rose's hand squeezing his thigh again, she was silently telling him, let Barbie talk, let the booze talk.

"When you called and wanted to talk with me in person," Barbie said, "I figured, if you're talking to everybody who was in the saloon the night of that murder, you've figured out a lot." She wheezed out cigaretted laughter and a hiccup, then silence.

Rose's turn, so Rose gave her a nudge, "We figured out you were waitressing for the football party in the saloon that night. We figured out you had downers."

More sounds of Barbie drinking. Sloppier. "Putting downers in your beer, only time I ever *ever* did anything like that. Randon figured out he needed to marry me to keep me quiet, along with having sex." Slurring worse. "I been waiting for you to show up. Waiting for years. Barbie's guilty conscience, feeling guiltier and guiltier."

Rose gripped his thigh communicating, that fracture we imagined between Barbie and Yates? It's not a fracture, it's the Grand Canyon.

He said, "Rose, how about showing Barbie the photo?" He heard rustling as Rose pulled out the big print of the best photo she'd extracted from the video evidence, the photo showing Barbie and Randon Yates and Perry Sebastian and Frank Meinhardt conspiring a few hours before the murder. He imagined Rose was handing the photo to Barbie. He heard Barbie sigh. A sigh of despair.

"You got it all right here," Barbie said. "Everything

figured out in this photo. *Right. The fuck. Here.*"

"Talk to us," Rose said. "You didn't want to do what they pressured you to do. It's time to put this to rest. Tell us what happened. You know you owe us."

"You and Nikki Fontaine on the cover of that football magazine," Barbie said to him, "like you represented *progress?* When Randon saw that, he started ranting."

Now Barbie started ranting, propelled by the alcohol and her conscience. "They laughed about how hard she fought them. *They laughed!* They told me Randon did the choking while Perry pinned her legs. I thought they were pulling a prank." More ice clinks and drinking. "Those guys don't even like each other! ... Randon, he's got to be the boss. ... Have you figured out Meinhardt rigged your first DNA test in the lab? Meinhardt started blackmailing Randon last year, such a greedy bastard. ... At least when Meinhardt went for that tipster reward, on top of his blackmailing, it got you out of prison." More clinking and drinking. "Have you figured out Randon wanted a video of snuffing you at the lake, so Randon could watch it and use it to promote White Pride? Have you figured out Randon planted the swastika and the photos in Perry's place? Randon is tricky — *tricky tricky tricky*, he also had a guy rig your pickup to crash ... I didn't give a shit when Perry drowned."

He heard Barbie's glass drop to the deck. And a new sound — *snoring?*

"Barbie?" Rose called out. "Barbie? ... Dawson, she

passed out."

Passed out? he thought. That wasn't in the plan.

He heard a helicopter in the distance.

"Uh oh," Rose said.

"Maybe it's not Yates," he told her. "Maybe it won't land here."

Together they focused on listening. The helicopter got closer and hovered and descended, judging by the *wup-wup-wup* of the blades and the engine roar. It landed and shut down, no more helicopter noise. He heard her walk to the edge of the deck so she could see the parked machine.

He heard her say, "It's him."

CHAPTER 52 / ROSE

She leaned over the deck's railing and watched Randon Yates scramble from the parked helicopter. "Yates walked into the house," she told Dawson. "Walking quickly. Probably he'll be up here on the deck any second. This could go very badly for us. Should we try to leave now?" She looked straight down and said, "There's a big snowdrift below the deck. Maybe we could jump into it. The drop would be about twenty feet, or twenty-five. I don't know ... depends on how deep the snow is, but if we survive the jump, we could try to steal one of their snowmobiles."

Her jangled nerves were talking more than her mind. She blew out her lungs and inhaled deeply trying to calm herself, leaned over the railing again and studied the snowdrift below for a few more precious seconds.

"Let's hold off on jumping," he said.

She looked at him sitting there on the weatherproof couch near the campfire in the big metal bowl, cooler than ever. "I need a gummy bear," she said. She patted her pockets, no gummies with her. "How could Yates be here now? His schedule said he'll be off the ranch all this week, up north by the border."

"Maybe somebody told him we were coming to see Barbie, before we got here," he said. "Or maybe Barbie talked about it in advance."

"This could go very very badly," she repeated, adding the second *very*. She grabbed the incriminating photo that Barbie had dropped on the deck, kind of arming herself for talking with Yates.

"We shouldn't tell Yates we're recording conversations," Dawson said. "He'd have the goons search us more thoroughly to get the recording of Barbie."

She heard the men approaching through the hallway. They burst into view. "Three men coming onto the deck," she told Dawson. "Yates and two of his goons. All wearing pistols in hip holsters." She stood ready as the White Priders fanned out along the railing, forcing her to back up against the log wall of the house. She tugged Dawson back against the house, next to her. "No pistols drawn yet."

"What are you doing here?" Yates demanded.

Not *who are you?* And not the media version of Yates, here was a real forty-three-year-old man who'd killed Nikki. Finally within reach. She sized him up. Maybe four inches taller and eighty pounds bulkier than her. Greenish eyes and brown hair slicked back. Handsome in a generic way, which made him scarier. He could be any White man, and any White man could be him. He'd costumed himself in a canvas rancher vest over the obligatory White Pride shirt, jeans and white cowboy boots. By the set of his face, he wanted more than he could ever have.

She concentrated on Yates while Dawson drifted to her left to become a distinctly separate target, harder to deal with than if he stayed close to her.

Dawson said, "You know why we're here, Yates."

Yates snapped his gaze toward Barbie, who was still passed out in the chair and snoring. He motioned for the goons to check Barbie's condition.

"She's out cold," one said.

Yates refocused on Dawson and her. "Get out. *Now*."

She couldn't turn her back and walk away from one of the men who'd killed Nikki. "Dawson," she said, "I'll show Yates the photo, OK?"

"Do it right and ... hell, you know the rest."

She flicked the photo over to Yates. "This sums it up." Yates trapped the spinning photo against his chest and took a look. She assessed his hands — thick fingers with big knuckles — and imagined those hands closing around Nikki's neck.

She heard Dawson prodding Yates, "You going to work that photo into your next White Pride rally?"

She could see Yates was surprised by the photo showing himself just before the murder, conspiring. "Les, Archie," Yates said to the goons, "take my wife to her bedroom. Close the security door in the hallway and lock it from the inside. I'll use my radio to stay in touch. Don't allow anybody else to leave the deck or come onto the deck unless I radio you my approval for it."

She glanced at Dawson, thinking his body language might indicate what he wanted to do, and he said to her, "We'll let the goons and Barbie go their way."

She took another deep breath that didn't ease her tension and watched the goons collect Barbie, who mumbled about being disturbed but didn't wake up. "If my wife starts to puke on you," Yates told the goons, "drag her by her ankles."

The goons kept Barbie erect as they dragged her through the open sliding-glass door. About five feet into the hallway they paused to close and lock the security door — a solid barrier made of metal or metal-clad wood, probably meant for defending the castle from barbarian hordes, or Anti-Defamation League hordes — and she heard them lugging Barbie deeper into the hallway.

She told Dawson the layout of the security door. "Yates wants no witnesses."

"Changes the odds, though," Dawson said. "Now it's one of him against two of us."

"One with a gun," Yates said.

She drifted to her right, even more space between her and Dawson, and told him, "Yates just drew his pistol. Like he's contemplating what to do with it. Semi-auto, not a big caliber. He's aiming at us, casual aiming. Actually he's aiming at you."

"Toss your cane over to me," Yates told Dawson.

Dawson tossed the cane only halfway to Yates and sniffed the air and said, "I smell *des-per-ation.*"

She looked at her hands trembling, and controlled the trembling by making fists, and said, "You won't shoot us until you know what we've figured out and who we've told about it." She cupped a hand over part of her mouth and pretended to confide in Dawson, "Sheesh, Yates is wearing white cowboy boots." Dawson laughed. "That's my man," she told Yates, "getting my joke."

She thought she might discourage Yates by describing their most damning evidence and how they'd tipped off Sheriff Kurt and the FBI. But as she began, Yates interrupted. "You're both angry over something that happened long ago. You came to my ranch to take advantage of my wife's alcoholism. I happened to cut my trip short due to a mechanical issue with my helicopter. I'll report that you attacked me when I got here. I'm standing my ground. I have no choice, I have to shoot both of you. Sounds believable, doesn't it? After I end your miserable lives, I'll shoot myself in the arm with a different gun I have in my ankle holster, and I'll make it appear that you shot me, forcing me to stand my ground."

She flinched at the blast of the pistol and the bullet slamming the log wall between her and Dawson.

"A warning shot," Yates said. "Who else has seen this photo? Your husband, the sheriff?"

She couldn't stop the trembling spreading through her

body. She drifted another few inches away from Dawson and managed to say to him, "This man promised to shoot us to death, then he fires a *warning shot?* I think he's more scared than we are."

"We don't care what wrecked you," Dawson said to Yates. "We don't care if your father kept you in a dog kennel when you were growing up. You and your lousy race war. *You killed Nikki!*"

"For White Pride," Yates said, his tone icy. "For the revolution."

The next shot hit Dawson. No more fucking around she leaped farther from Dawson — harder for Yates to pivot the gun to shoot her — and flung herself down as a bullet zinged over her and another bullet slammed the deck beside her. She sprang up and dived again and rolled to where she could kick the campfire bowl with both her legs at once and Yates yelled as the bowl tipped and scattered flaming wood at him. She wanted to check on Dawson but first she had to slam into Yates forcing him against the railing. She kept going and bulled Yates over the railing with some of the flaming wood caught in his clothing. As he began to fall he grabbed her and she had a sickening feeling losing her balance, yanked over the railing, grappling with Yates in thin air, plunging down, hoping to meet the snowdrift and hoping it would be deep.

CHAPTER 53 / Dawson

When he heard the gun go off a second time he felt an impact. Am I shot? Yeah. It staggered him but he stayed on his feet and heard another shot which didn't hit him and another shot and he heard Rose doing some wicked cheerleader move and Yates yelling and from the clatter he guessed one of them tipped over furniture or maybe the campfire bowl. He felt a surge of pain high on his right arm and tingling down the arm to his hand, a combination he'd experienced in prison when he got stabbed. Rose had said Yates's pistol was a small caliber ...

He heard her and Yates struggling more around the edge of the deck. He had to lean against the house gathering himself for a moment and the struggle disappeared in a way that told him, she and Yates had gone over the railing. He found his cane lying on the deck and tapped around quickly and went through hot low flames that must mean the campfire bowl had tipped over and he confirmed he was alone on the deck. Which wouldn't last.

He heard goons scrambling in the house, inside the locked security door. He groped the wound on his arm and felt what must be blood — good thing he'd been in the midst of taking another step to the left or the bullet would've hit his core. For now he had the use of both arms and could tolerate the pain and numbness. Playing while hurt was something he knew how to do.

Going faster he dropped his cane on the deck again and wiped his hands on his jacket so he wouldn't leave bloody handprints on the log post he'd scouted a few minutes ago and now he climbed the post cleanly and found the edge of the roof. Another surge of pain as he pulled himself up onto the roof that was slanted and covered in snow. Trying to stay motionless on the roof so as not to spill more snow onto the deck, he listened as the goons got the security door open and charged onto the deck immediately below him.

"Where are they?" one asked.

"How the fuck do I know?" one answered.

Maybe only two goons on the deck at the moment. He heard them moving around and the *where are they* voice said, "I see Randon and the girl down there in a snowdrift. The nigger must've jumped or fallen too. We better get down there."

Two goons, that's all.

Got to stop them from reaching her.

With no more thought he dropped off the roof aiming himself to where the goons seemed to be. He landed on one who collapsed under him. Sprawled on the deck he grabbed the other one's leg and pulled him down too. They rolled around in his clutches, striking him and trying to escape him and he smashed their heads on the deck again and again until they were both unconscious or dead. He stood up worrying about her and whether more goons would come through the open doorway.

He found the cane and tapped through the low flames to the railing and yelled, "Rose, are you down there? *Rose?*"

He heard a fight down there, probably her and Yates. A squawking voice somewhere on the deck startled him. Sounded like a handheld radio either dropped by Yates or associated with one of the knocked-out goons. The squawking voice was some other goon elsewhere on the ranch, telling everybody on the radio network, "The sheriff is at the gate. He says he's here to escort his ex-wife and Dawson Koloko off the ranch. What do I do?"

He heard a siren burst, *whoop whoop*, loud over the radio. The siren stopped and the fight continued below. He heard her cry out. He climbed over the railing and stood facing outward, heels on the edge, cane in his right hand, and yelled, "Watch out, Rose, here I come!"

He leaped into nothingness.

Down and down through those flashes of orange and red.

CHAPTER 54 / ROSE

She fought Yates in the deep snow that hampered her ability to make quick moves. Threw herself into him with her elbows jabbing, almost knocked him down, saw he still had the pistol in his right hand. She grabbed that hand and twisted the pistol loose but it dropped into the snow and as she scrambled to find it he grabbed her hair to hold her head still for a blow that staggered her and another blow while she hit his neck with her fists, again and again until he released her hair. She thought no use hitting the center of him because his canvas vest absorbs the hits. She punched his neck again as hard as she could. He yelled and doubled over and she realized he was reaching for the spare pistol he'd said was strapped to his ankle. She dove and yanked his hands from the ankle, went for that pistol herself and he kicked her hard and kept kicking until the pistol slipped from the loosened ankle strap and her hands. She sprang up and tried to knee him and he turned sideways and whipped an arm around her neck, got her in a headlock. She struggled to break the hold hitting any part of him she could reach and going for his wrist with her teeth. He applied his other arm and lowered the headlock to do a bear hug pinning her arms at her sides. She kept kneeing him as he used his strength and his weight forcing her backward and down under him, deeper in the drift. She felt herself getting buried in the snow as he applied both his hands around her neck and began choking her. The same hands that choked off Nikki's air. She got her hands out from under him and hit him again and again on his neck and his head, and he continued to bear down. She tried to pry his hands open but with him on top of her strangling her she breathed shallower running out of air, snow over her face now. She thought maybe if I pretend to be dead he'll let up and she made dying noises and stopped struggling and lay inert under him. He kept his grip both hands squeezing her neck his thumbs digging in hurting her until she only had a moment left and she began struggling again and hitting him more but she was honestly damn weak now, beginning to lose it, fading away.

Yates vanished.

She sat up coughing and sucking air with pain in her throat. She managed to stand up to see over the snowhole she was in and she spotted Yates over there in Dawson's grip, Dawson overpowering Yates. She dropped and groped in the snow thinking there are two pistols somewhere down here and found one. A small revolver, must be from Yates's ankle. She crawled from the hole toward them and yelled, "Dawson, I've got a gun!" and managed to stand and as Dawson held Yates upright in some hold, she told Dawson, "Don't move," and she grabbed Yates by his hair and shoved the pistol barrel into his mouth at which point he stopped moving.

"I've got him sucking the pistol," she told Dawson. "Keep your hold on him."

She heard snowmobiles and glanced toward the noise — four or five White Pride goons on the machines coming fast. They slowed assessing the situation and dismounted and kept coming on foot, assault rifles at their shoulders pointing at her.

She yelled at them, "We've got Yates sucking on a pistol! Stop or we'll blow his head off! This has nothing to do with you. Yates murdered my sister five years ago. We're taking him to the sheriff and the FBI."

She kept yelling that, and the goons did pause. But they kept the rifles aimed at her and Dawson, talking among themselves about what to do.

"Nice work," Dawson said to her quietly.

"Same to you. How's your bullet wound?"

"Dandy. I think the sheriff is at the gate. Maybe he'll do it right this time. Or maybe the goons are dealing with him too."

The goons here formed a semi-circle about thirty feet away containing her and Dawson and Yates. She ignored their commands as Yates moved a tiny bit and Dawson controlled Yates and she pushed the pistol barrel deeper into Yates's mouth and throat. Yates gagged and moaned and sucked air around the barrel, portions of his lips freezing to the cold steel. One of the many benefits from that, Yates couldn't say anything.

Bullets stitched the snow near her — one of the goons firing a burst to frighten her. More fired, a storm of bullets not quite hitting her, knocking particles of snow into her face. When her eyes cleared she saw the goons had edged closer. She heard another vehicle and looked past the goons and saw Sheriff Kurt's SUV coming around the side of the house, Kurt at the wheel, bogging down in the snow, stuck. He got out and trudged toward her, his pistol still in his holster, no rifle or shotgun in his hands. "Don't shoot the sheriff!" he yelled to the goons. "Don't shoot the sheriff!" as he came through the goons and reached her. "Hey, Babe."

She told him again, "You know I don't like you calling me Babe."

He turned to face the goons, standing between her and them, and told them, "If anybody shoots the sheriff, everybody else here will witness it. A lot of witnesses. My deputies and the FBI are on their way here. Boys, don't start a war over this. Lower your rifles and step back."

The goons held their ground.

Kurt told them, "Rose here, she's my ex-wife. You boys know how ex-wives can be? There's new evidence that Randon Yates was involved in the murder of her sister. I'm taking her and Dawson Koloko and Yates to my headquarters. We'll sort this out." He focused on one of them, "Bob Gibson, I guess you quit your job at Ace Hardware or is this your day off?" He repeated, "Lower your rifles and step back."

For a long moment nobody talked or moved.

A gust lifted snow from the drifts, nearly a whiteout. When it paused, the goon on the left said, "I'm not shooting the sheriff today." He snapped his rifle down, a military-like gesture. "You guys are seeing me back off." He stepped back.

Another gust and then another goon snapped his rifle down and stepped back. Then Bob from Ace Hardware and the other two. No doubt there were White Priders who'd shoot a sheriff who got in their way, but they weren't here right now. Or anyway the ones who were here wouldn't shoot a White sheriff and a White sheriff's ex-wife and a Black man in broad daylight in front of so many witnesses.

He liked the tropical air here on Isla Mujeres, the small Mexican island off the coast of Cancún where people rode horses more than driving cars. He liked the sunshine on his skin and the breeze rattling the leaves of the palm trees. If he could see, he'd probably feel silly in the straw hat Rose picked out for him, but since he couldn't see the hat he didn't mind wearing it. His bullet wound didn't hurt much under the bandage and pain meds.

He was good with almost everything now. Good with Sheriff Kurt taking credit for Barbie Connor's confession back in Montana, nailing Randon Yates and implicating Frank Meinhardt. Good with Rose's FBI friend working with Mexican cops to locate Meinhardt on this island, good with Rose charming the captain of the local cops to allow her a role in Meinhardt's arrest on this beach this morning. Mexican cops liked theatrical busts even more than U.S. cops did. And the captain honorably conveyed the bribe to the cartel in charge, so the cartel wouldn't kill Rose and him in some very theatrical way.

Standing next to her, he heard and sensed her swinging up onto the saddle on the rented horse named *Calabaza*, and the horse adjusting its stance on the sandy beach. "Pleased to meet you, *Calabaza*," she said. "Good girl."

"What's *Calabaza* mean?" he asked.

"Pumpkin. Swing up here, you can ride bareback behind the saddle."

This was the problem. She wanted him to ride double with her.

"Shrink the cane and clip it to your shorts," she said, "grab my hand and the back of the saddle, swing yourself up. Come on. I see the captain and his cops gathering on the street beside the beach. We need to finish this."

He raised his right hand and she grabbed his hand and guided him as he swung up on the horse. He almost slipped off the other side and his hat fell off.

"I lost my hat," he said.

"Meinhardt just showed up," she said. "He's about a football field away from us, claiming a wicker couch under palm trees. He's got a cooler and he's taking out food and beer. He's got his horse with him as usual — he tied the reins to one of the trees. We'll make sure Meinhardt doesn't get away on his horse, help the cops round him up. Easy-peasy."

He wrapped his arms around her, which was always

good with him, and she nudged *Calabaza* into gear, first a walking pace letting the horse grow accustomed to carrying two people. "You OK?" she asked over her shoulder, obviously loving it.

"Yeah," he said. "Go for it."

She nudged the horse for a faster pace that probably had a name, trot or gallop, something like that. As she sped up, the breeze became more of a wind.

He thought, Nikki would've loved this too.

Isla Mujeres — Island of Women, how cool is that?

He felt the wind on his face and the power of the horse thundering under him, with Rose in front.

www.ingramcontent.com/pod-product-compliance
Lightning Source LLC
Chambersburg PA
CBHW021224310726
48971CB00006B/1679